THE SUNNYSIDE CAFE

THE SUNNYSIDE CAFE

CHINLE MILLER

Cover by Chinle Miller.

For Nick Stokes
May your retirement be filled with good friends, warm campfires,
and shining stars way out in the Big Empty

CONTENTS

1

Bud Shumway slowly backed the shiny red Ford 350 dually up to the faded orange door of the old gas station, carefully watching his Uncle Hank in the rear-view mirror, waiting for him to make a fist as a signal to stop.

Unfortunately, his uncle was a tad late with the signal, and when Bud heard the crunch of metal, he quickly hit the brakes, pulled forward a bit, then got out to assess the damage.

Bud hated to borrow anything, especially an expensive truck, but he hadn't known of any other way to get the heavy commercial stove from the kitchen of his wife's cafe up to the old gas station, the future home of his aunt's new business, the Sunnyside Cafe.

And so, he'd reluctantly asked his fellow melon farmer, Larry Digham, if he could borrow his almost-new truck to haul the big six-burner double-oven stove the 50 or so miles from Green River to Sunnyside, Utah.

Larry owed Bud a favor or two, especially since Bud had headed him off at the pass when he'd been ready to plant peanuts on all 200 of his acres, having heard that Bud's deputy Howie McPherson had grown a successful crop the summer before.

Bud figured he'd saved Larry a fortune by informing him that

Howie's so-called crop had only amounted to enough for a single batch of peanut brittle, and Larry might not want to bet the farm on peanuts.

Since Larry was Bud's main competitor in the melon business, Bud wondered if he would've done the same for him, but it didn't matter, for Bud wasn't just a melon farmer, but was also Sheriff of Emery County, and his integrity wasn't conditional on what other people thought or did.

But Larry had been happy to loan Bud his truck, even though Bud hadn't really wanted to borrow it. The stove was more than Bud's old farm truck could handle, so he felt he didn't have much of a choice in the matter, as his wife had promised his Aunt Ginger they'd get it up to her.

And now, stepping out of the cab onto the Ford's shiny running board, Bud wondered if he wasn't going to have to pay a pretty penny to get Larry's truck fixed, maybe even more than all those seed peanuts would've cost. He was relieved when his uncle informed him the dent was in the stove, not the truck.

"Your wife's gonna be good and mad at me, Bud," his Uncle Hank said glumly. "It's a pretty good dent."

"Not as mad as *your* wife's gonna be, Henry Shumway," Bud's Aunt Ginger informed Hank, hands on her hips, having just emerged from the cafe upon hearing the crunching sound.

"It looks bad, but it won't affect how it works any," Hank said defensively. "It's stainless steel, and I think I can hammer it out."

"Well, it's a shame," Ginger replied. "I'm sure Wilma Jean paid a pretty penny for it. After all, it's a Wolf, and they're not cheap. And now for it to get all messed up because..."

Bud interrupted. "Now, Aunt Ginger, Wilma Jean won't worry about it one bit. She got it over in Grand Junction from some restaurant that was going out of business, and I don't think she paid all that much for it. Besides, you gave her a good excuse to replace it with a new one, and she's pretty happy about that. And your customers for sure won't care if the stove's dented, as long as they get good food. But anybody have any idea how we're going to get it off the truck? It's heavy."

Hank said, "My buddy Jimmy Johnson's bringing his lift truck over and should be here any minute. He'll get it off, then help us wrestle it inside. Let's go have a cup of coffee while we're waiting and catch up on what you and Wilma Jean have been up to."

They went inside the old building, where Bud was pleasantly surprised, for the interior was nothing like the dilapidated exterior but had been completely redone, with the walls a bright yellow and the bar-height tables and chairs all shiny black metal with orange seats and tabletops.

Framed pictures of sunflowers hung on the walls, and the concrete floor had been painted a subtle shade of what Bud figured some marketer would call seafoam green. It all reminded Bud of what he imagined a bistro in Paris to look like, though he'd never been to Paris, or even inside a bistro, as far as he knew.

"What exactly is a bistro?" Bud asked as Ginger put a coffee carafe and two cups in front of him and Hank, as well as a small carton of half-and-half.

"Oh, Bud, that's so nice of you," Ginger replied, squeezing his shoulder as she poured the coffee. "That's exactly the look I was going for. I got these tables up in Salt Lake for almost nothing from a little bistro that was remodeling. You boys want some coffee cake with your coffee?"

Bud nodded his head yes, though still not sure what a bistro was. Ginger soon returned from the kitchen, putting two platters of homemade coffee cake in front of them.

Bud scooted his chair up to the table, saying, "I really like these chairs, Aunt Ginger. They're easy on the knees, and with the table right up under my chin like this, I won't have to worry about spilling coffee on my shirt." He then asked, "How do you guys like living up here on the sunny side of the Books? You've been here about six months, right?"

"That's about right, Bud," Hank replied. "We really like it, but that's not where the name Sunnyside came from, you know."

Hank paused, then added, "There used to be a place called Sunnyside down along the tracks close to Mounds, where the sheepmen sheared their sheep. When the coal mine opened, the railroad built a new terminus up here and called it Sunnyside. The original Sunnyside wasn't on the sunny side of anything—it wasn't even on a side. Up here, we're on the sunny side of the Bookcliffs."

Ginger said, "That's exactly what he said, Hank—up here on the sunny side of the Books. But we like it up here a lot, Bud. We have to go down to Price for groceries and such, but it's not a big deal. It's a lot quieter up here, and I love the views. I'm hoping the cafe will become kind of a community meeting place, like Wilma Jean's."

Hank nodded, then added, "But so far, fixing up this old gas station has been a lot of work. Ginger here can work all she wants, but I'm going back to being retired after this stove is installed."

"I was getting bored," Ginger replied. "And I've always wanted my own cafe."

"That's great," Bud replied. "So, you're going to call it the Sunnyside Bistro?"

Hank laughed, saying, "Bistro? Nobody here would know it was a place to eat if you called it that. We're in eastern Utah, Bud, not France."

"It's the Sunnyside Cafe, Buddy," Ginger said. "But who knows, maybe I'll eventually call it the Sunnyside Bistro. It has a nice ring. And Hank underestimates the people here. Just because we live in the sticks doesn't mean we're ignorant. Tell Hank what a bistro is, Buddy."

"Can I get a refill?" Bud dodged.

Ginger poured him another cup from the carafe, then added, "But there is one thing up here I'm starting to really not like. Tell him about the weird noises we've been hearing, sweetie pie. You know, Bud, I'm kind of regretting renting that house right at the mouth of the canyon. It's too much on the edge of nothing."

"It was just a moose, Gingie, you know that," Hank said.

"There aren't any moose down here. It's too dry."

"There's lots of moose up on the Tavaputs," Hank replied. "One just wandered down, that's all."

"It didn't sound anything like a moose."

"What did it sound like?" Bud asked.

"One of those dinosaurs in that movie *Jurassic Park*," Ginger replied. "And it scared me to death. I've heard it several times now, and it's not all that far off. Somewhere up the canyon."

"Dinosaurs have been extinct for millions of years," Hank replied. "It's impossible to hear one, unless it's a ghost. Just ask the guy who runs the Cleveland-Lloyd dino quarry. He'd laugh to think you'd heard a dinosaur. Maybe it was a buffalo. The wildlife people moved some to the Tavaputs from that herd on the Henry Mountains a few years ago."

"They're called bison, sweetie pie," Ginger said.

"Tell the Indians that," Hank remarked. "But you didn't hear no dinosaur. I'd stake my life on it."

Just then, Hank's phone rang. After a moment of silence, he said softly, "OK, Sam, thanks for letting me know. I'll go get Freckles in a bit. He's in the yard, right?"

Hank said goodbye, then slowly put his phone back in his pocket. Looking into his coffee cup, he said, "I guess Jimmy's not coming after all. Sam said they just found his body over by the old mine."

Ginger gasped. "His body? You mean he's dead?"

"That appears to be the case," Hank replied solemnly.

"What happened?" Ginger asked.

"Sam said he was found lying on his stomach next to his truck. It appears he was crushed by something, something with three very large toes. It left a big track on his back."

"A dinosaur," Ginger whispered. "I knew it. A real live dinosaur."

Bud leaned back in his chair, and not being used to the higher center of gravity, almost tipped over backwards, spilling coffee on his shirt.

"Was that Sam Wiggins?" He asked. "Deputy Sam Wiggins?"

"It was," Hank said. "Jimmy doesn't have any family, and Sam knows Jimmy and I are good friends—*were* good friends. He wants me to go get his dog."

Bud now badly wanted to unload the big stove and head back home to Green River. He knew Sam Wiggins fairly well, as Sam had been a fledging deputy when Bud's grandfather was sheriff of Carbon County. If Sam found out he was in town, he'd be wanting him to help figure out what had happened to Jimmy Johnson, and the last thing Bud wanted was to get involved.

"Well, that's a real shame," Bud said. "I'm sorry to hear it, Hank. I know you need to go get his dog, but we've got to figure out how to unload that stove, as I have to get this truck back."

"You're lucky," Ginger replied. "You can go back to Green River. We should've moved there instead of up here."

She stood, and picking up their empty plates, gave Hank a look as she added, "Or anyplace where there aren't dinosaurs running around killing innocent people."

Hank frowned, then stood and followed Bud outside.

2

Bud pulled into the long drive in front of Larry Digham's big white farm house, parking the big Ford next to his own old Sandstorm Tan 1975 Toyota FJ40. Leaving the keys in the truck's ignition, like Larry had told him to do, he then put Wilma Jean's homemade apple pie, wrapped in aluminum foil, on the hood where Larry would see it.

He'd filled the truck's gas tank, even though it had been almost empty when he'd borrowed it, and had then taken it to the car wash, wanting to show his appreciation to Larry for letting him borrow it, though he hoped to never need it again.

Seeing Larry out in the field on his tractor, Bud waved, then got into his FJ, happy to be back in Green River. He'd head back to the bungalow, where their three dogs waited, put on a clean shirt, then go to the sheriff's office. He wondered for a moment about Jimmy Johnson's dog, Freckles, and what would become of it, though he knew Hank and Ginger would make sure it found a good home.

They'd managed to unload the stove by using the winch on Hank's truck to lower it, wrapping the cable around a defunct light pole above the old gas station. Hank had then commandeered a friend to help them push it into the cafe. Fortunately, it had rollers and moved easily across the concrete floor and on into the kitchen.

Now Bud noticed a note from Larry on the FJ's dash:

Bud, If you get a chance, go check the gate at the diversion dam. Seems like water's still coming down the ditches.

Bud knew the gate wasn't really his responsibility, but he'd go check it anyway, as it was in his best interest to not have the ditches running. The diversion dam provided the area's only supply of irrigation water, as Green River was basically a desert.

All the area farms, including his, had been buttoned up for winter, and about all that was left to do was plow the fields under, which Bud knew his farm manager, Kale, was doing that very moment. Having water in the ditches would complicate things.

Bud was glad to be back in Green River, surprised he'd managed to make it through several hours without hearing from his deputy, Howie McPherson. Just then, as if on cue, his cellphone rang.

"Yell-ow," Bud answered.

"Is that you, Sheriff?"

"Well, seeing how you dialed my number, I'd say the odds of it being me are pretty high, Howie," Bud replied.

"I'm hearing some strange news coming out of Sunnyside," Howie continued, unfazed. "There's talk of a dinosaur on the loose. Is that true?"

Bud groaned. "Well, the talk is true, but the reality isn't. Howie, I just barely got back in town. All I can say is I wish truth would travel as fast as rumors. I take it you called my Aunt Ginger?"

"I was wondering if you'd be back in time for me to go to my business meeting, so I called to see where you were. Are you coming into the office now?"

"You could've just called me, Howie. How'd you know to call Ginger?"

"Wilma Jean told me. I tried calling you, but you must've been out of cell range. Wilma Jean needs to get to this meeting, too, Bud. Are you coming into the office now?"

"I'm on my way, Howie. But what's this important meeting about? And why is my wife going?"

"She's my campaign manager—I thought you knew that. We're having a strategy meeting. It's pretty important, as we need to figure out how we're going to proceed with me running as mayor."

"Didn't you fill out the application for the election?" Bud asked. "I think that's about all you really need to do, other than shake a few hands in the meantime. Actually, that's not even necessary, since everyone already knows you."

Howie, sounding frustrated, replied, "I wish it was that simple, Bud, but there's a reason it's called a campaign. You have to be organized and have a battle plan, kind of like going to war, if you want to win. You need a strategy. We're going to barnstorm."

"Don't you mean brainstorm, Howie?"

"No, barnstorm. I've been reading up on this stuff. That's when you make a quick tour of an area as part of a political campaign. It came from when theatrical companies would tour rural districts giving performances, usually in barns."

Bud, now turning into the bungalow's drive, could see his three dogs—Hoppie, his Basset hound, Pierre, his wiener dog, and Lindie, his Carolina dingo—all waiting in the yard, wagging their tails.

"Howie, you're running for Mayor of Green River, not Sheriff of Emery County. You don't have any rural districts to barnstorm. I think you could barnstorm the town in an hour, maybe even less. Actually, brainstorming would be even quicker, as a lot of people here don't even use their brains."

Howie replied, "Well, we need to get organized. There are fliers to make and put up, and we need to figure out my campaign promises. Any ideas there, Sheriff?"

"You could promise that you'll never let dinosaurs wreak havoc on the town," Bud answered, getting out of his FJ. "That would be one promise you'd have no trouble keeping."

"Was that for real?" Howie asked.

"I'll tell you about it when I get there," Bud said, the dogs now jumping up and dancing around, happy to see him. "I have to go check the diversion dam first, so it may be awhile. Why don't you just have Wilma Jean come to the office there?"

"I guess that would work," Howie replied. "That way we wouldn't have to wait. I'll call her right now."

Bud said goodbye, then opened the front gate, where he was quickly inundated by excited dogs. Working his way into the kitchen, he started a pot of coffee, then gave each of the dogs a Barkie Biscuit.

He found a note on the table from Wilma Jean that read:

Hon, stay out of the pumpkin pie in the fridge. It's for dinner. We're having very special company. You can have some of the frosted pumpkin cookies in the cookie jar. XXOO

Bud poured himself a cup of coffee, then, thinking that since he'd have a couple of those cookies and probably shouldn't put his usual dollop of vanilla-bean ice cream in the coffee, he instead poured in a bit of cream. Grabbing several cookies, he then took everything out onto the back deck.

Drinking the coffee and munching on cookies, he half-heartedly kicked the ball for Lindie, who repeatedly retrieved it and dropped it at his feet. Pierre and Hoppie were busy sniffing along the fence line, checking to make sure there'd been no interlopers in the few minutes they'd been inside, especially one of the little cottontails that liked the two grassy acres surrounding the bungalow.

It was nice to take a little break, Bud thought, knowing he'd soon be back in the thick of things after checking the dam and going back to the sheriff's office, though he knew nothing much ever happened in Green River. Howie would be fine meeting with Wilma Jean there.

As he kicked back in the wicker chair, he thought back to delivering the stove, glad the chore was over with and done. He was glad it had all worked out, in spite of the dent.

He then thought of his Uncle Hank's friend, Jimmy Johnson, and the strange way he'd been killed—crushed by a dinosaur's foot? It seemed ludicrous to Bud, and he was sure there was a logical explanation, but for the life of him, he couldn't think of one.

And his Aunt Ginger hearing strange noises coming from the canyon? Bud knew the town of Sunnyside had been built at the mouth of Whitmore Canyon, named for George Whitmore, who had ranched there. Whitmore Canyon was famous for its bighorn sheep, but compared to most of the canyons cutting into the Bookcliffs, it wasn't all that long, though it did have several tributary canyons feeding into it. The Books were rugged, as was the Tavaputs Plateau high above, but it certainly wasn't some lost world where dinosaurs could go unnoticed for millions of years—or was it?

Coffee and cookies now gone, Bud gathered up the dogs. He'd take them for a little ride out to the diversion dam since the day was wearing on and they hadn't been out yet. Besides, if dinosaurs were invading the country, he might need them for protection—they could bite the beasts' ankles, giving him time to escape.

He again shook his head at the improbability of it all, then loaded everyone into the FJ and headed on down Long Street to the dam, wondering who Wilma Jean's very special dinner guests could be, hoping it was someone who didn't care much for pumpkin pie so there would be leftovers for a midnight snack.

3

Bud stood on the bank of the Green River, watching as the slow-moving water lazily made its way towards its eventual destination downstream at Glen Canyon Dam. It was October, the roar of spring snowmelt now just a memory, one that would get even more distant as winter froze the river's edges into ice and snow.

Before it could go on downstream, the water first had to negotiate the Tusher Diversion Dam, also known simply as the Green River Dam. To the locals, the dam kept the "green" in Green River—making it possible to irrigate the some 5,300 acres that produced the area's watermelons, cantaloupes, casabas, honeydews, alfalfa, and corn.

The original dam, a U-shaped rock-and-crib weir example of pioneer ingenuity, had been damaged by recent floods. The new updated dam included a boat passage as well as fish ladders, as the original structure had obstructed the flow of boats and fish both.

Before, boaters had to portage the dam or take out at Swasey's Beach, a few miles upstream, but now they could float all the way to the Green River State Park, another dozen river miles, miles with such a slow current that even canoes and kayaks could easily navigate it.

Even though it was now autumn, boating season pretty much over, Bud could see a trio of rafts coming down the river. He waved and they waved back. Watching as they floated the boat passage, Bud was surprised they made it through, as the water was so low.

Bud had never been much of a rafter, though he and his cousin Jewel had floated the Green a few times in his Uncle Chet's old raft. They'd put in at the state park and taken out a few miles downstream at Crystal Geyser, where Aunt Rhoda had met them. It was only because of Jewel's skill as a boatman that they hadn't missed the boat launch there and gone on downstream, with the next takeout miles away.

Part of the problem was that he wasn't much of a swimmer, having grown up mostly in Price, where he'd spent summers helping his grandfather run cattle on the big ranch he managed up Nine Mile Canyon before becoming sheriff. The only water there was Nine Mile Creek, which one could usually jump across, and even its potholes weren't deep or big enough for swimming.

Bud now took a good look at the canal gate, which looked like it was securely closed. The canal itself looked low, and he couldn't make out any kind of flow. The water in Larry's ditches must just be remnants.

It was then that he noticed something bobbing slowly up against the gate itself, something that looked like a small box. He wondered if it might be something that had fallen off a raft. Maybe he should retrieve it. If it was someone's gear, he could check down at Jay's Tavern where all the boaters ate and see if anyone had reported anything missing.

He walked along the bank upstream from the gate until he finally found a long stick from one of the many tamarisks along the river. He managed to fish the box out, though it was much heavier than he'd anticipated.

On closer inspection, he could see it was made of wood, and its musty odor accentuated the fact that it had been in the water for some time.

Dragging it through the sand on the riverbank, he noted it had faint lettering on its side. Wiping off the muck, he read:

Hercules Powder
High Explosives

He couldn't believe his eyes! He'd just recovered a Hercules dynamite box from back during the Cold War, probably dating from the 1950s or possibly even earlier, when dynamite was a common tool for uranium miners.

He knew such boxes were rare, and what was one doing floating down the river? It was seriously waterlogged, and he knew if he hadn't found it when he did it probably would've been doomed to sink in a day or two, gone forever into the depths of Davy Jones' Locker—or did that only apply to the ocean? He wasn't sure, and who the h-e-double-hockeysticks was Davy Jones, anyway?

Bud now pulled his harmonica from his pocket, fiddling with it as he wondered where the box had come from. As far as he knew, there weren't any uranium mines upriver, or any kinds of mines, for that matter. The river flowed through the deep canyons of the Tavaputs Plateau for many miles after leaving the basin country near the town of Ouray, Utah, named for the Ute chief.

He wasn't really sure he wanted to know what was in the box, but he did recall seeing one somewhere for sale for over $100. He wanted to take the box home, but didn't want it in the FJ until he thoroughly examined its contents.

He now looked carefully inside, expecting to find mud and leaves and other kinds of river detritus, but was instead surprised to find it was dry, with what looked to be a faded brown and green plaid jacket of some kind.

He gingerly pulled out the jacket, noting it appeared to be about his size. Looking through the pockets for some kind of clue as to its owner, he found a small folded piece of paper. Opening it, he read three simple words—or was it two?—*Choo-Choo Rock.*

Shaking his head, he looked in the other pocket, finding what appeared to be a small inch-long arrow made of aluminum with magnets glued onto the back. Engraved on the arrow were the letters *PM*.

He had no idea what he was looking at, but he carefully put both the note and aluminum arrow in his shirt pocket and continued looking through the box. He wanted to get going, as the dogs waited in the FJ.

Something wrinkly was under the jacket, and he was reluctant to touch it, as it was suspiciously flesh-colored. As he gingerly picked it up, he realized it was rubber, but upon seeing what it was, he immediately dropped it in the sand.

It was flesh-colored with white stringy hair, something like you'd see in a bad dream about your old high-school principal. He picked up the stick he'd used to reel in the box and carefully flipped the thing over.

He was now staring into the face of a rather benign-looking fellow, someone who could be your neighboring farmer or postman or even the grocery-store clerk, and this someone had white hair, and lots of it.

Bud reached down and picked it up, now knowing it was some kind of Halloween mask with fake hair attached. He put it back in the box with the jacket and loaded it into the back of his FJ, then got in and headed back to the bungalow, surprised at his own ability to be taken in by something so innocuous.

But then, he thought in his own defense, he'd been thinking about Davy Jones' Locker and such, and who knew what superstitions and secrets the waters at his feet held, the waters of the Mighty Green. Probably not too many, he decided.

Soon back at the bungalow, Bud gave the dogs each another biscuit, leaving them to snooze in the house until he got home later. He then unloaded the wet box by the front gate and headed for the sheriff's office, now fiddling with the aluminum arrow from his pocket, wondering where the box had come from and what its contents meant.

He would call Jay's Tavern and put the word out as to what he'd found, then hope no one would claim it. If nothing else, it would make a nifty side table for the office, and he could donate the plaid jacket and Halloween mask to the thrift store.

But as he pulled in front of the sheriff's office, he wondered if it might not be prudent to wait awhile before contacting Jay, for his intuition told him that the box and its strange contents might have some significance, as unlikely as it seemed.

4

Bud sat in his office, relishing the peace and quiet, knowing it could all change in a moment with a simple phone call from old Mrs. Jensen wanting him to chase the kids riding their bikes across her lawn or from Sherwyn down at the Melon Harvest Grocery wanting him to come give a kid a ride and lecture in his sheriff's vehicle for stealing bubble gum.

Anything could happen in Green River, Bud mused, though little seldom did. Howie must be meeting with Wilma Jean somewhere, he figured.

He now keyed the words *Davy Jones' Locker* into the search bar of his computer, reading:

> *Davy Jones' Locker refers to the seabed, the resting place of thousands of sailors drowned at sea. The phrase denotes seafarers or even objects including ships whose remains are consigned to the depths of the ocean, i.e., Davy Jones' Locker. The origin of the phrase is lost in time.*

Bud leaned back, not sure if he'd learned anything or not. He already knew that the term referred to the bottom of the sea, but what he was wondering was if one could use it to refer to the bottoms of rivers and other bodies of water.

Given the adaptability of the English language, he figured one would be understood, even if it was an erroneous usage, but given his aunt's comment about how the locals weren't so ignorant as to not know the meaning of the word *bistro*, he felt a little more motivated than usual to be sure he didn't fit into the ignorant category. If he was indeed ignorant, he didn't want it to be willful ignorance.

He now keyed in the word *bistro*.

A popular folk etymology of the word claims that it originated among Russian troops who occupied Paris following the Napoleonic Wars. In taverns they would shout the Russian býstro, which means "quickly," to the waiters, so that bistro took on the meaning of a place where food was served quickly.

This surprised Bud, for it didn't fit his impression of what the word meant, which he thought was maybe more connected to French sidewalk cafes. He now searched on *Russian bistro*.

In Russia restaurants are not traditionally called bistros, and the concept of the quick-serve restaurant is seen as a French import.

This really didn't explain much and was a tad circular, he thought, starting to click on another link, but realizing he was going down a deeper than usual rabbit hole, he instead keyed in *Hercules dynomite box.* The search found nothing, so he tried *Hercules dynamite box* and was surprised to see a dozen or more links, as well as photos of boxes that looked just like the one he'd found, though in various states of preservation. Several were listed for sale, and he noted prices ranging from $100 on up to around $175.

He was now sure he'd found something of possible value, though the trick might be finding a place to sell it, as he wasn't real keen on using an online site. Now thinking of the Halloween mask, he keyed in *Halloween mask Price UT*, knowing there was no place in Green River that sold Halloween supplies.

He was surprised when a store called *Wiggins Diggins* came up. He'd been in it a couple of times with Wilma Jean on shopping forays, but he hadn't noticed any Halloween supplies, though it was probably a seasonal thing.

He knew it was run by Deputy Sam Wiggins' wife, Dorothy, and was basically what he called a junk shop, though Wilma Jean had corrected him and said it was a collectibles shop. Since the only thing Bud really figured worth collecting were things like rocks and old Prince Albert tobacco tins, he hadn't been all that interested, though his wife had found a couple of nice sugar-glass bowls to go with her peacock glass collection. Trying to be helpful and clean them up a bit when they got home, he'd instead melted them, not realizing they were made of real sugar.

Bud leaned back, shutting down the computer, wondering again what the contents of the Hercules box was all about. It was one of the stranger things he'd ever found floating on the river, though his river findings were fairly limited so far, usually consisting of things like half-rotten melons and an occasional old tire, though he'd once found a carved pumpkin.

He looked at the clock on the wall, and seeing he had another half-hour before he was off-duty, leaned back and closed his eyes, wondering what they were having for dinner.

He then remembered his wife had said they were having company, and he felt mildly irritated. He enjoyed the special dinners she cooked the rare times they did have someone over, but he actually preferred going home and relaxing and not having to entertain anyone, instead playing ball and fetch with the dogs in the back yard.

Just as he was starting to drift off, his phone rang. Noting that he had two minutes until he was off duty, he almost didn't answer, letting it instead go to the answering machine, but he finally decided to pick it up.

"Sheriff's office, Bud Shumway," he answered.

"Bud, there's something really strange in a box out by the gate. Did you leave it there?"

It was Wilma Jean.

Bud replied, "What's in it?"

"It looks like a shrunken head or something. I'm afraid to pick it up. It's creepy. Is it something of yours?"

Bud laughed. "It's a Halloween mask I found on the river."

Wilma Jean sounded put off. "And you just left it there for me to find, knowing it would scare the bejeebers out of me? And what were you doing out on the river?"

Bud sat up straight, saying, "I wasn't on the river, it floated by. I thought it might be something important."

"So you brought it home, even though it wasn't?"

Bud asked, "Wasn't what?"

"Anything important."

"It was either that or send it straight to Davy Jones' Locker, and I didn't think it would go down willingly, since rubber floats."

"Whatever are you talking about? Anyway, I put it in the barn. Are you coming home soon? It would be nice if you were here when our company arrives."

"Who's coming?" Bud asked.

"It's a surprise."

"You know I hate surprises," Bud replied.

"You'll like this one."

"How'd the meeting with Howie go?" Bud asked.

"We postponed it. Come on home and get the dogs out from under my feet. I'm making your favorite dish."

"I could just pick up some fried chicken at the Melon Harvest, and we could go to the state park for a picnic, just the two of us," Bud said wishfully, but he was too late, as she'd hung up.

Now Bud suddenly felt apprehensive. She was cooking something special, his favorite, and there must be a reason. And she said she'd invited someone special over, though he had no idea who it could be —maybe their good friends Shorty and Cassie, or maybe even Howie and Maureen. It was beginning to sound like a party, and why would she be going to all this trouble? And she sounded a bit stressed or put out.

It must be a special day, Bud thought, feeling more and more unsettled. It was autumn, so it couldn't be his birthday, as he was born in the spring, or so he'd been told, not having any actual memory of the event. Was it Wilma Jean's birthday? No, hers was in the summer, and if it were, she'd be wanting him to take her out for dinner, not cooking him something special.

That left their anniversary.

Bud put on his jacket and locked the office, now feeling panicked. He'd done this same thing last year—completely forgotten it, and he swore he'd never do it again, yet here he was, no gift and not even a card.

He got in his FJ and slowly headed for the bungalow, now sweating a bit. Wilma Jean would be nice about it—she always was—but he really didn't want to make her feel bad. What he needed was a nice card and something like a good bottle of wine and a promise to take her shopping. But the state liquor store only sold cheap wine, if it had any at all, being simply the locked case in the Westwinds Truck Stop. They always had a bottle or two of whisky, but he knew she wouldn't like that.

As he drove slowly towards the bungalow, he had an idea. He'd swing over to the Wandering One B&B—its proprietor Jay Landowska always had nice stuff over there for his clients, and he'd surely have something Bud could buy or beg for Wilma Jean.

After a few pleasantries with Jay, Bud managed to secure a nice bottle of Merlot, and Jay had some nice stationary for Bud to make into a card. Jay wrote a note for him in a nice calligraphy as Bud dictated:

Hon,

Like this fine wine, you just get better with age. IOU one shopping trip to Price. Happy anniversary. Love, Bud

Jay had asked Bud if he didn't think maybe Wilma Jean might

take offense at him mentioning her aging like wine, but Bud was in too big of a hurry to really give it much thought, thanking Jay and quickly heading home.

He was relieved that he'd figured that one out, and as he pulled into the drive, he noticed Shorty and Cassie's car parked next to an older dark-brown Oldsmobile Cutlass Supreme that looked vaguely familiar, though he couldn't recall where he'd seen it.

Opening the door, he was hit by the delicious smell of enchiladas as well as by the impact of Pierre the wiener dog grabbing onto his pant cuff and growling as Lindie and Hoppie looked on, tails wagging.

Wilma Jean looked surprised as Bud handed her the colorful package Jay had wrapped the wine in, along with his homemade card. He then took out the aluminum arrow he'd found in the box and started fiddling with it.

"What's this?" She asked.

"Open it. Read the card," Bud commanded, grinning, feeling on top of things for once.

"A nice bottle of wine! Bud Shumway, what's got into you?"

As she read the card, Bud could tell she was trying not to laugh.

"Hon, this is really nice, but it's not our anniversary. That's next month."

"I didn't want to be late again," he said lamely, now noticing there were others in the room. "So I thought I'd give it to you early."

Sure enough, their friends Shorty and Cassie were there, Shorty trying to hide a big grin while Cassie talked with a small somewhat roundish woman who held hands with a man of similar build who wore jeans that hung down under his pot belly. Those jeans were held up by signature red-white-and-blue-striped American flag suspenders, and he also wore scuffed-up moccasins and an olive-green long-sleeved underwear shirt.

It was Bud's Uncle Junior and his wife, LuAnn, straight from Paradox, Colorado.

Junior stood, saying, "Buddy, Buddy, Buddy, you haven't changed a bit, you rascal."

Bud gave his uncle a big hug, just as little Pierre let go of his pant leg and went for Junior's moccasins, Junior letting out a yelp. His uncle was soon down on his hands and knees chasing Pierre around, the little dog running in circles, not sure what to do with this change of events.

"Looney as ever," LuAnn commented, laughing.

"Dinner's served," said Wilma Jean. "Who wants wine with their enchiladas?"

Bud picked up Pierre and took the dogs outside as everyone headed for the dining room. Standing at the back deck for a moment, watching the sun set in the distance over the watermelon fields, he grinned.

The anniversary thing had been a bit embarrassing, but he was glad to see his Uncle Junior and LuAnn again, and he wondered why they'd come to visit, though he knew he would soon find out.

5

"Buddy, we're going up to Sunnyside to help your aunt get her cafe going," Junior told Bud over a big slice of pumpkin pie with whipped cream as they all sat on the back deck, eating dessert. "You know LuAnn's a darn good cook, and having run the Paradox Cafe for ages she can show Ginger the ropes."

"And who's running the Paradox Cafe while you're gone?" Wilma Jean asked.

LuAnn answered, "We have some big news for you. Tell them the news, Junior."

Junior leaned back. "Well, see, this young couple came into the valley looking for something to do, so we're leasing the cafe and general store out to them. They want to buy them if they can swing a loan. The gal's dad is coming out from somewhere back East to check it out. I guess he's pretty well-heeled and is also their banker."

"I've never heard anyone refer to Denver as back East," LuAnn shook her head. "But if they end up buying everything, we're getting an RV. We're going to retire and be free birds."

Bud was surprised at this news. Even though he and Wilma Jean didn't get over there very often, he couldn't picture the Paradox

General Store without his uncle sitting in front watching the world go by while eating ice cream.

"What about your duties as mayor?" Bud asked.

"They won't even know I'm gone," Junior said. "Buddy, tell us what's going on up in Sunnyside. We heard there was a guy killed by a dinosaur."

"I'm amazed the news has already hit Paradox," Bud replied. "I doubt if Deputy Wiggins had that in mind when he told Uncle Hank. The cause of death isn't usually discussed with the public until the crime's been solved, if there is one."

"Oh, we didn't hear it from Hank," LuAnn replied.

"Then it was Ginger," Bud said matter of factly. "But she probably isn't aware of protocol. Sam told Hank, who told me and Ginger, who told you and Junior and Howie, and now Wilma Jean and Cassie and Shorty, so there you go. Word of mouth is usually exponential like that."

Now Wilma Jean asked, "A dinosaur? How could anyone be killed by something that no longer exists? And how did they know it was a dinosaur?"

Bud replied, "He was crushed, and whatever crushed him left a three-toed track. Only the coroner knows if that's what actually killed him."

He now turned to Shorty and Cassie. Shorty was a retired geologist, and Cassie, also a geologist, taught the high-school science classes in Green River. Bud said, "You guys should know if anyone does. Is it possible that some very hardy species of dinosaur survived?"

Cassie replied, "Well, of course, Bud. We know for a fact that a number of them did."

Junior said, "You're kidding, right?"

"No, they're the descendants of the avian dinosaurs," Cassie continued. "We don't call them dinosaurs now, we call them birds. Paleontologists have found dinosaurs with fossilized feathers, and they even have pigment in them. Some were beautiful, multicolored."

Junior let out a guffaw. "Birds? Birds are dinosaurs?"

Cassie patiently continued. "There are now more than 10,000 species that we think evolved from the avian dinosaurs, the only branch of dinosaurs that survived the mass extinction from the Chicxulub asteroid impact 66 million years ago. Paleontologists think they survived because they were small and could move around easily."

Shorty said, "If you were to scale something like a raven to the size of a tyrannosaur, it would be pretty scary, in my book. But the early birds did evolve from theropods, which were the fierce, three-toed predator family that also included Tyrannosaurus rex. Just like the mammals, with the rest of the dinosaurs gone, they then had less competition and flourished."

"The tiniest hummingbird is related to the T. rex?" LuAnn asked.

"It is," Shorty replied. "When the comet or asteroid hit, they're not sure which it was, the world was plunged into an impact winter and the forests were destroyed. The surviving species were more at home on scrubland or at sea, and the ones that depended on thickly wooded zones went extinct."

"OK," Junior said, balancing his now-empty plate on the arm of his wicker chair. "But could some of the big guys have survived, living in some protected niche, someplace where nobody knew about them?"

Cassie replied, "No one's found any evidence of it. It's been the subject of a lot of B-grade movies, like *Valley of Gwangi*, but it's highly unlikely."

"Kind of like in that Scooby Doo movie, *Legend of the Phantosaur*," Bud added. "This guy tells everyone about the Phantosaur, the ghost of this dinosaur..."

Wilma Jean interrupted, laughing, "You and Scooby Doo."

Shorty added, "If a non-avian dinosaur species were to survive, it would have to be someplace really hidden. We humans are very invasive. We've been about everywhere on the planet."

LuAnn now asked, "How about like in *Jurassic Park*, where some scientist clones them from DNA?"

Cassie replied, "You need viable DNA, and so far, no paleontologist has ever found any."

"So, you're saying it's pretty much scientifically impossible for a dinosaur to have killed Jimmy Johnson," Bud said.

Shorty replied, "Not impossible, but highly improbable. Actually, extremely unlikely and improbable."

LuAnn leaned back next to Junior, and putting her arm around his shoulders, said, "Well, that's good to hear, especially after Ginger told me she'd heard a dinosaur or something up the canyon from their house and that's where we'll be staying. Whatever do you think that could be?"

Junior snorted. "Her imagination. Or maybe the sound of a distant train echoing off the canyon walls. Any number of things."

It was late, and as they all sat in silence, pondering a huge T. rex mucking around in the fields or even walking up the drive, Bud finally said, "I'm going to have to hit the hay. I take it you guys are staying out in the Airstream?"

LuAnn replied, "Wilma Jean offered for us to stay at her Melon View B&B. It sounds really nice, and that way, you won't have to put up with us for breakfast."

Everyone now said their goodbyes, and Bud and Wilma Jean stood on the front porch, watching the taillights of LuAnn's Olds Cutlass turn one direction towards the B&B and Shorty and Cassie's vehicle go the other, out to their ranch.

Wilma Jean put her arm around Bud's waist, saying, "That was really nice of you to bring wine, hon, but do you really think I'm aging like that? And I am going to take you up on that shopping trip, even though it's not our anniversary."

Bud groaned, took her by the hand, and they went inside, dogs at their heels.

6

Bud sat in his office, feet on his desk, reading an old issue of *Outdoors Photography*, engrossed in an article about organizing your photos which claimed that this was one of the most challenging aspects of being a photographer.

He wasn't sure how that could be, since you couldn't have photos to organize without equipment and a certain level of know-how, but when he got to the part called, "Use these tips to tame your photo library," the page had been torn out.

So much for getting stuff from the free box at the library, he thought, putting the magazine down. Maybe he could put in a hint for Wilma Jean to get him his own subscription for their anniversary.

Just then, a small wiry man dressed like a cowboy came into the office. Bud was surprised—not at seeing the guy, but at seeing him dressed in Levis, cowboy boots, a Wrangler shirt, and a baseball cap with the word *Cinch* on it.

"Morning, Carl. Haven't seen you for awhile," Bud said. "You working undercover, or is your uniform at the cleaners?"

"Morning, Bud. Actually, I'm trying to keep a low profile. Your wife and the dogs doing OK?"

"Fine, fine, thanks for asking," Bud replied. "But what brings you up here?"

Carl leaned back in his chair, saying, "Well, Bud, we've had a report of a boat being stolen. A rafting party was camped at Range Creek Rapids and when they got up, one of their rafts was gone."

"Are they sure they tied it up good enough?"

"They are. These guys are seasoned rafters and would never make a rookie mistake like that. Here's a photo of it, if you don't mind keeping an eye out."

Carl handed Bud a photo of a yellow raft holding several boaters going down the Green. He studied it for a moment, then handed it back.

"Looks like every other raft I've ever seen. Any idea who took it?"

"Another group was down the river and saw a white-haired man in it. I think he must've taken out at the geyser, as nobody saw him at the state park."

Bud replied, "The BLM sent you all the way up here from Radium to investigate a stolen raft? And undercover? Things must be pretty slow, eh?"

Carl replied, "Bud, you know with over two million acres in our jurisdiction and only two rangers things are never slow. That raft may be part of something bigger—or maybe it's simply just a stolen raft. But I'm getting ready to deploy to Range Creek, and I need your help."

"Deploy? Are you bringing in troops or something?"

Carl laughed. "That's just my ex-military experience rearing its head. You know what I mean."

"Actually, Carl, I don't. What's going on in Range Creek?"

"Looting. There's always been looting in the area since Harvey sold it to the state, even though it's all gated—actually, there was looting even when he had it, but it was minor, as people knew they'd get shot if he caught them. But we now have evidence of some wholesale big-time stuff going on."

Bud replied, "It's too bad the media caught wind of it. Nobody even knew it existed before that. But is that in your jurisdiction if the state owns it?"

"Range Creek Canyon includes Bureau of Land Management properties as well as state lands, Bud. The BLM lands are part of a wilderness study area, so no mechanized travel is allowed. Actually the lands managed by other agencies also prohibit vehicular travel except down the main road, and you can't even get a vehicle in there without a key to the gate. You can't even hike in without a permit. As a law-enforcement officer, I have a key, as does the state guy and the archaeologists working in there and staying at the old ranch headquarters, but it appears someone else managed to get one. There's evidence someone's digging in there and taking out antiquities."

"Fremont relics?" Bud asked.

"Yes, and the stuff's over a thousand years old and very valuable on the black market."

"But how do you know all this?"

"We have an informant on the other end of the pipeline, where it's being sold. That's all I can say about that."

"I understand," Bud replied. "But what do you want me to do? Even though Range Creek's in Emery County, it might as well be on the moon in terms of accessibility. I'd have to go up by Sunnyside to even get into the canyon, up over Horse Creek, and it's quite a trek, as you know. I'd be glad to provide backup if you need me for an arrest, but I can't be spending a lot of time in there, as much as I'd like to, as I have the usual stuff to tend to around here."

"Are you still into photography? Hum told me you were getting pretty good at it."

Bud replied, "I don't know how good I am, but I enjoy it."

"Well, Range Creek is a photographer's paradise. Those deep canyons in the Bookcliffs are hard to get into, and very few have roads going down them like Range Creek does. Of course, Harvey ran cattle and grew hay on the bottomland—he had over 4,000 acres—but most of the canyon is pristine. There's even a couple of nice arches in there. Don't you have a deputy who could cover for you for a few days?"

"You're saying I could go in there with you? Would we camp?"

"We'd stay at one of the cabins down at the ranch headquarters. Bud, I'll be honest with you. I really don't want to go in there alone. When you start getting into these kinds of deals, people know they can end up in prison and get violent."

"So, does that mean you're going to stand behind me if someone starts shooting?" Bud joked.

Carl replied, "Well, I'll stand behind you, but not literally. We'll hide behind rocks. There's lots of rocks in there. But Bud, you can pose as a photographer, and I'll be your sidekick. It's a good cover. Maybe you could work for *National Geographic* or something. We don't even want the archaeologists knowing we're LEOs, as some of them might be involved."

"Man, I need some better equipment if I'm going to be a NatGeo photographer."

"I can arrange that," Carl replied.

"And they won't know I'm sheriff?" Bud now took the aluminum arrow from his pocket and began fiddling with it.

"It's unlikely, since they're all out of the university in Salt Lake, as far as I know."

"Where would you get this equipment?" Bud asked.

"I don't know, but I can coordinate with the official BLM photographer. Probably rent it."

"A NatGeo assignment into the famous Fremont Indian ruins of Range Creek. How much does it pay?" Bud joked.

"Well, the pay will be in good will. If we can put these guys in jail, it will illustrate that the Feds and local sheriffs can work together. You know as well as I do that there's been a lot of ill will in those departments, locals feeling the Feds were overstepping their jurisdictions on public lands, even though it's our job to protect them—and it's a thankless job, too."

Bud was silent, then said, "I know. I've never felt that way, you know that, but I do know some of the fellows down in Radium have had some opinions on it. Not Sheriff Hum, but a deputy or two."

"I know who they are, Bud. Hum's a good sheriff. He's always been someone we can rely on. But couldn't your deputy cover things for you?"

"Well, speak of the devil and here he comes," Bud grinned as Howie opened the door. "We can ask him in person."

Bud was surprised to see that even though he was in uniform, Howie had his hair combed up above his forehead, slicked up into a pompadour.

"Howdy, hep cats," Howie said, grinning.

Bud groaned silently, then said, "Howie, I'd like you to meet Carl Chapman. He's from Radium and will be accompanying me to take some photos, assuming you agree to cover things while I take a few days off."

Howie replied amiably, "You can do anything you want, but stay off of my blue suede shoes. I'd be glad to, Sheriff, though I hope you can get back before the big rockabilly car show, 'cause me and the Ramblin' Road Rangers are going to play for it."

Carl stood, saying, "It's nice meeting you, Deputy McPherson. I need to get going. I'll be in touch, Bud. It'll probably take a week or so to get everything organized."

With that, he walked out the door and was gone.

"Who exactly was that?" Howie asked, taking Carl's chair.

"He's a BLM law-enforcement ranger, Howie. He's undercover. He's one hep cat you want on your side. But you know him only as a photographer who's going out with me for a few days. Mum's the word."

"I can keep a secret with the best of them," Howie replied. "I'm earthbound."

"What's that?"

"That's rockabilly talk for reliable. I hope he wasn't offended by me calling him a hep cat, Bud, but I need to get into this rockabilly thing if we're going to be a hit."

"Howie, I'm not even sure what a rockabilly is, but if that's what you need to do, I'm sure Carl understands."

Howie replied, "It's pretty simple, Sheriff. It's everything that goes with stuff from the 1950s and '60s, you know, hot rods and muscle cars, Bill Haley, Wanda Jackson, Buddy Holly, all that. It mixed country with blues and was the start of classic rock—rock plus hillbilly—rockabilly. It's really popular, and I think it'll help my mayoral campaign. Which reminds me, I still need to meet with Wilma Jean. But why do I know Carl only as a photographer going out with you? What's going on?"

"I'll tell you later, Howie," Bud replied. "Right now I need to get over to the Shriner's Club luncheon, since they're wanting me to give a talk on our new ride-along program, unless you want to do it."

"How can you give a talk on something we don't even have?" Howie asked. "Since when do we have a ride-along program?"

"I just thought it would be a good way to show people what we do, Deputy," Bud replied. "People can sign up and ride around with one of us for an hour or so, whoever happens to be on duty."

"What if there's nothing going on? Will they sit around and read old magazines with us?" Howie laughed.

"I guess they could if they wanted," Bud replied, "Though that would be more of a sit-along."

With that, he said goodbye and headed out the door.

7

Bud sat by the irrigation ditch, playing stick with the dogs, even though there was no water for them to play in. Other than Carl, the BLM agent, showing up, and his meeting with the Shriners, it had been a quiet uneventful day, the kind Bud liked.

He was used to stopping by the bungalow after work and picking up the dogs, bringing them out to the farm where they could play and get some exercise and he could relax, even though he was seldom wound up enough to need to unwind.

He absent-mindedly threw a stick to Hoppie, who caught it and started dragging it in circles, Pierre close behind. Bud knew that once Pierre grabbed it, the game was over, for Hoppie would passively let him have it, and then Pierre would just guard it and refuse to return it to Bud. Somehow, Bud mused, dachshunds had lost the retriever gene—or they probably never had it, was more like it.

Lindie sat quietly by his side, as usual acting a bit aloof, as if she were somewhat contemptuous of the others' lack of self-awareness to chase sticks around, even though she herself loved chasing balls.

Bud's day had gone pretty well, and he was looking forward to going home to leftover enchiladas, as he knew Wilma Jean would be working at the bowling alley that evening, leaving him to his own devices. He was fine with that, for tonight he felt like he needed some alone time. Something didn't feel quite right, and he wanted to try to figure out exactly what it was, though he knew it had to do with Carl asking him to go into Range Creek.

Or maybe it was the death of Jimmy Johnson up in Sunnyside that was bothering him, he thought. Nobody was killed by a dinosaur, it just couldn't happen, and yet Sam Wiggins had told his Uncle Hank that Jimmy was crushed and had a big footprint in his back.

Bud was kind of surprised that Deputy Sam Wiggins hadn't tried to contact him. He was pretty sure that Hank had told Sam he was there in Sunnyside. Sam knew Bud's reputation for solving crimes, and Bud knew him well enough to know he would just as soon have Bud do the heavy lifting, even though it hadn't even happened in Bud's county. There was a reason Sam had never been elected sheriff, even though he'd been on the force for many years. He hadn't exactly been known for his enthusiasm for the job.

Pierre now dragged the stick under a big cottonwood tree, so Bud stood and picked up another, throwing it to Hoppie. Seeing that Hoppie had a new stick, Pierre dropped his and grabbed onto the new one, making Hoppie drop it, who then picked up the old stick. Pierre now went for that one, and Bud, feeling distracted and not wanting to deal with Pierre's shenanigans, picked up both sticks and threw them across the ditch, then gathered the dogs into the FJ.

He might as well go home, as he wasn't enjoying being out like he usually did. He knew there was plenty of Merlot left, as no one seemed to want wine with their enchiladas, and it occurred to him that maybe a glass would cheer him up some, even though he wasn't much of a drinker.

Now driving back home, it dawned on him that his problem was that he was feeling unsettled. Even though he didn't believe it could've been a dinosaur, something or someone had killed Jimmy, and what about his Aunt Ginger saying she'd heard something like a dinosaur's roar coming down the canyon?

Pulling into the drive, he chided himself as he let the dogs out and herded them into the dark house, turning on lights as he went. He gave them each their dinners of kibble mashed into a little canned food, then took out the enchiladas. They suddenly didn't sound all that good, so he instead took out the wine and poured himself a glass.

Going into the living room, he sat in his big leather recliner, tipping it back and nearly spilling the wine as Pierre tried to jump up onto his lap. Bud put the wine down and lifted the little wiener dog up, then took a sip, grimacing.

He wasn't sure how anyone ever acquired a taste for the stuff, but he was committed to finishing the glass, hoping it would relax him. In his mind, his worries had little substance, and he needed to just forget them. He tried another sip, but couldn't pull it off, as the wine tasted too bitter, so he instead chugged the entire glass at once, something he hadn't done since drinking beer back in high school.

Now he leaned back, head resting against the cool leather, and thought again about Carl's proposal for him to go into Range Creek. In retrospect, maybe this was what was really bothering him, maybe even more than Jimmy's death.

First, Bud had little to no interest in most archaeology, as to him it seemed a lot like grave robbing, a practice he'd been thoroughly indoctrinated against by his grandfather, who had actually arrested several members of the famous Peabody Museum archaeology dig in Nine Mile Canyon, a canyon even more famous for its Fremont ruins than Range Creek. None of those arrested had been archaeologists, but were instead locals hired as assistants who had taken a mummy home and hid it in their basement.

Bud knew that archaeologists were scientists and were careful to record their finds, and he also knew they'd played an important part in recreating the culture and lives of the Fremont, who the Utes claimed as their ancestors. But he was squeamish when it came to such things, especially skeletons, and he'd never been big on reading articles about early hominids, kind of preferring to think humans had just been dropped from the sky as they are or something, as he found early humans kind of homely.

For him to go wander around Range Creek, where an ancient civilization had once flourished and was now buried, pretending to be a photographer, well, it just didn't feel right. And he wasn't sure he could do a good job as a plainclothesman or whatever one might call it. He was used to being a straight shooter, not a spy.

He'd have to call Carl and back out of the deal, an action that also didn't set right with him, as he'd said he would do it. But he'd never signed on to be a spy, and he'd never been good at keeping secrets. In fact, his job as sheriff kind of precluded such activities, as he wanted his constituents to trust him and know he upheld the law, not spied on them.

Bud was getting sleepy, and he now started thinking about the few times he and Howie had set up stakeouts, sitting in the bushes, keeping an eye on who was coming and going, mostly when they knew underage kids were drinking. Wasn't that a form of spying?

And what about that time he'd sat under a tree up on the Swell in the dark by the Ghost Rock Cafe, waiting to see who would come back to the scene of what he'd thought had been Joe Swasey's murder? Hadn't that also been spying? What was different about that and what Carl wanted him to do? When someone's breaking the law, it *is* rather helpful to catch them in the act, as it sure saves on speculating and having to build up a case against them.

Bud was now asleep, snoring lightly, when his phone rang, the ringer startling him awake. It took him a minute to figure out what the sound was, but he eventually answered.

"Yell-ow."

"Bud, it's Aunt Ginger. I'm sorry if I woke you, but is there any way you can come up here?"

"You mean right now?" Bud asked, barely awake, the wine having taken effect.

"Yes. I'm sorry. That thing's making noise up in the canyon again, and Hank's down in Price with his nephew in the hospital with a broken leg. I'm all alone here, Buddy, and I'm scared to death."

"Hank has a broken leg?"

"No, his nephew."

"How'd Hank's nephew break his leg?"

"He was out bow hunting for a deer, his very first time, and he smeared himself up with something that hides your scent. A young mountain lion attacked him. They think it was inexperienced and thought he was a deer."

"It broke his leg?"

"No, he was just scratched up a little, but he was so shook up that he drove his pickup into the ditch on his way out and wrecked it."

"That's too bad, but you're saying you want me to drive up there right now?" Bud repeated groggily.

"Bud, it sounds like it's coming down the canyon."

"Aunt Ginger, I'm really sorry, but I don't think it would be a good idea for me to drive right now. And Wilma Jean's running the bowling alley and can't leave. Where are Junior and LuAnn? Aren't they there?"

"No, they went to Salt Lake to get supplies for the cafe."

"Why don't you go to Price and stay with Hank?"

Ginger now sounded like she was about to cry. "Oh, Buddy, I can't. I have that dog, Freckles, and I guess you didn't hear me say that Hank's nephew's in the hospital. I don't know what to do. And I need to be here to open the cafe in the morning."

Bud, now more awake, said, "Come on down here. Put Freckles in the car with you and bring some overnight clothes and come stay in our Airstream. Nobody will bother you here. Come on down, Aunt Ginger. I'll be waiting. We'll figure out the cafe after you get here. You can get up early and drive back. It's less than an hour."

Bud put his phone back in his pocket, going into the kitchen to make some coffee. He didn't want to make a whole pot, so he just poured a cup of water into a saucepan, put several tablespoons of grounds in it, and let it boil for a minute. It was strong, but it did the job, and he was soon fully awake, now thinking he should've gone up to Sunnyside instead of making his aunt drive down there.

After about an hour, he went out onto the front porch, watching for his aunt, wearing his heavy jacket, as the night was getting nippy with autumn coming on. He'd left the dogs inside so they wouldn't overwhelm Freckles when they showed up.

He couldn't believe the effect one small glass of wine had had on him, but maybe it was because he drank it so fast, he thought. Or maybe it was because he had no tolerance for alcohol, having never been much of a drinker.

The coffee and night chill had quickly sobered him up, and he again wondered about the sound his aunt had heard. What could it possibly be?

He could now see car lights coming down the lane, and he hoped it was Ginger, but as the vehicle came closer, he could see it was Wilma Jean, back from the bowling alley.

"What are you doing standing out here in the cold?" She asked, coming up the small set of stairs onto the front porch.

As Bud explained that his Aunt Ginger was on her way, he could see another car coming up the lane and knew it was her from the gray shadow, as she had a gray Ford Taurus.

"Bud Shumway, have you been drinking?" Wilma Jean, now standing next to him, asked. "You smell like wine."

"I had one glass," Bud replied, hoping his aunt wouldn't notice. "It sure knocked me for a loop. That's why Ginger's coming here—I didn't think it would be prudent for the Sheriff of Emery County to get a DUI. But I'm pretty much over it now."

"You go inside and go to bed. I'll take care of your aunt," Wilma Jean said, opening the door and gently pushing him inside.

"She has a dog." Bud's voice trailed off, and he was soon in the bedroom, putting on his PJs, door closed so the dogs wouldn't bother Freckles.

He crawled down under the covers, the dogs all piled onto the bed with him, and as he listened to the muffled sound of voices in the living room, he was soon fast asleep, knowing tomorrow was his day off and he could sleep in as late as he wanted, which was a very good thing.

8

Bud sat at a bistro table in the back of the Sunnyside Cafe, wishing that his aunt had put in a booth or two, as the bar-height chairs weren't all that comfortable after awhile. He liked kicking back as he drank his coffee, and as he'd learned earlier, kicking back in a bar chair was a recipe for disaster.

He'd decided to come up to Sunnyside with his aunt and would stay overnight if necessary, though Junior and LuAnn were due back possibly today, but for sure tomorrow. He'd brought Lindie to help entertain Freckles, who had turned out to be a beautiful Australian Shepherd with black spots all over his face. He and Lindy were at Ginger's, hopefully playing with each other or sleeping, staying out of mischief.

His aunt was busy serving customers, of which there were a dozen or more, word quickly getting out that the cafe was now open. The town had a small grocery store, but the cafe was the only place in Sunnyside where one could get cooked food.

Bud studied the people as they came and went, wondering what it would be like to live in a town like Sunnyside with only a hundred or so inhabitants. Of course, Dragerton was just down the road, maybe a mile away, if that, and a few more miles to the south was the hamlet of Columbia, which Bud guessed had a hundred people at the most.

The three towns together might have a thousand people, and all three towns had been built to house coal miners. At one point they'd incorporated into a single entity called East Carbon in what Bud figured had been for management reasons to save money, but the locals still called the towns by their original names, ignoring the supposed unification.

Bud had been here before as a kid when his parents had come over from Price a few times—he didn't recall why, but maybe to visit friends. He remembered the towns as being somewhat prosperous with well-kept lawns and houses, and nice cars in the driveways.

All three towns had been settled primarily by immigrants, many from Italy, as well as coal miners from the Appalachians looking for better lives. The towns were now in various states of decay from the closing of the mines. A big coal generation plant near Sunnyside kept that town alive, but barely.

Bud now thought of Ranger Carl and what he'd said about someone looting antiquities from Range Creek. Given the current state of the towns, he could see any number of possible suspects, people desperate for money. It seemed every third or fourth house looked abandoned, paint chipped and worn from the clapboard sides with dying trees and weeds in the yards, and Bud was sometimes surprised to see such places were inhabited. He knew that poverty was rearing its ugly head, the jobs long gone. The nearest town was Price, some 25 or so miles away, and jobs there were also scarce for the same reason—coal mining was a dying industry.

Now a man and woman came into the cafe, greeting everyone, and Bud soon surmised their names were Earl and Pearl. He could tell they were probably cattle ranchers from the way they were dressed and how they carried themselves.

Bud had grown up with ranchers and to him, it seemed they had a distinct manner and way of dress. The older ones were usually fairly broken down from the hard work, and the lines in their faces reflected the many hours they'd spent outdoors in the sun and weather. In addition, they were typically no-nonsense people who were as solid and reliable as they come.

As the couple sat down and ordered coffee and hamburgers, another fellow walked into the cafe, greeting everyone just as the ranchers had done, but with a big smile. He wore jeans with six-inch rolled-up cuffs, shiny black engineer boots, a plain blue cotton shirt, and a turquoise jacket with the name *Rod Ruff* embossed on the front in yellow. His white hair was combed back in a pompadour just like Howie's, and he had a white mustache with a white beard that went halfway down his chest.

A small blonde woman greeted him from her perch high on a barstool chair. "Hey, Rod, whatcha workin' on today?"

Rod replied, "Hey there, Terri. Come on down to the shop sometime. I've got an old '51 Lincoln I found over in Cisco in the ditch on its side. It's in rough shape, but I'm puttin' a '54 Chevy grill on it and painting it a salmon color. It's gonna be a purdy thing when I'm done."

Terri laughed as Rod walked by, squeezing her shoulder, then made his way towards Bud, nodding at him and smiling.

"Hello," Rod said. "I'm Rod Ruff. I have that garage just down the street. Mind if I join you? This place is fillin' up fast."

"Sure," Bud replied congenially. "Pull up a chair."

Rod sat down, then said, "I love and build custom cars. God gave me the mind to think that way. If I was on an island and even if there was nobody else around, I would build me a car. I just dig doin' it. My daddy was a coal miner, but that wasn't for me. So who are you and what were you put on Earth to do?"

Bud laughed. "I'm Bud Shumway. My Aunt Ginger started this cafe. I was put on Earth to drink coffee and grow Green River melons."

Rod laughed, "Well, bless you and your aunt both. You must both come from a fine family. We needed a place like this. And as for Green River, man, I love those melons. We go down there every fall and get a pickup load and bring 'em back for the folks here and in

Dragerton. We're having a car show down your way soon, white-hub customs. You won't want to miss it."

Bud grinned. "It sounds great. I'll be there."

Rod continued, "This town was a boom town right in the middle of the custom car times, and a lot of people here still think we're in that era. Dragerton probably has around 70 show cars, most of them built by myself. I used to bring cars in that were so rusted my dad would ask me if I'd had my tetanus shot. I love these old cars. Sometimes I cut 'em up into a bunch of pieces and put 'em back together until they look good, and sometimes I make sanitary—that means original—look good."

Rod laughed as Ginger came over to take his order, and Bud suspected he'd just met the hep cat who had inspired Howie's latest shenanigans, including possibly becoming Green River's first rockabilly mayor.

Coffee finished, he said goodbye to Rod and decided to take a drive up Whitmore Canyon before heading back to Green River. Maybe he could get a few good photos of the canyon, as well as a shot or two of a bighorn sheep.

As he opened the cafe door, he heard Rod saying to someone in the cafe, "Sure, I can make you a custom car. I lower, shave, nose, deck, and louver 'em, whatever you want. I drop 'em and chop 'em."

Bud grinned and walked out the door.

9

Bud drove slowly up Whitmore Canyon, scanning the steep rocky walls as he went, looking for bighorn sheep. The canyon was famous for bighorns, and he'd been told they weren't afraid of people and were thereby easy to photograph. He'd already taken a photo of the sign at the mouth of the canyon that read, *Caution! Bighorn Sheep Crossing*.

He had Lindie and Freckles with him, both riding in the back seat with their heads hanging out the windows. Lindie usually rode in the front with Bud, but when he'd put Freckles in the back, she'd wanted to ride back there, too. Bud was glad to see that she and Freckles were becoming good buddies, once again wondering what would become of the dog.

The town of Sunnyside set up against a spur of the Bookcliffs called the West Ridge, and Bud had noted how Ginger and Hank's rental house had been built on the cliff's toe, with huge rocks all around and above it, detritus from the cliffs above. Ginger had expressed concern about those rocks coming on down into the house, a concern that Bud felt was well-founded, even though the house had been built a good hundred years ago.

The house was brick, one of the original structures in the town, Bud suspected, and almost the last building before entering the canyon itself, if you didn't count the maintenance building and the old dugout shack that had been the home of an old guy who'd only recently passed on.

Next to the shack were a series of stock tanks, which the old man had kept filled with water for wildlife when he was still alive. Bighorn, deer, and even bears came to the tanks for water, as the creek that flowed through the canyon, Grassy Trail Creek, often became dry towards the end of summer.

Bud now passed the Sunnyside maintenance shop with its old yellow fire engine sitting out front, then passed an old road with a bridge that had been blocked off. He could see the remnants of foundations on the hillside, and he knew he was near the old abandoned Sunnyside Mine, the original reason for the town's existence. He thought of Jimmy Johnson, knowing this was where he'd been killed.

Whitmore Canyon was a quintessential Bookcliffs canyon, etching its way into the West Tavaputs Plateau, and as Bud drove along, the canyon tightened. His map showed a reservoir on up the canyon some five or six miles, so he decided to go have a look.

It was a beautiful fall day, and Bud was beginning to really enjoy himself, stopping every so often to take photos of the golden cottonwoods along the creek with the buff-colored canyon walls and blue sky in the background. The Bookcliffs were vastly different from the canyons of the Big Empty, what he called the area around Green River. Instead of being sheer, the Books stairstepped back with slopes covered with junipers that ended in cliffbands making it impossible to continue upwards, unless you were a bighorn.

After five or six miles, the road narrowed even more, a branch now taking off to the right. Bud knew this was the road up Water Canyon, where an asphalt mine had once struggled, part of its tramway still hanging high above the road even after the mine had gone bankrupt. It was also the road that climbed high to Bruin Point, home to various communication towers, then dropped down into Dry

Canyon to eventually meet up with the famous Nine Mile Canyon, home to Fremont rock art and ruins.

Bud had seen photos of the road up to Bruin Point, and it was steep and narrow, wide enough in places for only one vehicle and not a place one would want to be when it was wet or icy.

He took the left fork and was soon at a pleasant looking small lake, a perfect place to kick back. He suspected he was at Grassy Trail Reservoir, which served as the water source for Sunnyside and the rest of East Carbon.

He pulled over and let the dogs out, who immediately slid down into the lake and paddled around for a bit while he had a cup of thermos coffee and mused at his good fortune at having such a pretty spot all to himself.

He hadn't seen another soul, except for the white pickup parked on the road farther down which had *East Carbon Water Dept.* on the door, though he hadn't seen its driver.

Finally, dogs now wet and tired, he decided to head on back down canyon and look again for bighorn, as he hadn't spotted a single one coming up. Gathering the dogs, he took off and was soon back down to where the road widened, where he noticed something he hadn't seen on the way up—a gate. A closed gate. He was puzzled—it definitely wasn't there on the way up or he was sure he would've noticed.

Bud got out to open the gate and discovered it was not only a closed gate, but it was a closed and *locked* gate. And not just any type of lock, but a very big lock set in a really big cylinder that couldn't be easily monkey wrenched. And there was no way around this locked gate with a 20 foot drop-off on one side and huge rocks on the other. He slipped under the gate and saw the words *No Trespassing* written on the front in big white letters.

He now suspected that the lock was meant to keep people (and dogs) out of the town's water source, and the only reason he hadn't noticed the gate going in was because it had been open, swung against the bushes. The water guy had opened it so he could go take samples from the creek, and not knowing Bud had gone on up to the reservoir, had locked it on his way back out.

Bud sighed. It was hard to describe the feeling of being locked into the wilderness in an area of immense forest and cliffs and those primal things humans guard against with vehicles and food and shelter and all. He had a vehicle that could take him nowhere, one small box of Barkie Biscuits, plenty of water in the car and nearby stream, and a warm sleeping bag, but he needed to get out. Ginger would miss him, but worse, he had no food, yet alone coffee.

He'd explored a lot of country, and he'd been locked out of places, but never locked in. It was a unique feeling. Maybe, if he'd had the supplies he needed, it would be a great experience, camping in a beautiful canyon with nobody else around, having a reservoir all to himself, but right now, he wasn't at all prepared. He checked his cellphone, but there was no signal, which wasn't surprising.

Getting back into the FJ, he sat there, thinking. It was late afternoon, and it appeared he had two choices—he could walk the six or seven miles out, some of it in the dark, then spend the night at Ginger's, contacting the water guy in the morning to come unlock the gate, or he could spend the night in the FJ, then walk out the next day, maybe even hitching a ride back.

As he sat, he thought of Jimmy Johnson's death, then of the strange noises Ginger had claimed to hear, and he felt conflicted. The shadows were lengthening, and he suddenly wanted nothing more than to be back home in Green River, or heck, even at Ginger's. He decided to start walking, but then hesitated, deciding to spend the night in the safety of the FJ.

He vacillated—it was autumn and would get cold. He had his emergency sleeping bag, but the dogs would suffer, even with their fur coats. And his stomach would probably suffer even more.

He got out, grabbed the box of dog biscuits, the dog's leashes, and his flashlight, then put on his jacket, locked the FJ, and crawled under the gate, the dogs climbing over the big rocks. He hoped to get to Ginger's before it was pitch dark, though he knew deep inside there was no way he could walk that fast.

Setting out, he mused on how quickly one's luck can change,

though he knew it wasn't really luck at all, but fit more into the category of just not paying attention. He knew he'd have plenty of time to think, and he hoped that whatever had made the strange noises was long gone.

10

Bud and the dogs had made good time, and he estimated they were only a couple of miles from Sunnyside when it finally became dark enough that he needed his flashlight. He was encouraged by the good progress they were making, the dogs dutifully trotting at his side, no need for their leashes, seeming to enjoy being out.

He'd hoped that maybe someone was coming back down from Bruin Point and would stop and give him a ride, but he'd seen nobody. He knew that the road was a popular drive for locals, and the leaf peepers should be out and about this time of year, enjoying the fall colors.

He'd enjoyed the walk, for it gave him a more up close and personal view of the canyon, and he'd even managed to see a few bighorn high on the walls, though they'd eyed the dogs warily and were soon gone in the rocks. He'd even seen a few deer down by the creek, including one big buck, but it was gone before he could count how many points it had.

But now it was dark, and he began to have an uneasy feeling, glad he had the dogs nearby. He knew their senses were much better than his in the dark, and they would alert him to anything unusual, or at least so he hoped.

He was now having to pay attention to where he walked, shining the light at his feet, as the canyon took on that inky blackness that only a deep desert canyon can have. Stopping for a moment, he turned off the light and let his eyes become accustomed to the dark, hoping he could continue without it, worried about the batteries dying.

He looked upwards to see a section of Milky Way high above, truncated on each end by the canyon walls. The stars glittered like a Porter Wagoner necktie, and though Bud found it otherworldly beautiful, he couldn't kick the unsettled feeling.

He never felt like this out in the Big Empty, and he knew it was a primal fear from having canyon walls on each side, places where a mountain lion or some other creature could easily waylay him. He figured the dogs must feel it, too, for they instinctively stayed close.

It had been easy to gauge distance when there was light, but now, in the dark, he lost all perception of how far he was going. It just felt like an endless procession of footsteps into the blackness with no real forward movement.

Finally, he could see something light-colored on the other side of the road, and he veered over to it, as he suspected he was seeing the white pipe fencing at the grounds for the Grassy Trail Rodeo Club, where Pasture Canyon met Whitmore, which meant he was definitely less than two miles from Sunnyside.

Tired, Bud decided to take a break, crawling through the fence into the rodeo grounds, the small reminder of humankind giving him a comforting feeling, the fence making him feel more secure.

He sat back on his heels, now giving the dogs biscuits, which they wolfed down. Bud was hungry, too, but he knew he'd be back at Ginger's in an hour or less, so he figured he probably wouldn't die.

It was then he again began thinking of Jimmy Johnson and the dino track. Even though he knew it was impossible, a chill went up his back with the thought that a dinosaur might exist, and if it did, it could very well be right here in this canyon right now, watching him.

Maybe he should go spend the night in one of the nearby horse shelters, Bud thought, giving the dogs the rest of the biscuits and folding up the cardboard box and sticking it in his pocket.

Just then, he heard the sound of an engine—someone was coming down the canyon! He could hopefully get a ride into town. He stood, ready to crawl back through the fence and wave them down, when he heard the sound of another engine, this one coming up the canyon. As both vehicles stopped near where he stood, he instinctively put the dogs on their leashes and crouched back down. It appeared to be a rendezvous of some type, and Bud wasn't exactly sure what anyone would be doing out this time of night.

Both engines now off, Bud heard a voice he thought he recognized.

"You brought me out here for this? Are you out of your minds?"

Now, a second voice, one new to Bud, replied, "But these are the best there are, Rod! You can use them on your old cars when you get them all spiffed up."

"I thought you were talking about some old car body you'd found out here when you said you had something I'd want, you lugnuts. Now I know why you wanted to come out after dark. Where did you get these?"

Bud couldn't quite make out the answer, but he could clearly hear Rod reply, "You boys are walkin' a mighty fine line here, thinkin' I won't turn you in. I know where you got these whitewalls—from behind my shop! You stole them, and now you have the gall to try to sell them back to me! You can just put them right here in my pickup, muy pronto before I whack you both on the head."

Bud heard the sound of something being loaded, then Rod said, "Everyone knows you two are stealing things, but I had no idea how truly stupid you are. Now get out of here, and don't ever come into my shop. If I ever see you again, I'm calling the sheriff."

With that, Bud heard a car door slam and an engine start up, which he figured was Rod Ruff's, then peel out into the dark. He knew he definitely didn't want whoever was in the second vehicle to know he was there, and when Lindie decided to growl, he quickly put his hand over her mouth.

"What was that?" The first voice asked.

Now a new voice said, "Sounded like a coyote. Let's get out of here."

Now the second vehicle drove off, going back up the canyon, and Bud strained to make out what it looked like, but it was too dark. He wasn't sure what had just gone down, but he knew he was glad he hadn't been seen. It would be better to walk the last two miles to town.

He slipped back through the fence and again headed down the road, wondering who the pair were. It seemed pretty cheeky to Bud to try to sell something to the same guy you stole them from in the first place.

Now he was surprised to see another vehicle coming up the road. He knew the pair who'd talked to Rod had gone on up the canyon, so he thought maybe it was Rod coming back, and he decided to flag him down.

But instead of Rod, a white SUV with the words *Carbon County Sheriff* on the side stopped.

"Where's your vehicle, Bud?" A voice asked, and Bud immediately knew he was talking to Deputy Sam Wiggins.

Sam continued. "Your aunt said you told her you were going up the canyon for a drive, and she called me when you were so late. Put the dogs in the back and hop in. Nice seeing you again."

11

Bud loaded the dogs into the back of Sam's vehicle, then got in front somewhat reluctantly, though he was careful to not show it. He was appreciative of the ride, but he wasn't sure it would be worth the price, as he knew Sam would now try to involve him in the Jimmy Johnson case.

Bud knew Sam was good at offloading his responsibilities onto whoever was nearby, and Bud would've preferred to walk those last two miles to town over getting on Sam's helper list. He generally enjoyed helping people out, but he knew Sam would probably try to defer the entire case to him while he found more amenable things to do, like skeet shooting out in the desert.

"What happened to your FJ?" Sam now asked.

"It got itself in a little trouble up at the gate to the reservoir," Bud replied.

"Trouble? What kind of trouble?"

"It got locked in," Bud said. "We need to go get the key from the water guy."

"He's probably in bed," Sam replied. "We'll have to get it tomorrow. But how did your FJ get itself locked in? Weren't you there with it?"

"I was, but I myself wasn't locked in," Bud replied.

"What, you drove up when the gate was open, and when you came back, it was locked? Don't you know that's off limits up there? Were you fishing?"

"No, and I didn't know it was off limits," Bud replied defensively.

Sam said, "It's clearly marked *No Trespassing*. Maybe you were tired or something and didn't see it—or looking for bighorns. Have you had anything to eat?"

"You can't see it when the gate's swung back. Maybe a separate sign would work better. But thanks for the ride, Sam. I had these for dinner, so I'm OK." He pulled the crumpled-up box of Barkie Biscuits from his pocket.

Sam looked skeptical. "You ate dog biscuits for dinner?"

"If you look at the ingredients, they're more nutritious than a lot of people food," Bud said. "Kind of tasty, too, if you pretend you're a dog."

Sam interrupted. "There's somebody else out here walking down the road. Must be the thing to do."

He slowed as they came upon a man carrying what looked like a boombox, slowly walking alongside the road. As they got closer, their headlights revealed he was wearing some kind of large headphones that covered his ears.

His arm hanging half out the window, Sam asked, "Everything OK? You need a ride?"

Bud could now make out the man's face in the headlights. He seemed to have an intelligent look about him.

"I'm fine. Thanks for asking, though." The man smiled, then waved them on by.

As they sped back up, Sam said, "I've seen him out here a bunch lately. Not sure what he's up to. Maybe just a walker, out getting some exercise."

"Someone should tell him about MP3 players," Bud replied. "Lots lighter than carrying a boombox."

"I hate to tell you, Bud, but MP3 players are pretty old school. People use iPods these days."

"Even better," Bud replied. "But I take it you pretty much cover this end of the county, is that right?" Bud was now hoping to keep Sam distracted until they got back to Ginger's so he wouldn't ask about Jimmy Johnson. "But don't you live in Price? You have to run out here every time anything happens?"

"It gets old, Bud," Sam replied. "Especially when I need to help my wife at Wiggins Diggins. But I told the sheriff I'd cover out here since I know everybody."

"And since there's hardly ever anything going on," Bud thought silently to himself.

Sam continued. "But man, Bud, you should come by the store sometime. We're getting a lot of nice stuff lately, things you might like."

"What kind of stuff?"

"Well, for example, we got an entire jar full of old marbles the other day. I mean old ones from the '50s, the kind made of glass, not plastic. Cat's eyes, mostly. Some marbles are worth thousands of dollars, Bud."

"You're kidding me. Marbles worth that much?"

"Yeah, though I've never seen one. But some cat's eyes are worth a lot."

"Those are the ones with the streaks, right?" Bud asked, still trying to divert Sam.

"Right. They took clear marbles and injected streaks of colors into their centers. While some cat's eyes are rare, most were mass-produced."

Bud asked, "What other kinds of stuff are you selling these days, Sam? Any Halloween masks?"

Sam replied, "No, that's a seasonal thing, though we did have some come in as part of a lot from an estate."

"Halloween masks as part of an estate?"

"Yeah, lots of junk with that one. Surprisingly, they sold right away."

"Who wants masks this time of year?"

Sam replied, "Well, I don't know. Halloween's not that far off, really. Just a guy who said he was going to have a party down on the river."

"Which river? Price doesn't really have much of a beach, does it?"

"I don't know," Sam said. "What was really odd was when a woman came in and bought a bunch of plastic life-sized skulls. But back to the marbles. Playing marbles was a big thing from about the 1920s into the '40s and '50s. There was a popular style called a corkscrew, which had different colors of glass spiraling on top of another color. One even featured the colors of Superman's suit. Bet you can't guess what it was called."

Bud saw they were now nearing Ginger and Hank's house. He answered, "The Superman?"

"Good guess," Sam replied, pulling over by the gate. "Man, I wouldn't want to live in this house. One of those big rocks is gonna roll right through it one of these days. All it would take is one small tremor."

Bud got out, and letting the dogs into the yard, asked, "Does Sunnyside get earthquakes, Sam? Thanks for the ride. I'll call the city tomorrow and get the key. My Uncle Hank can take me up there. Looks like he's back."

Bud felt like he'd dodged a bullet with the Jimmy Johnson thing and was eager to go inside.

Sam replied, "This area does get earthquakes once in a blue moon, though they're small ones. They think they're linked to the coal mining. But since most of the mines are shut down, that should end."

Bud was now almost in the front door when Sam yelled, "Hey, Bud, let me pick you up in the morning. I'll get the key and take you up there. I'd like for you to help me check out where Jimmy Johnson died. I'll come by at eight. We can have breakfast at your aunt's new cafe."

Bud groaned, nodded his head in agreement, then went inside, dogs at his heels.

12

Bud wanted to turn over, but he knew if he did, he'd fall into the immense canyon on one side of him or into the open maw of the deep ravine on the other. He was perched high above both on a narrow ridge that was barely wide enough for his cot, though he had no idea how he'd gotten there.

And now, he was cold. He wanted badly to pull the covers up over his head, but he knew he was somehow inextricably wound up in them, and unwinding also meant he would fall off into the abyss. He knew he was in a precarious situation, and he had no idea how to get out of it.

And to make things worse, he could hear something strange coming up the ridge, and it sounded big from the way it was breathing in and out, in and out. Since it was dark, he couldn't see it, but he somehow knew it had three toes on each of its huge feet, feet that could easily crush him.

He thought of trying to hide under the cot, but the ridge was too narrow, and he knew he'd fall into the empty blackness below. The creature now let out a shrill call, like some kind of giant bird, and Bud knew it was looking for him.

Before he could even try to duck, it was on him, its giant three-toed foot coming down hard, crushing him into the cot until everything collapsed and he went hurtling into the inky black space below.

He woke with a start, still wrapped in blankets, Lindie on top of him and the collapsed cot beneath. He could see Freckles standing nearby, on alert, wondering what was going on.

Bud managed to get Lindie off, then unwound himself from the blankets and got up, turning on the small battery-powered lantern his aunt had put on a nearby chair.

Since Junior and LuAnn had come back from their supply trip, Ginger and Hank's spare room was taken, so Bud had ended up sleeping on an old army cot in the screened-in porch, the dogs on blankets Ginger had folded up into dog beds.

He'd wondered if the cot would hold him, but even though his arms hung over the edge if he tried to sleep on his back, he'd managed to make do on his side until Lindie, who'd probably gotten cold, had decided to sleep with him, jumping up on top and making everything collapse.

Bud had badly wanted to just go home after Sam had dropped him off, but with his FJ indisposed behind a locked gate, he was stuck in Sunnyside for the night, or even longer if Sam couldn't get the key. He'd tried calling the town's number, but everything was closed, and he knew he'd just have to wait for Sam Wiggins to come and get him the next morning.

The night had started out comfortable enough, but at a little over 6,000 feet in altitude, Sunnyside was a good 2,000 feet higher than Green River, and it had eventually cooled off enough that he wished for his warm sleeping bag—the one in the FJ.

He now righted the cot, then tried sleeping on the settee Ginger had on the porch, but it was too short and he couldn't get comfortable. He finally ended up taking the cushions off and putting them on the floor, but they kept scooting apart when he'd lie down, leaving a gap in the middle.

Finally looking at his watch, he saw it was four a.m., and figuring he'd gotten at least a few hours of sleep and wouldn't be getting any more, he slipped into the kitchen to try to round up a cup of coffee.

Not wanting to turn on the light and wake anyone, he held the little lantern up to the kitchen cupboards until he found a small saucepan and a glass container with what looked to be coffee. Turning on a burner, he set the pan on the flames and poured enough water into it for a couple of cups, then let it come to a boil. He then poured several tablespoons of the black stuff in and let it boil for awhile, then turned off the burner just before it boiled over.

Brewing cowboy coffee was a fine art—one had to know just how long to let it boil, though there were some old-timers who said you shouldn't let it boil at all, but just bubble a little, and others who said you couldn't boil it long enough. And if you failed to get it off the fire at just the right time, you'd have a big mess on your hands of coffee grounds all over.

Pouring the dark brew into a cup, Bud looked for some cream in the fridge, but finding none, resigned himself to drinking it black and went back onto the porch where the dogs waited. He sat on the settee and wrapped himself in the blankets Ginger had given him, Lindie and Freckles next to him under another blanket.

As he sipped the strong brew, he contemplated this new turn of events. Not only was he suffering in the sleep department, but he was now forced to drink his coffee black, a state that signaled about the lowest one could fall in his book, though he guessed no coffee at all was much worse.

He'd once read an article that said only psychopaths, tortured artists, and English majors drank their coffee black, which had confirmed his belief that coffee had been somehow genetically engineered to taste good only with cream, or better yet, with a dollop of vanilla-bean ice cream. He thought of Wilma Jean's cafe back home and how she'd added the Shumway Latte to the menu, which was coffee with a dollop of ice cream.

So far, it had been a big hit, and Wilma Jean had even gotten a fan letter from some mysterious person signed simply W.E.B. who'd been traveling through and said they'd enjoyed it. Maybe he should mention it to his Aunt Ginger, he mused, noting that, now that it had cooled enough to drink, the coffee had a somewhat odd taste.

Finishing it, he noted the coffee grounds looked more like tea leaves and the coffee tasted a bit nutty, but too tired to think about it, he decided to again try the cot. He pulled it over next to the settee, hoping that Lindie would be happy sleeping next to him instead of on top of him.

Even though it had an odd taste, Bud had to admit that Ginger's coffee packed a wallop in the caffeine department, for he was unable to get back to sleep, even though he was still tired. He lay there, listening to the night sounds, the screens on the porch the only things keeping him from technically being outside.

He was surprised at how noisy it was. He could hear the tiny pings of bat radar skipping off things, as well as the occasional burbles of Grassy Trail Creek, even though it was across the highway and running low.

And, of course, the constant hum of the coal generation power plant not far away provided a background sound that changed intensity when the breeze changed, bringing the sound closer or farther away. And he sometimes heard the footsteps and snorts of the many mule deer who made the yards and fields of the area their home.

But now he heard something different. It started low, then, like a siren, gradually changed pitch, rising to a crescendo, then went back to low again. Bud sat up, turning on the lantern, and he could see the dogs were agitated. The sound had lasted an incredible length of time—maybe a good 20 or 30 seconds, and he knew of no animal with that kind of lung capacity.

Still wrapped in blankets against the night's chill, he got up and leaned back on the settee, mystified. He could see shadows forming in the nearby canyon walls and the trees along the watercourse as dawn moved in.

He shivered, thinking about going inside, but didn't want to wake anyone. He now heard a new sound, a distant *thwock*. It had a bony sound to it, and he could picture two dinosaurs fighting, heads slamming against one another. And then again, another *thwock*.

He listened, but soon the sounds of car engines starting and dogs barking in the distance told him the little town of Sunnyside was waking, and it would soon be time to go meet Sam at the Sunnyside Cafe.

But somehow, he knew he'd heard Ginger's dinosaur or whatever it could be.

13

"I've heard of being locked *out* of the wilderness, but not locked *into* it."

Sam Wiggins balanced precariously on one of the tall chairs in the Sunnyside Cafe across from Bud, who was appreciative to be drinking what he considered real coffee.

"Next time I'll go prepared and stay awhile and enjoy it," Bud countered. "Maybe never come back out."

"Well," Sam replied, "You're lucky I have the key so you *can* come back out. It took awhile to chase down the water treatment guy, and he wasn't real happy to hear someone had been in there."

"His FJ is *still* in there, breaking the law," said Junior, who sat at the table next to theirs along with Bud's Uncle Hank.

"How's your nephew?" Bud asked Hank.

"Well, he's still in the hospital, but I think he'll be out soon, even if he has to walk out," Hank replied.

"Can he walk with a broken leg?" Bud asked.

"He'll be walking out if they don't stop bugging him. I mean, they're really nice people, but they keep waking him up in the middle of the night to make sure he hasn't died in his sleep."

Now Junior said, "Buddy, remember this?" He handed Bud a photo of his rusted-out old Ford F-100 pickup, a truck Bud had fond memories of, as Junior had bought it new in 1953, and Bud had ridden in it many times.

"Of course I do," Bud replied. "What color was it when you bought it?"

"A beautiful powder blue," Junior replied. "And man, that was the year. Can you believe it's still running?"

"Hard to believe," Sam said, studying the photo. "It's sure rusted out. Where do you have it stored, Florida?"

Junior snatched the photo back, saying, "I believe in letting old vehicles rust in peace, young man."

Sam, not sure whether to be offended at having the photo snatched from him or pleased at being called a young man, replied, "Well, better keep it away from Rod Ruff, or it'll be rusting in a million pieces."

Now Ginger was there, taking their order.

"I'll have two eggs sunnyside up," Sam said. "With a glass of orange juice and whole-wheat toast."

Ginger smiled. "Good call. This *is* the Sunnyside Cafe, after all."

Bud said, "Can I get some biscuits and gravy? And a refill?" He held up his coffee cup.

"I didn't know you were a maté drinker, Buddy," Ginger said, filling his cup.

"A what?" Bud asked.

"You got into the maté last night. I drink it for my arthritis."

"What's maté?" Sam asked.

Ginger replied, "It's a drink from South America, kind of a tea-coffee kind of thing, from the yerba maté plant. Has a nutty taste and tons of caffeine."

"Every fine bistro serves it," Bud said knowingly.

"You're right!" Ginger replied enthusiastically. "I need to put it on the menu."

"Along with a Shumway Latte," Bud replied. "Wilma Jean can tell you how to make it, though it's just coffee and ice cream."

"You pour coffee over a dish of ice cream?" Ginger asked. "Doesn't it melt?"

"I'll have to try it that way," Bud replied. "Though usually you put a dollop of ice cream in the coffee."

"I can put all kinds of specialty espresso drinks on the menu. Great idea, Bud!"

Ginger walked away, taking their order to the kitchen, where Bud assumed LuAnn was cooking.

Just then, Rod Ruff walked in the door, and seeing Bud and Sam, nodded hello, then, noting the photo Junior was holding, looked at it for a moment and said, "I'll be darned. Is that a '53 F-100? That old beauty's quite a barn find. Is it yours?"

Junior replied, "It is, but it's not all that old, not really. I mean, I bought it when I was 22, and I'm still young enough, as long as you don't ask young enough for what."

"Mind if I join you?" Rod asked.

"Go ahead," Junior said. "But let's keep the word *old* out of the conversation."

Bud grinned, knowing Junior had no idea who Rod was or what he was getting himself into. Actually, Bud thought, one could say the same about Rod not knowing what *he* was getting into with Junior.

"Done," Rod replied. "We'll use the word *classic*. Is that thing original?"

"Yup, just like me," Junior said proudly. "A classic."

"I'd love to do a frame-up restoration on that beauty," Rod said.

"Speak English," Junior demanded.

"That's when you restore the paint, chrome, interior, and mechanicals to the original specs. You can only do it with one like this, that's all original, otherwise you end up doing a frame-off, which is where you take the darn thing apart and completely restore everything. You can still drive it?"

"I can, though it's currently not in my possession."

"Did you hock it or something?" Rod asked.

"Are you out of your mind?" Junior replied. "No, it's just a few hundred miles away, that's all, over in Paradox, Colorado."

"But you *do* own it?" Rod asked.

"I do. Paid cash for it back in '53."

"What color was it?"

"Powder blue."

Ginger now brought their breakfast, and Bud lost track of the conversation, hungry, not having had any dinner the night before. Sam seemed also to focus on eating, and after a couple of cups of coffee, he said, "Well, Bud, you ready to go get your FJ?"

"I'm about as ready as one can be," Bud replied. "I can't go home without it."

Sam, now looking worried, said, "You said you'd help me check out where Jimmy Johnson died. Don't forget."

"I haven't forgotten, Sam. But didn't anyone else check it out when he was found?"

"Well, I called Sheriff Davis and he came out and looked over everything with me. He agrees that it was weird. We got the medical examiner out of Salt Lake involved and he did an autopsy and said Jimmy died from being crushed. But there was nothing around that could've crushed him, and you'd think it would've still been there on his back. Like I said, weird."

"Are you thinking I'll find something you guys didn't?" Bud asked. "Where's his lift truck now?"

"It's parked over at his house. He doesn't have any family, no will, so it's going through probate and everything will probably become the state's. Not that he had much."

"What about his dog?"

"I dunno, Bud. I guess Hank's going to find him a home. He said they can't keep him. I'm not sure why."

Bud thought of how Freckles and Lindie had taken to each other. He wouldn't mind taking the dog, but having four might be a bit much, and Wilma Jean probably wouldn't go for it, as kind-hearted as she was, as there wouldn't be any place in the car for her to ride.

Bud stood, anxious to get his FJ before anything else came up, leaving the money for their breakfasts on the table for Ginger.

He said, "Let's go open that gate, then I'll follow you over to the mine where Jimmy was killed. But I need to get home, Sam, back to my own job. I had yesterday off, but now my deputy's covering things until I get back, and it's supposed to be *his* day off."

As they walked outside, Sam asked, "Is that Deputy Howie McPherson? I hear he's running for mayor. Are you going to have an opening then?"

Bud groaned silently. Sam Wiggins was the last person he'd want working for him, primarily because he wouldn't be working.

"You thinking of moving to Green River?" Bud asked.

"I don't know, Bud. What I'd really like is to just retire, but we couldn't make it without my income. But one of these days maybe someone would want to buy the store. I wouldn't mind retiring in Green River. It's a nice town."

"That it is," Bud agreed. "And I need to get back down there. Let's go."

14

Bud followed Sam down Whitmore Canyon, happy to again have his FJ. They would stop where Jimmy Johnson's body had been found, look around, then he would head back home to Green River, hopefully getting in before lunch so Howie could have at least part of the day off.

Bud was pretty sure there was nothing he could do to help Sam solve the case, partly because of the elapsed time since Jimmy's death, and partly because he still couldn't get his head around the fact that he'd been crushed by something with three toes—*big* toes—and Bud knew it was impossible for it to have been a dinosaur. He thought of the sound he'd heard the previous night and knew it had to have a logical explanation, strange as it was.

Nearing the mouth of the canyon, Sam stopped at a locked gate and opened it, and Bud followed him across an old bridge that crossed Grassy Trail Creek. They stopped at an open area with old concrete foundations.

As they got out, Sam said, "You won't see the mine anymore, as it's been reclaimed. It was bored back into the cliffs over there. Actually, there were two mines, Sunnyside #1 and Sunnyside #2. They have a long history, but eventually Kaiser Steel bought them for coke production to run their steel mill in California. This area had the best coke-producing coal of anywhere in the United States. Have you been over to the coke ovens?"

Bud nodded his head no. He enjoyed learning about the history of a place, but right then, he was anxious to get going. He followed Sam across an open area as Sam continued talking. "There's about 400 coke ovens left, over on the road to Columbia. You really should go see them, as they're quite the sight, stretching clear across the countryside. There were originally over 800."

"Sounds like quite the deal," Bud commented. "A good place to store stuff. But where did you find Jimmy?"

Sam pointed to a small pile of what looked to be broken-up chunks of coal. "His truck was parked right there, by that pile, and he was right next to it."

Bud walked over to the pile, which was mostly small chunks of coal, though there were a few slabs. He looked around, but found nothing unusual.

"What do you think he was doing out here?" Bud asked. "He must've had a key to get in here. Where would he have gotten it?"

"The town keeps the key, except I had one made so I could investigate more. But the lock was sawed off. Jimmy broke himself in here, or so it looks like to me. Kind of the opposite of what you did up the road."

Bud was now walking around the grassy area, not sure what he was looking for, but trying to be thorough.

"Me and Sheriff Davis already searched everywhere," Sam said. "But Jimmy wasn't the only person to die here."

Bud, surprised, asked, "There was someone else?"

"Yeah, in 1945, 23 coal miners died here, though they were down in the mine. An electrical spark ignited methane gas down underground and blew everything to kingdom come. It was a real tragedy. Two of the guys are still buried, as they never found them."

Bud replied, "What a shame. Seems like Carbon County's had its share of coal mining disasters." He again asked, "But what do you think Jimmy was doing up here? Was his lift truck his only vehicle, or do you think he brought it up here to retrieve something?"

Bud now thought of the two fellows he'd overheard talking to Rod Ruff. Had Jimmy been in on some kind of illegal activity with them?

Sam said, "That lift truck was his only vehicle. He was retired from the power plant and, as far as I know, just liked to go around looking at stuff. He has quite a collection of old junk at his house. But his truck did have some coal in the back, though there wasn't much room to haul anything with that lift on it."

"Did he load 16 tons?" Bud joked, then asked, "So you think he was maybe after some coal? Did he have a coal-burning furnace?"

Sam replied, "Everybody around here has a coal-burning furnace. It's possible, though there's not enough coal here to merit breaking in and ruining the lock. There's plenty of other places he could get coal without risking a trespassing charge."

Bud now sat on a large chunk of coal, taking the aluminum arrow from his pocket and fiddling with it, thinking. After awhile, he said, "I'm afraid I don't have anything to add to your investigation, Sam. I wish I could help, but I really do need to get going."

As he stood, the slab of coal tipped back and forth, then settled back onto the ground.

"It seems like there's something under here," Bud said, going to the FJ and retrieving his flashlight. He then got down on his stomach and shone the light under the slab, trying to see what it was balanced on.

"Probably just a rock acting like a fulcrum," Sam offered. "That slab probably weighs a couple of hundred pounds or more. Too heavy for us to lift."

Bud stood back up. "Looks like a bump of coal underneath, like it wasn't cut smooth. But I need to get going, Sam."

Sam, looking disappointed, said, "Well, it's sure a mystery. What's really odd is that if Jimmy was killed by a dinosaur or something big like that, you'd think we'd find more tracks, but there's not a thing. I hiked a good half-mile all around, looking. Nothing."

Bud was surprised. Maybe Sam wasn't as much of a slacker as he'd thought.

"Sam, it's impossible for there to be a dinosaur out here. First of all, enough people come out here and go up on Bruin Point that something that big would've been seen by someone. And second, it's impossible for a dinosaur species to have lived for millions of years and not be noticed by humans."

"Humans haven't been around for millions of years," Sam replied somewhat petulantly. "And there's lots of places dinosaurs could hide around here. The Books and Tavaputs have some really rugged canyons that nobody ever goes into. And what if it's a pterodactyl? It wouldn't leave any tracks if it could fly."

Bud asked, "Do pterodactyls have three toes?"

"Beats me. They could have."

As Bud walked to his FJ, he said, "Sam, I'm not discounting anything, but if you see something that looks like a dinosaur around, let me know and I'll come back up. But for now, Jimmy's death is going to have to remain a mystery."

"Thanks, Bud," Sam replied. "I appreciate your help, but Jimmy Johnson was killed by a dinosaur. I know it in my gut."

Bud nodded goodbye and headed for Ginger's, where he would pick up Lindie and go on home, all the while thinking of the *thwock* noises he'd heard early that morning and wondering if somehow Sam could be right, as crazy as it sounded.

15

Bud left Freckles and Lindie in the yard at the Green River bungalow, along with Pierre and Hoppie, who were strutting around and sniffing the poor Australian shepherd like they were twice his size, when the opposite was true.

Bud had brought the dog along at the request of his aunt, who'd said his uncle was doing nothing to find the dog a home and that she was worried they'd end up with it. When Bud had asked her why that would be a bad thing, she'd said something about how he was able to open gates, then handed Freckles' leash to Bud and added a comment about free food at the cafe for the rest of his life, which Bud couldn't take lightly.

He knew he'd stand a better chance of finding the dog a good home in Green River, for he knew everyone and could easily put the word out, though he was quickly becoming fond of him.

Pulling out of the drive, he could see Lindie and Freckles playing stick while the two boys ran around in circles, and he knew they'd be busy while he was gone. It was kind of nice to see Lindie with a companion more her peer.

Bud was soon at the office, where he found Howie waiting, out of uniform and instead wearing blue jeans turned up at the cuffs with his hair still up in a pompadour. He wore a t-shirt with bowling pins on it that read, *This is My Spare Shirt, Tumbleweed Lanes, Green River, Utah.*

"Howdy, Big Daddy," Howie grinned.

"Are you still doing that hep cat thing?" Bud asked.

"It's part of my new gestalt, Sheriff—confidence with style. It's more than just playing for the car show coming to town. I've discovered a new way of being—I'm a cool, carefree cat with no worries. Well, except for one thing, that is."

"What would that be, Deputy?"

"I want to order some kind of gel for my wave, something that will hold it in place a bit better. I've heard you can get stuff with glitter in it, but I can't find any."

"I thought it was called a pompadour," Bud said.

Howie replied, "I don't know for sure, but I think the wave is the pompadour part that kind of looks like surf, well if you do it right, anyway. Or maybe it's called a quiff. You know we don't have much culture in this little town, Bud. It's hard to know what's what."

"Culture's kind of a subjective term, Howie, and I'd think wave would describe it better. But we don't have any dress codes, either," Bud said, sounding serious. "At least not in writing."

Howie, now chagrined, asked, "Sheriff, if LEOs can have beards, why not me have a wave? It's kind of the same, just on opposite parts of the head. You know me, I've always been kind of the strong silent type, and now I'm ready to cut loose a little. I was thinking about bleaching it blonde, but Maureen says that's a big no can do. I think this rockabilly show is going to be great."

"I don't have a problem with it, Howie. You can have both a beard and a pompadour if you want, as long as you do your job. I was just pulling your chain." Bud grinned. "Your hair kind of reminds me of a dinosaur's crest. But did you ever meet with Wilma Jean? Do you think Green River wants a rockabilly mayor?"

Howie sighed. "I don't know, Sheriff. This town can be pretty conservative. A lot of people here live in the past."

"Well, think about it, Howie. Rockabilly *is* conservative—it's from *way* in the past. I mean, the '50s were awhile ago. That could be your election slogan—take Green River back to the good old days, or something like that."

Howie grinned, gingerly patting his pompadour. "Bud, you're a genius! I'm meeting with Wilma Jean in about 20 minutes, and I think you're on to something."

Howie opened the door to leave, then added, "Oh, by the way, a box came for you. It's in the corner. Express delivery from UPS, insured and registered. I signed for you. Ed knows I'm not you, but he said it was OK, seeing how I'm a deputy and all. Later, gator."

Bud grinned as Howie walked out the door, then went and picked up the box, setting it on his desk. It wasn't that big, yet was relatively heavy for its size. He looked at the return label:

Pixel Magic Camera Rentals
50 N. West Temple
Salt Lake City, UT 84150

As it gradually dawned on him as to what might be in the box, Bud felt a combination of dread and excitement. He loved camera gear and was anxious to see what he was getting, yet he felt totally inadequate to pose as a NatGeo photographer.

Carefully opening the lid, he could see nothing but bubble wrap. Whoever had packed it had done a good job, he thought, or maybe they'd forgotten to put the camera gear inside. Half-hoping for the latter, he slowly pulled out a box that had the word *Nikon* on the top, then two more boxes, each with the word *Nikkor,* which Bud recognized as Nikon's name for its lenses.

Opening the boxes, he first found what looked to be a very expensive Nikon DSLR camera, then wide-angle and telephoto lenses. Bud had once wanted to buy Nikon gear, but, realizing it was out of his price range, opted instead for Canon.

While doing his research on cameras, he'd discovered that Nikkor was from the early version of the company's name, which was originally Nikko, and means *sunlight* in Japanese. He thought of how

Canon's cameras all used the name *EOS*, which was the Greek goddess of dawn.

He was now both excited and disappointed. He was a Canon guy, and it would take some doing to untrain his fingers from Canon's placement of its buttons and retrain them to Nikon's. He'd never used Nikon gear, and he was now even more uncertain about his ability to pose as a knowledgeable photographer.

He turned the camera on, and noting the battery was fully charged, mounted the wide-angle lens onto the body. There was nothing else to do but go try it out, he decided. He'd forward the 911 line to the State Patrol's office, and if anyone asked, he was at work, for it was imperative that he learn how to use this new gear before going on what he was now thinking of as a spy mission up Range Creek.

He'd head down to Crystal Geyser, down by the river. If he was lucky, he'd catch it erupting and maybe get some good photos, and if not, well, he was sure he'd find something or other to practice on.

Later, in retrospect, he wondered how he'd managed to time everything so perfectly as to capture exactly what he did, though it was probably blind luck and had nothing to do with either sunlight or the goddess of dawn.

16

Bud sat near Crystal Geyser, one of the world's few cold-water carbon dioxide geysers, the result of a failed attempt to drill for oil back around 1935. Instead of oil, the driller had found carbon dioxide, which created pressure that forced the groundwater to the surface. The geyser once shot up a good hundred-plus feet into the air, but was now much smaller due to people throwing rocks into it to try to make it erupt.

The geyser was next to the Green River some five or so miles downstream from the town itself, and thick tamarisk grew along the shore. And now, with autumn at hand, Bud noted that the tiny leaves of the tammies were turning a pale yellow, nothing at all like the intense colors of the aspen and scrub oak in the high country.

He'd gotten what looked to be some good photos of the red and yellow travertine surrounding the geyser, and even though it still felt foreign to him, Bud felt he was gradually getting the feel for the new Nikon. It was heavier than his Canon, but he knew it had many more features just from the number of knobs and buttons on the body, though he had no idea what most of them were for.

As the sun began its journey to far-away places, its obtuse light began turning everything a blazing gold, the tammies now reflecting in the deep blue waters of the river. Bud thought it would make an interesting composition to capture the gold against the deep ruby of the travertine, and if he crawled down into the shrubs, stickers and all, and wiggled himself into just the right angle, he could even get a stretch of river in the shot, making for a contrast in colors.

Contentedly taking photo after photo, he was eventually surprised to hear voices. He'd been the only one at the geyser, and he knew he would hear if a vehicle came in, but there had been no such sound.

It had to be someone on the river, he thought, pulling the tammies aside enough to see better. Sure enough, a yellow raft was slowly floating down the river, its boatman turning it towards the geyser, which had a rustic boat launch just past it.

Bud had parked his FJ up the road past the geyser a ways near the little mudpots that bubbled before each eruption. He couldn't really make out the people in the raft, but he could see that there were two, both looking like the typical river rats that hung around the river.

Seeing the raft was coming straight for where he stood in the tammies, Bud stepped back. He wondered why they weren't heading for the takeout. The last thing he wanted to do was get run over by a raft.

Now the raft bumped up against the river bank just below him, and he could hear one of the guys say, "Why are we stopping here?"

A second voice said, "There's someone here. There's a vehicle over there."

The first voice said, "What should we do?"

The second voice replied, "We should probably wait them out. They'll leave before long, as the geyser's not going to erupt. It's not even bubbling. They'll get tired of waiting."

"Dang it, I'm hungry," moaned the first voice. "I just want to get this done and get out of here. Let's just unload anyway. They won't see anything."

Bud now crouched even lower. Whatever the pair was up to, it didn't sound good. He thought he recognized the voices as being the same he'd heard while hiding in the corral in Whitmore Canyon the night he'd walked out.

He reached into his jacket and touched his Ruger in its shoulder harness, then pulled the aluminum arrow from his shirt pocket and began fiddling with it.

"Dang it, Trevor, I don't like this at all. I think I know that FJ sitting over there. It's Sheriff Shumway's."

"What would he be doing out here, Cory? There's nothing going on. He should be back in town where there's crime and stuff happening."

Cory replied sarcastically, "You think so, Trevor? Why don't you tell him that? Go ahead, just stand up and yell for him to go where the crooks are. Nothing to see here. Idiot."

Bud could hear the raft bumping up against the river bank and wondered when they'd go on down to the boat ramp. His knees were starting to lock up from crouching, and it was now getting dark. He tried to recall knowing anyone named Cory and Trevor, but couldn't.

He then realized he hadn't seen a vehicle when he'd arrived. Was someone coming to pick them and the raft up? He was getting more and more nervous, wanting to get out of there, yet he knew he needed to stick around and figure out what the pair was up to. But if there were more coming, he'd be seriously outgunned if they discovered him.

He then remembered he was holding a camera. He could take photos of everything and then sneak away, but he would have to hurry, as the light was quickly fading. He fiddled with the camera settings, wanting to change the ISO to better shoot in low light, but he wasn't sure how. Finally, he carefully pulled the tammies aside enough to clear the camera lens and took a photo.

"What was that, Cory?"

"It sounded like a camera going off."

Bud groaned to himself. He hadn't set the camera to silent mode, one he frequently used on his Canon to not scare wildlife. He now crouched even lower, holding his breath.

"It was probably just a bug of some kind, like a cricket," Trevor said. "Let's go on down and unload. Lucy will be here soon. It's gonna be too dark to see anything if we wait any longer."

"Look, Trevor, I'm willing to sit here all night until Shumway leaves. That guy's got a reputation."

"Granted, Cory," Trevor was now pleading. "But it's getting dark, man. We'll end up floating on down to Cataract Rapids and die."

"Where's the flashlight?"

There was now complete silence, and Bud could see the back part of the raft floating on by. He quickly held up the camera and took another shot, but it was so dark he was sure he didn't get anything.

When he could hear the men's voices in the distance, he slipped out of the tammies, ran across the travertine to where his FJ waited, then got inside, key in hand, just as the headlights from a vehicle pulled in on the downriver side of the geyser where the boat ramp was.

Bud was conflicted. He had no idea what was going on, yet he knew it was probably something illegal. He also had no idea if the pair and this Lucy person were armed or not. If so, he would be putting his life in danger if he confronted them, and there wasn't much he could do without a search warrant anyway.

He waited in the FJ, listening as a woman's voice joined the conversation, though unable to make out what anyone was saying. He finally saw something drifting on down the river, and pulling out his camera, he zoomed in enough to see it was the yellow raft, but didn't appear to have anyone in it, which he found odd.

Finally deciding going home was the better part of valor, he started the FJ and drove over to the boat ramp, shone his lights on a black SUV, wrote down the license plate number, then backed around and took off into the blackness of the desert, heading home, his taillights fading into the night.

17

Bud was just about at the truck stop on the edge of town when his cellphone rang. He could see from the caller ID it was his wife.

"Yell-ow," he answered.

"Bud, where are you?" Wilma Jean asked, and he could immediately tell from the tone of her voice that something was wrong. He thought he could hear faint howling in the background.

"I'm just getting into town," he replied. "What's wrong?"

"We have a little problem here at the cafe. Can you swing by?"

"Sure. What's going on?"

"Just come by, and hurry."

Bud had no idea what was happening, but he knew it somehow involved him, and not necessarily in a good way.

As he pulled up in front, he could see several dogs tied, all wagging their tails upon seeing him. As he got out, he could see it was Hoppie, Pierre, and Lindie. Had Wilma Jean brought them to work for some reason? And where was Freckles?

Bud untied the dogs and put them in the FJ, then went inside, where Wilma Jean was behind the counter, serving someone a milkshake. Seeing Bud, she came over and said in a quiet yet tense voice, "The dogs actually came into the cafe. I thought you were out walking them or something, then I realized they were on their own. I tied them outside, and they've been howling so much a couple of customers threatened to call the sheriff."

Bud replied, "They should have. He would've been right on it. But why not put them in your car?"

"Maureen took it to get some stuff for me at the Melon Harvest. Did they get out of the FJ or something?"

"I left them in the yard. They somehow escaped. That's quite a walk into town, and I'm glad they didn't get lost. It shows how much they love you," Bud said, recalling his aunt saying Freckles knew how to open gates. "But where's Freckles?"

"Who's Freckles?" Wilma Jean asked, eyeing him suspiciously.

"He's the ring leader. You know, the instigator, mastermind, troublemaker. He belongs to a guy who died up in Sunnyside. My aunt and uncle were supposed to find him a home and instead sent him home with me."

"And you're adopting him without even asking me?" Wilma Jean now seemed even more perturbed.

"No, because you can't adopt a dog when he's lost," Bud replied.

He now put his arm around her waist and said, "I told Aunt Ginger I'd find him a good home down here. Any idea where he went?"

"He pushed the cafe door open and they all came in, then he grabbed part of a hamburger someone left on their plate and took off out the door when another customer went out. He's smart, that's for sure. If he comes back here, I'm going to have him arrested," Wilma Jean added as Bud walked out the door.

It was now dark, and Bud wanted to go home and see if he'd gotten any good photos on his new camera, especially of the travertine glowing in the sunset, but he knew he needed to find Freckles.

He felt bad, for he was sure Freckles wouldn't have any idea how to get back to the bungalow, and he knew he didn't even have a collar, yet alone tags. He started driving up and down the streets of Green River, looking, even though he knew the odds of finding the dog in the dark were slim.

He was driving down Farrar Street when he saw Shorty Doyle's pickup. Slowing, he waved for Shorty to pull over, then got out to talk to him.

"Hey, Shorty, you haven't seen an Australian shepherd running around, have you?"

Bud explained the situation, and Shorty replied, "I need to go take these papers to Jay, then I'll help you look for him."

"Meet me at my place," Bud said. "I need to feed the dogs."

Bud was soon at the bungalow, hoping that Freckles was there, but since there was no sign of him, he took the dogs inside and gave them their dinner.

Now waiting for Shorty to show up, he quickly booted up his computer and did a search on *Nikon silent shooting mode*. Finding a short tutorial on quiet shutter-release, he turned off the shutter sound on the camera.

Shorty still not there, he next keyed in *pterodactyl toes*.

A short summary read,

> *Pterodactyls are a member of the pterosaur family. Pterosaurs are the earliest vertebrates known to have evolved flight. Their first to fourth toes were long, and they had elaborate head crests.*

Now thinking of Howie, Bud scanned down farther, and seeing the question, *Would a pterodactyl eat a human?* He clicked and read,

> *New fossil finds show that some large pterosaurs ate prey as large as a horse, including dinosaurs.*

Glad he didn't live back then, he continued reading.

> *Pterosaurs, which technically are not dinosaurs, could have wingspans of up to 36 feet. Standing, such giants could reach the height of a modern giraffe. Some estimate the pterosaur could weigh up to 550 pounds.*

Bud whistled. Something that big could easily kill you if it landed on you, but other than the fact that they no longer existed, they also had more than three toes, so the track on Jimmy Johnson's back had to be from something else.

There was no way Sam was right by insisting Jimmy had been killed by a pterodactyl. Bud leaned back away from the computer, now feeling silly for even entertaining the possibility.

He now wondered where Shorty was, then thinking he might have time to check out the photos he'd taken out by the geyser, he began downloading them.

The colors were somewhat different from what his Canon took and the focus seemed a little crisper, but in general, Bud had gotten some pretty nice shots, at least in his book. He slowly scrolled through them, studying the nice contrast between the reds of the travertine and the yellows of the tamarisk, thinking he might have a few keepers, when he finally got to the last two photos of the bunch.

The lighting was poor, but the camera had managed to capture the raft, though the yellow seemed a little blurry. The first photo showed several boxes and what looked like someone's feet, as if a guy was sleeping in the bottom of the raft, though his feet seemed rather long and skinny.

But when Bud pulled up the last photo, he sat back in shock and disbelief, for he could see the back half of the raft, and on it was a face that had seen too many years of sun, a face that was dried and desiccated like a prune, a face that belonged to the elongated feet in the first photo.

Bud knew without doubt that he was looking at the face of an ancient Fremont mummy.

18

"Kind of a homely fellow, isn't he?" Shorty remarked, studying the photo.

"I'm sure he looked better when he was younger," Bud replied. "But Shorty, where in hellsbells did you find Freckles?"

The dog was now in the kitchen, pushing everyone's dog bowls around the floor with his nose, hoping to find a morsel of food left behind, even though Bud had given him a good dinner.

Shorty replied, "He was at Jay's. He has a good nose and followed it right to Jay's lasagna. Jay sent some home with me. Hungry?"

Bud replied, "Cassie might appreciate having some instead of you feeding me."

"Cassie's out of town for a couple of weeks visiting her folks in Michigan. I'm batchin' it. Get some plates. Any of that Merlot left?"

As Shorty took a covered dish from a sack, Bud put the almost-empty bottle of wine on the table next to two plates, saying, "Drink it all. I give the stuff a bad reputation. But what do you think of that photo?"

"Well, it makes me want to use more sunscreen."

"Do you think it's a real mummy?" Bud asked.

"Looks real to me. But why would they want to take it rafting on the Green? It would probably like the Dead Sea better. And I guess mummies don't need life jackets."

Bud laughed. "Shorty, I think that mummy came from Range Creek. Mum's the word, but a BLM ranger came into my office the other day and wants me to go on a sting operation up there with him."

"A mummy sting? Like a mummy wasp? But why didn't the Fremont wrap their dead?"

"I don't know. Is this another bad mummy joke?"

Shorty now poured himself a glass of wine. "OK, I'll get serious now that I'm drinking. No more bad jokes. It's a genuine question."

Bud replied, "Maybe they wrapped them in deer skins. I don't know if they were able to weave clothes, but in this dry environment, they probably just put their dead in alcoves or in trees as is. That's what the Utes used to do."

"So you think whoever's in the raft is smuggling mummies? That would sure stump a *What's My Line* panel—remember that old TV show? But who would want to buy a mummy?"

"Maybe some museum."

"Don't museums vet where their stuff comes from?" Shorty asked.

"I would hope so," Bud replied. "But the BLM ranger told me there's a big black market for Fremont stuff, just like Egyptian antiquities, though those people are more interested in the sarcophaguses than the mummies themselves."

"That would be sarcophagi," Shorty said. "Who would want a mummy hanging around?"

"Some wealthy people build their own private museums. But Shorty, a BLM ranger wants me to go up there with him, posing as a NatGeo photographer. There's a team of archaeologists working in there, and I'm not real confident I could pull off being a pro like that. Archaeologists are usually fairly intelligent people, and I'm sure some of them are photographers themselves. It's actually keeping me up nights. He even rented me some nice equipment."

"What's he going to pose as?"

"I think maybe also a photographer."

"Well, would you be more comfortable posing as a geologist's assistant?"

"You mean you might go along?"

"Ever since we were talking about dinosaurs the other night, I've been thinking about going up into the Books and looking for the iridium layer. We could go up there and kill two birds with one stone —look for the layer and also for thieves, assuming the ranger agrees, of curse, I mean, of course. Get it—mummy curse?"

Bud groaned. "What's the iridium layer?"

"Well, when the meteor hit that caused the dinosaurs to go extinct —this wasn't all that long ago in geologic time, only about 66 million years—it had a huge impact, as you can guess. By the way, just so you sound like you know what you're talking about, if anyone asks, Chic-xu-lub, the impact crater, is pronounced *chick-shoe-lube*. It's a Mayan word that means *tail of the devil*."

"Who would ask?" Bud asked.

"If you're posing as a geologist, you might get caught if you said it wrong. Anyway, the impact affected the planet so much that it caused what we call the K-T Extinction Event. K is for Cretaceous, after the German spelling for chalk, and T is for Tertiary. It's the boundary between these two geologic periods. It was the end of what we call the Dinosaur Era, and lots more than dinosaurs went extinct—it's estimated that more than three-fourths of all plant and animal species living on Earth died off."

"And it left this iridium layer?" Bud asked.

"Yes, it left a layer of airborne debris all around the earth that has iridium in it, which is evidence of an extraterrestrial impact event. That's how the whole thing was discovered, a geologist named Alvarez discovered this layer in Italy. Nobody had a clue why this extinction event occurred until then. The impact caused a nuclear-type winter which stopped photosynthesis, and most of the plants died. It caused an ecological collapse. They eventually found the impact crater, partly undersea, in the Yucatan."

"That's what you were talking about the other night, when the avian dinosaurs survived, as well as some mammals."

Shorty replied, "Exactly. Iridium is extremely rare on Earth, but is common in meteors. The iridium layer contains 100 times what a normal concentration would be, and it also contains shocked quartz, which occurs only with a meteor strike or atomic blast. There have now been more than 100 iridium sites discovered worldwide. One is maybe only 50 miles or so from here, over by the town of Emery."

"So it could also exist in this part of the Books?"

"It's very possible," Shorty replied, now finishing the wine. "I need to study where the layers occur. It was in the North Horn formation over there. But I'd love to go look for it. If nothing else, I'd get more familiar with the geology in Range Creek."

"I'll talk to the ranger and see what he thinks. I'd much rather go with you. I barely even know this guy, Shorty, and he strikes me as being pretty—what's the word..."

"Rigid?" Shorty asked. "Some law-enforcement types are."

"That works," Bud said. "Do you think I'm like that?"

Shorty laughed, toasted Bud with his glass, then finished the last of the wine.

Bud grinned. "You and I, we go way back, Shorty. I'd feel much better if you came along. After our escapades in the Klondike, I'd trust you with my life."

"Likewise," Shorty said thoughtfully. "Actually, I *did* trust you with my life, Bud. You saved me from disaster up there in more ways than one." He stood, adding, "But I need to go home. Call me when you find out what the plan is."

Bud also stood. "You're OK to drive?"

Shorty laughed. "Bud, there was barely a glass in that bottle. I'm fine."

"You're a better man than I am," Bud said.

Shorty now called Freckles. "You mind if I take him home? Me and Cassie have been talking about getting a dog. He's a dandy, if we can get him to stick around. Let me foster him for awhile and see how it works out."

Freckles was now at Shorty's feet, wagging his tail. Shorty put a leash on him and said goodnight, and they were soon gone.

Bud was thinking about getting ready for bed when he heard Wilma Jean drive up, and the dogs all rushed to the door to greet her.

As she walked in, he could tell she was tired, and she said, "Bud, I'm still upset about you not telling me about this new dog."

Bud helped her take off her jacket as she added, "And what's this? New photography equipment? Nikon? With all these lenses? This must've cost a fortune."

Bud groaned, gave her a hug, put some leftover lasagna in the microwave for her, then headed for the bedroom, slipping into his Scooby Do PJs and crawling into bed, pulling the covers up over his head.

Wilma Jean was soon at his side.

"Hon, I'm sorry. I'm just exhausted, but it's no excuse to take it out on you. Iris has been gone, and I just can't do the bowling alley on top of the cafe any more. We're going to have to get someone to help when she's gone. The lasagna is delicious. Did you make it?"

Sticking his head out of the covers, Bud said, "No, Shorty brought it by from Jay's."

"I'm going to have to get his recipe," she said. "But where's the new dog?"

"Shorty's going to foster him."

She replied, "Oh, that's good. And hon, if you think you need more camera gear, well, I guess it's OK, but I *am* going to take you up on that shopping trip, and I plan to go hog wild, just so you know."

Bud didn't want to tell her the gear was a rental, as he was too tired to explain his spy venture. He knew she would worry, so he just squeezed her arm and put his head back under the covers, hoping he wouldn't dream about mummies.

19

It was the next morning, and Bud was in his office, talking on the phone while Howie sat reading an old copy of *Lost Treasure Magazine*, half listening to Bud's end of the conversation. Bud had called Ranger Carl after emailing him copies of the photos of the raft with the mummy in it.

"I'm really sorry to hear about your mom, Carl. Hopefully she'll recover quickly and you'll be back on the job soon," Bud said. He began fiddling with the aluminum arrow from his pocket, listening, then replied, "I agree that the mummy photo's pretty disconcerting. I have the plates of the truck that picked it up, but I haven't had a chance to run them yet."

Howie now looked up with interest as Bud paused, listening to Carl, then continued.

"I know you'd probably rather wait until you got back, but I do have a friend who could go in there with me. He's a geologist, one-hundred percent reliable. We could go look around for a couple of days. Whoever's looting things isn't going to wait for you to return, you know that."

More silence, then Bud said, "I'd rather wait for you, too, Carl. I don't know any of those people up there, but I guess that would be a bonus if I'm going undercover. But send the key to the gate up, and we'll make arrangements to go stay a few days. I'll be in touch if anything comes of it."

Finally, after a moment, Bud said, "OK, and yes, I did get the photo equipment. That's what I used to take those pictures with. It'll work fine. Stay in touch."

With that, he hung up the phone. Howie immediately asked, "Bud, you have a photo of a mummy? Where did you get that?"

"This is all confidential, Deputy. You can't even tell Maureen."

Howie replied with chagrin, "I know that, Sheriff—unless you saw it in a carnival or something, then it wouldn't matter, right?"

"I suspect it's illegal to have a mummy on display anywhere except in a museum. But what happened to your pompadour?" Bud asked, noting that Howie's hair now looked normal.

"It's still there, Sheriff, it's just resting. I didn't have time to pomp it up this morning. Malcolm kept us up half the night."

"Is he OK?"

"Oh, yeah, he's teething, is all. But what's this about a mummy?"

Bud began explaining his photographic foray down by the geyser while trying to run the plates at the same time. Finally, he said, "I'll be darned. The database says the plates of the rig that picked up the mummy belong to Maureen."

Howie now sat up straight, asking, "My Maureen? Maureen McPherson?"

"Yup, and they say the vehicle is stolen."

Bud laughed. "Just kidding, Howie, keeping you on your toes. They belong to someone named Rita Brown, who lives in Salt Lake."

"Isn't she some kind of singer? Blues, maybe?"

"I don't know, Howie. I'm not in that circle."

"You never get the blues?" Howie kidded, then added, "But Sheriff, I didn't get a chance to tell you, but we had a report of another stolen raft while you were gone. If you count the one the ranger mentioned, this would be the third one."

"Where was it stolen?"

"Range Creek Rapids, just like the other two. Same story—the rafters got up the next morning and found it gone."

Bud asked, "Did they see a white-haired man?"

"If so, they didn't mention it, Sheriff. But there's something else…"

Now Howie began flipping through the *Lost Treasure Magazine*, saying, "Say, I forgot to show you this picture of this huge gold nugget some guy found down in Arizona. They said it weighed five pounds. I'm thinking maybe I should go down there with my metal detector on my next vacation."

Bud said patiently, "Howie, what was that something else you were mentioning?"

"What?"

"You know, we were talking about stolen rafts."

"Oh, that. Well, Marty, he guides for Green River Waterways, he also came in while you were gone and said he's found several rafts down the river, all beached, and he was wondering if anyone had reported some lost rafts. But Sheriff, do you think it's disrespectful to call someone Big Daddy, or is it more of a compliment, like they're a cool cat or something?"

"I really don't know, Howie," Bud replied. "Maybe it would depend on who they are. But I need to go talk to Marty, I guess. Do you know anything about marbles?"

Howie grinned. "Not much, except I can usually recognize when someone's lost a few."

"Well, there's this store up in Price called Wiggins Diggins, and it has some collectible marbles. I'm wondering if these could be something illegal, collected from BLM land, like from old mining camps or such. If so, maybe the looters are the same ones taking Fremont antiquities."

"Did the Fremont have marbles?" Howie asked. "But Bud, I do know this about marbles, though it might not be much help. Atoms are so small, that if you made a proton the size of a marble, a hydrogen atom would be the size of a football stadium."

"That would be one big daddy of an atom, eh?" Bud grinned.

Just then, the office door opened and in came Junior, followed by Rod Ruff.

"Howdy, Buddy," Junior said, putting a small sack on Bud's desk. "We're just passing through on our way to go get my pickup. Rod's going to customize it and paint it, and me and Hank are going to be his gofers. If we hurry, we might be able to enter it in the car show. Ginger wanted me to drop this by. How's Freckles doing?"

"He's found a pretty good foster home for now," Bud replied. "But what's in the sack?"

"I don't know, something Ginger said you'd like."

"Any new dinosaur activity up your way?" Bud asked, grinning.

"Laugh all you want, Buddy, but I myself actually heard the darn thing last night. It was downright spooky."

"Did it sound like a siren?" Bud asked. "Or did you hear *thwock* noises?"

"Neither. It sounded like a dinosaur. I can tell you about it later. We need to get going. Next time you see my old truck, Buddy boy, it'll be a nice powder blue again."

Junior and Rod said goodbye, then headed out.

"Was Rod the guy who hired you guys to play at the rockabilly car show?" Bud asked Howie.

"Yes," Howie said. "And darn it, Sheriff, I wanted to have my hair all pomped up next time I saw him."

"He can tell you're cool without all that," Bud replied. "Coolness is an inherent trait, not something that depends on outward appearance."

"You think so? Well, right now, my coolness needs some sleep."

"Howie, take the rest of the day off. Go home and get some rest," Bud said.

"Thanks, Sheriff. I think I'll do that," Howie replied, heading out the door. Turning back, he said, "Maybe I can write a song or two for the show."

Bud nodded, saying, "Well, if you write songs in your sleep, you do a better job of it than most people do when awake. See you tomorrow."

As Howie closed the door behind him, Bud looked in the sack Junior had left. It held a box of *Wisdom of the Ancients Yerba Maté Looseleaf Tea* and a note from Ginger:

Bud,

Since you like this stuff, have at it.

Love,

Aunt Ginger

Bud shook his head. Apparently she didn't like it any better than he did. Putting the tea in his desk drawer, out of mind and sight, he locked up and headed for the offices of Green River Waterways, down by the river behind the museum.

20

Bud had talked to Marty down at Green River Waterways, who told him he'd managed to drag the rafts he'd recovered back to their warehouse. Bud then went back to the office and contacted each of the parties who'd reported stolen rafts, telling them where to find them. Unfortunately, two of the three parties were now on their way back home to different states, and Bud suspected Marty was going to inherit the rafts.

Bud had just fired up his computer to try to find out more information on who Rita Brown might be when his phone rang.

"Sheriff's Office, Bud speaking," he answered.

"Sheriff Shumway?"

"Speaking."

"This is Eileen Jensen. You remember me, don't you?"

Bud groaned silently, then said, "Well, it has been awhile since we've heard from you, Mrs. Jensen, but of course I remember you." It was hard to forget someone who gave you so much to remember, he thought to himself.

"I know, I know, I used to always call you and Deputy McPherson, and I do realize some of it was, well, what you might call frivolous. And I'm sure you miss my frosted sugar cookies."

Bud shook his head. Calling to report things like supposed lies in textbooks and kids walking across your lawn were beyond frivolous to him, and he always suspected the cookies were more of a peace offering than appreciation for the officers of the peace.

He said, "Well, we know things can seem more important when you're not able to get out much, Mrs. Jensen. Are you still hanging out with the BOB-Os?"

The BOB-Os, or Bucket of Bolts Overlanders, required that people on their forays dress like what they called the good old days, which was anytime at least a good 50 years past or more. Bud was still having trouble picturing Mrs. Jensen in a vintage leisure suit, though in some ways it seemed to go with other things about her, like the way she curled her hair into tight rings.

Mrs. Jensen replied, "If you mean am I still dating Frosty Merriott, yes, I am, though he sometimes doesn't act like it. But Bud, do you have a minute?"

Now Bud was on high alert, for Mrs. Jensen never called him Bud —it was always Sheriff Shumway. He wasn't sure what was coming, but he knew he should be ready to duck.

"Of course. I always have a minute for you, Mrs. Jensen."

Now her voice cracked and she sounded like she was going to cry. "Call me Eileen. Bud, you know my husband passed away some time ago. We were happy together, and I still miss him. I thought maybe Frosty and I would end up doing more things together—we are a good match after all—but he's always out running around the country with Eldon."

"Well, why don't you go run around the country with them?" Bud asked, not sure what the problem was.

"They invited me, and I tried, but I just don't have the stamina for it. They go out all day, and I need to have my tea."

Bud wondered if she would like the maté Ginger had sent.

Mrs. Jensen continued, "But you see, Bud, what little running around I did do, well, it ruined me."

Bud wasn't sure what to say. "Did it mess up your back or something?"

"No, no, it's not that. It ruined me mentally. It made me see how much I don't do, or maybe I should say how much I sit around the house."

"But you have a beautiful garden," Bud reassured her. "You can't accomplish something like that sitting around the house. And you bake those delicious sugar cookies."

"Thank you, but all that no longer cuts the mustard. Running around with Frosty and Eldon made me see how boring my life was."

Bud was now beginning to question his role as a counsellor. It didn't seem like they were getting anywhere, and he really needed to get busy and see if he could figure out who Rita Brown was. And he needed to get ready for he and Shorty's foray into Range Creek, for Carl had said he'd mailed the gate key that morning.

Finally, Bud said, "Well, if you're finding life's boring, maybe you need a new hobby or something. But I really need to get back to work. Is there anything I can do?"

Mrs. Jensen now sounded more upbeat. "There is, Bud. I'm wondering if I could maybe ride along with you in your cruiser for a few hours now and then. It would really perk up my life, and when Frosty and Eldon ask me what I've been doing, I'll have something interesting to talk about."

Bud replied, "Well, you might be overestimating things here in town a bit, as there's usually not much going on. But it's funny you mention it, as I've been thinking of starting a ride-along program to get people more familiar with what we do."

Bud wasn't sure why he'd just said that, even though it was true, as Mrs. Jensen wasn't who he'd had in mind for taking on a ride-along. He'd thought it might be more of a way to build confidence and trust with the town's teens and keep them from going bad, though few ever did.

"That sounds perfect! When can you come by?" Mrs. Jensen asked.

Bud now wondered what he was getting himself into, yet hadn't his oath as a lawman said to serve and protect? Maybe taking a bored old gal on a ride-along would be a form of serving. It wouldn't be too bad for an hour or so, then he knew she'd be tired and want to go home. Maybe she'd start making those frosted sugar cookies for them again.

He asked, "How about right after lunch?"

"One o'clock?"

Bud groaned. He hated committing to firm schedules. It made him uncomfortable, and he never knew what might come up preventing him from being on time.

"You do realize that if I need to cover something, I'll have to drop you off," he said.

"Why can't I cover it with you?"

"Because sometimes there's gunplay and things like that," Bud replied, though he couldn't recall the last time he'd been involved in gunplay, probably never.

"Oh, that would be exciting! I'd really have something to tell Frosty."

Bud wondered if he'd groaned out loud upon hearing that, because she then added, "Come at one and I'll have some of those cookies you like so much. Don't be late."

With that, she hung up.

Deciding it might not be too bad taking her for a ride-along, Bud decided to check his email before going to lunch. He had one message:

> *A donation of $920,000.00 USD has been made in your favor, Kindly contact the donor Mr. Charles W Jackson Jr via email for more details on your donation funds.*

He shut it down and headed for lunch at the Melon Rind Cafe.

21

Bud pulled up in front of Mrs. Jensen's silver Prairie Schooner trailer at the Palatial Estates Trailer Park, noting how neat and tidy her yard was, the front walk lined with orange and red chrysanthemums that were fading with the autumn frosts.

The flowers were the domesticated cousins of the rabbitbrush that was currently blooming all across the desert in vivid yellow, and Bud had to say he preferred the wild variety, as did the numerous birds who fed on its seeds all winter.

As he rang the doorbell, he could see that the front door had a sticker on it that read: *The neighbors have better stuff.*

As she answered the door, Bud said, "Afternoon, Mrs. Jensen. You ready for our ride-along?"

"Call me Eileen, Bud," she said, handing him a small box.

"What's this?" He asked with surprise.

"Frosted sugar cookies. These have orange frosting, since it's fall. I also put some orange zest in the cookies themselves. They turned out really good. Go ahead and have one."

"What's orange zest?" Bud asked, opening the door of the sheriff's Land Cruiser for her and wondering what oranges had to do with autumn. He noted she was dressed in a nice pair of gray wool slacks and a red sweater that looked to be made of cashmere. Her hair was all fluffed up instead of in ringlets, and it looked like she was letting it grow longer.

She replied, "Orange zest is just orange peel all zested up."

As they settled into the front, Bud said, "Your hair looks nice."

"Thanks," she replied. "You probably noticed that I've dyed it blonde. I'm not trying to be racy or anything, that's what color it was before it went gray."

"Back to the good old days, eh?" Bud said, immediately hoping he hadn't said something insulting.

"It was *platinum* blonde, not just any old blonde. I'm just trying to revive my life again before I die. I'm only 75, you know."

"Seventy-five's the new fifty-five, from what I've been told," Bud replied, now heading out on Green River Boulevard. He'd decided to just drive around town for awhile, then maybe take her for coffee at the Melon Rind, then back to her trailer.

"How well do you know Frosty?" She asked, handing Bud a cookie.

Bud frowned. He was hoping to avoid talking about his constituents, especially since such talk could come back to haunt him.

"Frosty's a good guy. I've been on a couple of BOB-O expeditions with him and Eldon."

"Did you know he's been divorced? His wife ran off with some guy from Radium. It was all about money, according to him."

Bud took a bite of cookie. "These are delicious. Where did you get the recipe? My wife's going to want it."

"Oh, they're pretty simple. Hey, look, there's a stray dog. Shouldn't you arrest it?"

Bud looked to where she was pointing, then groaned. It was Freckles. The dog looked intent, like he was on a mission, half-loping down the sidewalk in the direction of Jay's B&B.

Bud pulled over next to him, opened the back door of the Land Cruiser, and the dog jumped in, panting.

"This is Freckles," he told Mrs. Jensen. "Let's take him home."

"You know the names of all the dogs in town and where they live?" Mrs. Jensen asked.

"Pretty much," Bud replied, heading down Long Street. They were soon at Shorty and Cassies' ranch, where Shorty stood on the front step of the adobe-style house.

"I was just getting ready to go look for him," Shorty said, shaking his head. "I don't know about fostering him, Bud, if he's going to run all over creation. I put him in the yard for a few minutes, and he opened the latch on the gate."

Shorty let the dog inside, then said, "Afternoon, Mrs. Jensen. You two come on in for some iced tea."

Eileen grabbed the cookies, and she and Bud went inside, where Shorty showed them to a nice sunroom.

"This is a beautiful house," Mrs. Jensen said. "It reminds me of the house I grew up in as a kid. Lots of light and natural colors."

"Where did you grow up?" Shorty asked congenially, now munching on a cookie.

"Green River," she replied, sipping her iced tea.

Bud was surprised. "I thought you moved here with your husband. Didn't he work at the missile base?"

"He did, but we were both locals. Most of the families associated with the base came from other places, mostly from California, but my husband and I both grew up here. In fact, I knew your parents, Shorty. My mom was good friends with your mom, and we used to go out to the Doyle Farm to visit. I was fascinated by your mom's Canadian accent."

"Where was I?" Shorty asked.

"Oh, I don't know. I don't think you were born yet. I was just a kid, and I'm somewhat older than you."

Bud tipped back in his chair. "So, you're a local, Mrs. Jensen. I sure didn't know that."

"Oh yes," she replied. "I'm actually fourth generation Green River. Frosty and Eldon and I all went to grade school together—actually, all the way through high school. My best friend, Bonnie

Driggs, actually married Eldon, though she passed a number of years ago."

"Driggs? Was she related to Harvey Driggs up in Range Creek?" Bud asked.

"That was her uncle," Mrs. Jensen said. "He didn't have any kids, and he always encouraged me and Bonnie to come up to the ranch. He enjoyed showing us around. We rode horses all over that place, spent most of our summers up there. Bonnie's mom, Harvey's sister, would go up and cook for him and his crew, and we'd stay at a little cabin there on the ranch. Oh, those were the days. I'd give anything to go in there again."

"*Could* you go in there again?" Shorty asked.

"Oh, no. Harvey sold it to the state years ago, and it's gated now. It's an archaeologist's paradise. I can't begin to tell you how much stuff we saw in there. Harvey wouldn't let us touch any of it. He said it was bad luck, that we needed to respect the old ones."

"Actually," Shorty said, "What I was asking was, would you be able to physically go in there if someone were to take you? Could you show someone the stuff you know about?"

Now Mrs. Jensen looked doubtful. "I don't know. Some of that's rough hiking. I don't even have any hiking boots any more, and I'm not in that great of shape."

"Could you ride a horse?" Bud asked.

"I don't know—maybe. It's been years, but I was a good rider. I might need help getting on and off. But why are you asking?"

"We're thinking of going in there," Bud replied. "It might be nice to have a guide."

He immediately wondered if he wasn't again acting without thinking things through, which he'd been known to do before, in fact just hours before when he'd mentioned the ride-along. He had no idea how this was all going to work out, and getting Mrs. Jensen involved, especially out in what he knew was rough country, could be a mistake, one that could even possibly be deadly.

He then wondered what Ranger Carl would think, but he'd pretty much handed the investigation off to Bud and was currently on his way to Oregon to help his ailing mother, so Bud knew it was his decision as to how to handle things. He took the little aluminum arrow from his pocket and began fiddling with it.

Shorty watched Bud fiddle, then said, "There's a cabin there we've been offered, and you could stay in it while we pitch our tents nearby. It's probably the same one you stayed in as a kid. The ranch house is being used by the archaeologists."

Mrs. Jensen looked hesitant, then said, "I'd sure have something interesting to tell Frosty, wouldn't I?"

Shorty now asked Bud, "What's that you're fiddling with, anyway? It looks like a magnetic north arrow."

Bud handed the piece to Shorty, who examined it and said, "That's exactly what it is, a north arrow. These are used by geologists and archaeologists when photographing stuff to show its orientation. They're made of weighted aluminum with magnetic strips glued on in case you need to attach it to something metal. Kind of a handy thing to carry around, I guess. But who's *PM*?"

Bud shrugged his shoulders as Shorty handed the arrow back to him, putting it back in his pocket along with the note that read *Choo-Choo Rock.*

Turning back to Mrs. Jensen, Shorty said, "I'm not sure where we could get horses, but it could probably be done. Do you think you'd be up to something like that?"

Mrs. Jensen sipped her tea, patting Freckles' head, then said, "I think so. I could show you all kinds of interesting stuff. I even know where there's a mummy."

Bud gave Shorty a knowing look. "How soon could you go in with us?" He asked.

"Anytime you want," she answered. "But I'll need to get some riding clothes."

"I think we can arrange that," Bud replied. "My wife and I are going to Price tomorrow. I'll have her call you and find out what you need, the sizes and all that."

"It sounds wonderful," Mrs. Jensen said. "It'll be a *real* ride-along. I can't wait."

Bud nodded his head congenially while wondering if he'd regret inviting her along.

22

Bud sat in Wilma Jean's big pink Mary Kay Lincoln Continental, waiting as she cruised the aisles in the nearby clothing store, looking for something for Mrs. Jensen's upcoming riding foray, as well as for a new outfit or two for herself.

The dogs were sleeping on the back seat, and Bud himself was having trouble staying awake, especially since he was full of dolmades and tzatziki sauce from the Greek Streak, his favorite Price restaurant.

"Waiting in the car is the price you pay for not keeping track of important dates like your anniversary," Bud thought to himself, now jerking wide awake as he recalled what Wilma Jean had said about going hog wild. His fears seemed to be realized as he saw her coming out the door, piled high with sacks of clothing. He quickly jumped out and opened the car door, helping her.

"Don't worry, hon," she said. "You'll be happy to know they've added a gently-used section to the store, which is where most of this came from. And some of it's for Mrs. Jensen. But why again am I buying her bluejeans and cotton shirts and outdoors stuff?"

"She's going to take up horseback riding again. I guess she used to ride a lot. She said she wants to revive her life before she dies."

Bud wanted to change the subject, as he wasn't ready to tell his wife about his upcoming spy assignment, which was how he was starting to view it, kind of a *Mission Impossible* kind of thing. He tried to recall how the show had started each episode.

Good morning, Mr. Shumway. Your assignment, should you decide to accept it...

"Let's go get an ice cream," Wilma Jean said. "Then I need to go to Peezee Printing."

Bud was still thinking about the TV show when she said, "Hon, you're really distracted when the words *ice cream* don't put you in motion. Is everything OK?"

"I'm fine," Bud said, now starting the car and heading for the local drive-in. "After the printer, let's go over to Wiggins Diggins."

They sat in the car at the drive-in, eating ice cream, then Bud got into the back with the dogs and let them take turns licking the cone he'd bought for them.

As always, should you or any of your force be caught or killed, the Secretary will disavow any knowledge of your actions.

"Bud, let's go! Are you awake?" Wilma Jean sounded frustrated. "I swear, you seem like you're on another planet."

Bud was beginning to wish he *was* on another planet. Seeing the sacks of clothes for Mrs. Jensen was making his decision all too real. What had he been thinking? He didn't know what kind of shape or condition she was in or whether or not she would be a liability or benefit for the spy mission. What if it killed her? Or worse yet, what if they got into a situation where she wanted to kill him?

Wilma Jean had now slipped into the driver's seat and started the car, heading across town to the printer, Bud still in the back. Once there, she disappeared inside, then came back with a stack of what looked to be signs.

"What's all that?"

"Howie's campaign signs."

"What slogan did you guys decide on?"

"Back to the rockin' good old days. Howie McPherson."

Bud grinned, still in the back. Wilma Jean now headed for Wiggins Diggins as he leaned back, thinking how nice it would be to have a chauffeur.

That's how it had all started with Mrs. Jensen, he thought, he'd been chauffeuring her around in the sheriff's Land Cruiser, and one thing had led to another with him inviting her to go along to Range Creek, though he had Shorty to thank for not only encouraging it, but also for not shutting it down.

This tape will self-destruct in five seconds. Good luck, Bud.

Now at Wiggins Diggins, Wilma Jean got out, and holding the rear door open for him, Bud wondered if his new chauffeur could be a counterspy and if any of them would survive the mission.

They went into the store, which was actually just a series of long shelves piled high with all kinds of stuff, some in decent shape, but most of it what Bud would call junk.

Sam Wiggins' wife, Dorothy, greeted them.

"Well, I'll be go to heck," she exclaimed. "It's the Shumways! Gosh, I haven't seen you guys in a decade or two."

"Oh, Dottie, it couldn't possibly be that long," Wilma Jean laughed. "You and Sam were in my cafe just a few years ago."

Bud made his way towards the far recesses of the store, not wanting to get caught up in the conversation, as Dottie and Wilma Jean began discussing this and that.

As he wandered around, he saw old 8-track tapes, old baskets and wreaths, an old Wockoder turntable in its own case, a used garage door opener, an old BBQ grill, a plastic baby gate, a dusty arrangement of plastic flowers in a cowboy boot, and various old diet and exercise books.

He absent-mindedly picked up one of the books, thinking maybe it would help him get started on a new fitness regime, when he noticed a shelf behind the books that looked much more interesting, for it held what looked to be mining memorabilia such as old hardhats and lanterns and even a couple of coal buckets.

He slipped over to the shelf, examining what to him looked to be museum-quality mining gear, from old round metal lunchboxes to carbide cap lamps. He even found a methane gas detector and an old antique oak-handled pick.

Now, to his surprise, he saw a small clay figurine sitting next to a bucket, and carefully picking it up, saw a price tag of $25, a fortune for something from Wiggins Diggins. The figurine had several beautifully made necklaces and belts, the beads all perfectly round, with a strange concentric design on its torso.

He had a sudden urge to get out of the store, and carrying the figurine back to the front, he carefully put it on the counter.

Dottie, picking it up, said, "I told Sam he was asking way too much for this. Some little kid made it out of clay, and they didn't do a very good job, in my opinion. It's not even fired. It kind of looks like a flat chess piece. I'll give it to you for $15, which is still too much, but I don't want Sam getting upset."

She took the figurine and wrapped it in tissue paper and put it in a small sack.

"Do you know where Sam got it? Can I get a receipt?" Bud asked, taking the sack and handing Dottie $15.

"Oh, there's these two guys who've been bringing in some nice stuff, like all that mining junk you were looking at. They say they inherited it from their grandpa. But Sam tells me you're going to help solve the case of the dinosaur murder."

Bud groaned, then mumbled, "I'll do my best." He then turned to Wilma Jean and said, "Let's go. The dogs are getting tired of sitting in the car."

"But I haven't even had a chance to look around," she protested.

Bud now took her arm and began gently pulling. "Hon, we need to go."

Sensing something was wrong, she said goodbye to Dottie and

followed Bud out the door. Once in the car, she asked, "Bud, what was that all about? And why did you buy that strange clay thing?"

Now starting the car, Bud said, "Hon, I think I just found one of the Pilling figurines. And I'm thinking all that mining stuff may have come from a museum. If so, Dottie and Sam are buying and reselling stuff that's possibly stolen."

"Oh my gosh!" Wilma Jean said. "I'm not sure what a Pilling figurine is, but do you think they know the stuff might be stolen?"

"I don't know," Bud replied. "Knowing them, I doubt it. But our next stop's going to be the museum. I want to show it to the archaeologist there."

"But the Utah Symphony is having a 'Music Sways the World' concert here in the park, and it starts soon. Peggy Giannakopoulos is going to be there, and I was hoping we could go. It's nice and cool. The dogs will be OK in the car for awhile."

"Who's Peggy whatever?"

"She's a contrabass balalaika player. World famous."

Bud replied, "Well, since there's so many Greeks here in Price, it should be a big hit. But you know you're Greek when nobody can pronounce your last name, eh?"

"Don't be silly. Greek names are easy to pronounce, they just have a lot of syllables and you have to sound them out. But the balalaika's from Russia. You're thinking of the bouzouki, which is Greek."

Bud grinned. "Drop me off at the museum and I'll walk over and find you at the park. It won't take long."

23

Bud sat in the office of the interim museum director, an auburn-haired woman with an air of confidence who had immediately taken over the conversation. A skull sat on the corner of her desk, its gaping eyes staring at Bud.

The woman sitting next to him, the archaeology curator named Bailey Miles, was the one who he'd originally shown the piece to. She'd wanted him to show the figurine to the interim director, though he hadn't particularly wanted to. He wasn't looking to donate the piece to the museum or anything just yet, but rather wanted an opinion on what it could be.

To him, it looked like one of the Pilling figurines, a set of eleven Fremont clay figurines discovered in 1950 by Utah rancher Clarence Pilling under a rock overhang. The figurines were believed to be around 1,000 years old and were currently housed in the museum. Bud had seen them many times when he'd visited as a kid in Price, and knew the figurines had been discovered in a side canyon along Range Creek.

The figurines were famous, examples of how the Fremont dressed and decorated themselves. Each was around six inches long and made of unbaked clay with tiny clay ornaments painted red, buff, and black. They seemed to have been made in matching male and female pairs, though one female figurine didn't have a mate.

Bud thought he had what could very well be that mate, which would be quite a find, for the figurines were considered to be among the most important pieces of ancient art ever discovered in this part of America. Bud knew they'd been found on public lands back before picking up such things was taboo, but Pilling had been generous enough to donate them to the museum.

Now the interim director, who'd introduced herself as Renee Barstow, said, "And where exactly did you find this, Mr. Shumway?"

Bud, now beginning to feel unsettled, replied, "I didn't find it anywhere. I'm here only to verify if it's one of the Pilling figurines, that's all."

Renee raised her eyebrows, saying, "If Bailey here felt it was important enough to show me, then it's quite possibly of some importance."

Bud wondered if she realized how circular her sentence was—someone said it was important, so therefore it was important—but he said nothing. Maybe he should take it to someone else, like one of the BLM archaeologists down in Radium.

"Mr. Shumway bought it, Renee. He didn't find it, or at least that's what he told me," Bailey said.

"And where exactly did you buy it?" Renee demanded.

Unwilling to possibly implicate Sam and Dottie, Bud shook his head. "I need to get going. Maybe I can come back another day. My wife's waiting."

He stood to go, picking up the figurine and putting it back in the sack.

Now Renee also stood. "You have to be really careful with something like that! You really should leave it here for safekeeping. You could be arrested for having antiquities, you know."

Bud shook his head in agreement and walked out the door, Bailey the curator close behind. She followed him through the museum and then outside, saying in a low voice, "I'm really sorry, Mr. Shumway. I had no idea she would act like that. She spends a lot of time in the museum and seems really interested in all the stuff here, and I thought she might be willing to let me take your figurine and examine it. But she controls the budget."

Bud asked, "It would be expensive?"

Bailey replied, "Yes. It would take multiple chemical tests to ensure its authenticity. I'd send it off to the University of Utah, and they'd use a technique called X-ray fluorescence to identify the source of the clay used to make the figurine to see if it was the same as the others, as well as looking to see if the trace elements matched. They would also compare the techniques used to make the figurines to see if it was the same artist."

"Wow," Bud replied. "I had no idea it was that complicated. But I really don't like being treated like a criminal."

Now Bailey shook her head. "I know. She was out of hand. Just between you and me, she's not going to last much longer. She was hired as interim director based on some promises she made to the committee."

"Do you mind if I ask what kind of promises?"

"She says she's the granddaughter of Harvey Driggs, the guy who sold Range Creek. She told them she had connections and could not only get funding for the museum, but could also get us access into Range Creek, but so far she hasn't come through. She's an archaeologist and does know a lot about things, but not much about how people work together. She's always saying the archaeologists in Range Creek are inept and don't know what they're doing."

"Why can't you guys go in there?"

"It's pretty much tied up by the university because it's such an important place. They want to keep a close eye on everything, which makes sense to me. I've been in there a few times, but always with supervision. I don't know if you remember when they found a flute in there or not, but that's the kind of controversy that's going on. It's mostly political, or maybe I should say territorial."

Bud said, "I kind of recall the flute, but refresh my memory."

"The flute was found by a Department of Wildlife Resources officer who was patrolling the canyon. It was stuck in a crack. And the

GPS coordinates indicated it was actually on BLM land, so there was a controversy over who should have possession of it. I don't have a problem with who runs it at all, but it rankles Renee. Since it's in our backyard and once belonged to her family, she thinks we should control it."

Bud paused, then said, "Bailey, if I leave this figurine with you, would you try to get it examined?"

He almost told Bailey he was an LEO, but something made him hesitate.

Bailey replied, "I'm good friends with the head archaeologist in Range Creek. I can have him take it up to the university. Maybe he can get them to run the tests for free. But they're going to want to know where it came from."

"Just tell them I prefer to remain anonymous for now," Bud said. "I can prove it's not illegal when the time comes. I'll leave my number. Call me when you know anything, and much appreciated."

"I'll do my best. But did you notice the strange circular designs on it? None of the others have that."

"So you think it may not be the mate?"

"It could still be, but that design is definitely different. I've never seen it before, those yellow concentric rings with the red odd-shaped middle that looks like a crab," Bailey replied.

"Well, I hope it's the mate," Bud said, now feeling like he needed to get going, as he could hear some kind of odd music coming from nearby that sounded vaguely like *Found a Peanut*, and he thought he also heard the sound of dogs howling.

He wrote his cellphone number on the sack with the figurine and handed it to Bailey, then hurried towards the park.

24

"Bud, she wasn't playing *Found a Peanut*," Wilma Jean said. "It was some Greek ballad about her lover leaving on a train. But you should've seen her instrument. It's called a contrabass balalaika, and it's this giant triangle that's so big you have to rest one corner on the ground. It sounds like a double bass, but it has more volume."

Bud and Wilma Jean sat at a table in the Sunnyside Cafe, Ginger with them, drinking coffee.

"Now I'll have that silly song stuck in my head all day," Ginger said.

"Just like I do," Bud grinned. "By the way, thanks for the maté, though I'm not really that big of a fan. But where are Hank and Junior?"

Now LuAnn came from the kitchen and sat down with them, saying, "We haven't seen hide nor hair of them since they got Junior's old pickup. They're down in Rod Ruff's shop restoring it. But how's Freckles doing?"

"He has a good home if he'll just stay there," Bud replied. "A really good home."

"I saw him running around town here even when Jimmy was still alive," Ginger said. "Some dogs are just runners, kind of like some people are wanderers."

Bud thought of his Uncle Junior and how he'd once ridden the rails before settling down and marrying LuAnn. He knew their plans to go RVing were the result of his hoboing tendencies and hoped LuAnn was on board for the adventure.

"Did you hear about the Sunnyside Museum here?" Ginger now asked. "They just found out it was robbed."

"Who just found out it was robbed?" Bud asked.

"Sam, of course. Who else would it be?"

"You made it sound like it was robbed some time ago and they just found out," Bud said.

"That's exactly what happened," Ginger replied. "The museum's been closed for several months now from a lack of funds, and someone robbed it, though they don't know when."

Bud now thought of the nice mining stuff he'd seen down at Wiggins Diggins.

"What kind of stuff was taken?" He asked.

"Mining memorabilia. They had some really old stuff from the original Sunnyside Mine."

"Did they have anything Fremont? Like a small figurine or anything?"

"Not that I recall. It was just mining stuff," Ginger replied. "But I was only in there once. Sam's supposed to be investigating it, so watch out. He'll be calling you if he finds out you're in town."

"Fair warning," Bud replied.

Now Wilma Jean said, "Ginger, was Hank able to pound out that dent in the stove?"

"He did a pretty good job," Ginger replied, now picking up their empty cups. "Come on back and take a look. I have a question about the convection oven."

Ginger, Wilma Jean, and LuAnn all disappeared into the back of the cafe, leaving Bud alone. He was about ready to go take the dogs for a short walk when a balding man came into the cafe.

Bud was somewhat surprised to see it was the man he and Sam

had seen walking down the road in Whitmore Canyon carrying a boombox.

"Mind if I join you?" The man asked.

"Sure, have a seat," Bud replied, wondering why everyone always wanted to sit by him, wishing he'd had that problem with the girls back in high school.

"My name's Sandy," the man offered. "You live here?"

Bud replied, "No, but my aunt and uncle do. I'm just visiting. Are you a local? I saw you out walking the other night."

"Oh, I'm just here for awhile. I'm working on a jukebox."

Bud wasn't sure what that would entail, so asked, "Not too many of those left any more, are there? I wonder if my aunt would want one for the cafe here. Would liven things up."

"Your aunt runs this cafe? It's nice, has good food. But I think a mechanical jukebox would ruin the atmosphere. I like it quiet."

Bud, wondering why the guy would work on jukeboxes if he liked silence, replied, "You're right. It is nicer when it's quiet. A jukebox has the potential to be irritating if you didn't like the kind of music it plays or if you want a nice quiet conversation, like we're having."

"Exactly," Sandy replied. "Lao Tzu said that silence is a source of great strength. And wasn't it Arthur Conan Doyle who told Watson that he had a grand gift for silence, which made him an invaluable companion? But silence is kind of on the road to extinction these days, though it's pretty quiet around here, except for the power plant—that gets pretty noisy. But I'm not into total silence, like in a vacuum. I like nature's soundscapes."

"You mean like when you hear birds or coyotes or stuff like that?"

"Exactly. The sounds that you can hear when human noise disappears—the opposite of the mechanical, beeping world."

Bud now wondered why the man had been wearing huge earphones and carrying a boombox if he liked the quiet so much. Maybe he was listening to white noise or pre-recorded nature sounds while he walked.

Sandy asked, "You ever been in the bottom of the Grand Canyon? Total utter silence. It's wonderful. All religions revere silence."

Bud started to lean back, then, thinking better of it, said, "I know what you mean. Sometimes it's like that out in the Big Empty. It's so quiet you could be the last human on the planet."

"Sometimes I wish I was," Sandy replied. "But where's the Big Empty?"

"It's that country around Green River. That's where I live."

"Maybe I should go down there next," Sandy said thoughtfully. "That's why I came into the cafe. I wanted to talk to someone, ask about some of the country around here. When I finish with this jukebox, I want to go somewhere different and work on some more. I've pretty much been in all the canyons around here I can get to—Slaughter, Whitmore, Pasture, Water, Bear, Turtle—there's a lot around here, though I still have Range Creek."

Bud was now on high alert. Range Creek? What was he doing in Range Creek?

But as he formed the question, his phone rang. Sandy stood, waved goodbye, and headed out the door.

"Yell-ow," Bud answered, mildly irritated, though trying not to show it.

"Sheriff, are you coming back soon? I'm getting worn out by everything happening around here and could use some backup."

"We're on our way in a few minutes," Bud sighed. "As soon as Wilma Jean finishes showing my aunt how to use the stove. What's going on?"

Howie replied, "Well, first, I got stopped by a couple wanting me to help them find a vacation home. Bud, I'm not a tourism guy or anything, but I did try to steer them to Wilma Jean's B&B, but then they acted all frustrated, so I told them they were going to have to find their own place. But come to find out, they already had a place booked but were just lost. How one gets lost in Green River is beyond me."

Bud shook his head as Howie continued.

"So I told them how to get to it, then I stopped this car that was speeding, and as I was giving them a warning, a guy came by on his bicycle and chewed me out, saying that my flashing lights were disturbing him, and I should turn them off right after I stop people. I tried to explain that I leave them on as a deterrent, but he just rode off. And to top things off, there's someone with 'Vote for Digham' painted on their car who's driving all around town honking at everyone."

"So I take it Larry Digham's running for mayor after all?" Bud asked.

"Yes, and it's really irritating because he told Wilma Jean he didn't think he would. But that's one reason I want you guys to come back. I need to get those signs put up ASAP. You did pick them up, didn't you?"

"We did, Howie,“ Bud replied. "And here comes Wilma Jean now. We'll see you soon."

25

Bud was again sleeping on a cot, but this one was a bit sturdier than the old army cot at Ginger's. Lindy was sleeping soundly under the cot on her plush dog bed that he'd brought from the bungalow in Green River, which Bud hoped would keep her from trying to get in bed with him. If she did and this cot collapsed, at least they'd have something soft to land on this time, he figured.

This cot was much wider than the one he'd tried sleeping on at Ginger's and was one he'd bought right after his last expedition with the BOB-O's when he'd ended up sleeping on a hard vintage pad. He'd decided he wasn't getting any younger and needed something a bit more comfortable, plus it was hard on his knees getting up off the ground.

He could make out the faint outline of the full moon shining through his nylon tent, and he could also hear Shorty's faint snoring. Freckles was bedded down in Shorty's tent, though he'd wanted to be with Lindie. Bud was amenable to the idea, but Shorty wanted the dog to start bonding with him. Since Cassie was gone, they hadn't had any choice but to bring Freckles, and Bud hoped the dog would stick around. Howie had agreed to check on Whiskerbiscuit, Cassie's cat.

Bud felt restless, and since his sleeping bag wouldn't let him toss and turn, he instead began wiggling his toes, which he figured would serve the dual purpose of keeping his toes warm plus help satisfy his need to fiddle in order to think. He thought about getting his harmonica from his shirt pocket, but he knew playing it might wake Shorty, plus he'd forgotten to bring it.

It was late October, and the canyons were typically warm during the day through November, but the nights could get chilly, and here in the Books, winter was close at hand because of the higher altitude.

It seemed strange to actually be in Range Creek, camped in front of the old cabin where Mrs. Jensen now slept in a comfortable bed. If he hadn't invited her along, he and Shorty would be in that warm cabin, Bud mused, though the thought of actually sharing a place with Shorty wasn't very appealing because of his snoring.

Bud thought back to how he'd checked the weather and, seeing how a storm would be coming through in a few days, decided they should get into Range Creek as soon as possible. The road was basically impassible when wet, and he knew the archaeology field team would be closing things down soon. He and Shorty had hurriedly gotten their supplies and gear ready, then picked up Mrs. Jensen and hit the road, the key to the gate having arrived in the mail.

It wasn't a long drive, even in Bud's slow-going FJ, and about an hour later, they turned off the main road south of Sunnyside at a sign that read *Horse Canyon*, heading towards the imposing ramparts of the Books.

Bud had been on what the locals simply called "the pass" a number of times, but he never relished the drive, even though the views were spectacular. To him, it was more of a gap than a pass, a good place to take far-reaching photos in both directions—looking west to the desert and San Rafael Swell and east into the deep canyons of Range Creek and the Tavaputs Plateau. It was also a good place to take a break from the dizzying switchbacks up the side of Horse Canyon.

As a lad, he'd gone into Range Creek with his grandpa a number of times looking for stray cattle that had wandered over from Nine

Mile, and he recalled one summer day when they'd been caught in a gullywasher and had nearly gone off the edge near the pass, all while pulling a stock trailer. He'd developed a deep respect for the Horse Canyon Road, which was the only road into Range Creek Canyon.

Wiggling his toes while thinking about it, he remembered that one could also drive into the lower end of the canyon through Turtle Canyon, but the road wasn't maintained, and he'd heard it was in pretty bad shape. And there was the road coming down off the top of the Tavaputs, Sheep Creek Road, which had been built by Harvey in 1951, but was even steeper and shorter than the Horse Canyon Road with its 3,000-foot drop and ten narrow switchbacks.

As they'd topped out on the pass and started down the Range Creek side, Bud had kept an eye on Mrs. Jensen, who rode in the passenger seat while Shorty rode in the back with the dogs and their gear. She looked like someone out of a Zane Gray novel in her straw cowgirl hat, button-down billowy cotton blouse, jeans, and hand-beaded vest with what looked to be Aztec suns, all courtesy of the gently-used store in Price.

She'd noted his concern and said, "Bud, I can't tell you how many times I've been over this road with my friend and her mom, coming in to stay at the ranch with Harvey. This sure brings back fond memories."

"And this road doesn't make you nervous or anything?" Bud had asked, wishing they were down the other side.

She'd given him an exasperated look, then began telling stories of her escapades in the canyon as a kid, which Bud enjoyed hearing, as they helped keep his mind off the steep road.

Finally down at the bottom, they passed a primitive campground where visitors to the canyon could camp, as long as they had permits. It held only one vehicle, a white Chevy pickup with a nice camper on the back and Utah plates.

Shorty had unlocked the gate and waved Bud through, and they'd soon gone the dozen miles down the valley to the old ranch headquarters, which now housed the archaeologists and support people exploring the canyon's ruins.

Ranger Carl had called ahead, and the lead archaeologist, a white-headed man named Phil, greeted them, showing them to the old cabin, which sat a small distance from the main ranch house, connected by an expansive lawn.

After pitching their tents and getting Mrs. Jensen settled in, they'd gone to the ranch house, where they'd been invited to dinner with the crew. Bud had told Mrs. Jensen not to tell anyone he was the sheriff. She hadn't understood why, so Bud had said it was too complicated and he would explain later, but to just go along with them being geologists looking for the iridium layer, which was partly true, at least the part that was Shorty.

Dinner was homemade chili and cornbread, and upon finding out Mrs. Jensen had spent part of her childhood in the canyon, the crew had asked her myriad questions, which she seemed to enjoy. Bud was marveling at the change in her, comparing her to the little old lady who'd become somewhat of a thorn in his and Howie's sides and who now seemed like someone completely different.

And now, still trying to go to sleep on the cot, Bud felt unsettled. He was wondering how he'd come to be camping in Range Creek, trying to foil looters, and as he listened to the breeze pick up, blowing dried cottonwood leaves from the trees onto his tent, he finally had a hunch as to why he was feeling so uneasy.

In spite of being congenial and welcoming enough, Phil, the head archaeologist, had seemed to eye him somewhat suspiciously when he thought Bud wasn't looking.

That in itself made Bud uncomfortable, but what really made him take note was how much Phil looked like the Halloween mask he'd found in the Hercules Dynamite box floating on the river, which he found really odd.

He had no idea how things would work out, but he knew in just a few days he'd be back home. Now getting sleepy, he finally drifted off, dreaming about Howie showing a Fremont how to plant peanuts by wiggling his toes.

26

"I'm sorry, but we're under strict rules to not let anyone in the canyon without a guide," a guy named Lonnie informed them, who looked to Bud like he could enforce whatever rules he wanted, especially since he carried a rifle in a scabbard on his saddle.

Lonnie had helped them wrangle up and saddle several horses and a mule from the pasture next to the ranch house, and now Bud knew why he'd caught four instead of three—he intended to ride with them, to Bud's chagrin. How could they spy on looters with Lonnie along, and worse yet, what if he was one of them?

"We have permission from the BLM and the Utah wildlife folks to be in here," Shorty said curtly. "We don't need a guide—well, actually, we do, if you know where the iridium layer is."

"The what?" Asked Lonnie, now trying to mount his horse, a small black and white paint that looked to Bud to have a disposition matching Lonnie's from the way he sidestepped to keep him from getting on.

"Dang it, Tucker, stand still," Lonnie commanded.

Bud now rode his horse, a rangy sorrel named Spirit, next to Tucker so he couldn't sidestep.

Shorty replied, “We’re here geologizing, not looking for artifacts.”

“What exactly does geologizing entail?” Lonnie asked, now up on Tucker, who looked like he might start bucking any moment while eyeing Lindie and Freckles, who stood near Bud looking with trepidation at the large beasts.

“We’re here studying the formations, the layers, in the canyon,” Shorty replied. “You’re going to get awfully bored riding with us, because we’re not going to be doing much riding. Our forte is digging in the dirt.”

“Just like the archaeologists around here,” Lonnie replied. “Which is illegal, unless you’re here officially.”

“Which we are,” Bud added. “And we’re not digging looking for stuff, we’re digging to see what kind of rocks are there. And minerals.” He now looked at Shorty, hoping he hadn’t revealed his lack of knowledge about geology.

“Rocks are made of minerals, as we all know,” Shorty said. “And we’re actually more like pokers, not diggers. We take our rock hammers and poke around.” He then changed the subject, to Bud’s relief, asking, “Are you an archaeologist, Lonnie?”

Lonnie was now sidetracked, trying to get Tucker headed out, who’d decided he wanted to go back to the pasture.

“Dang horse,” he said, kicking Tucker’s sides while trying to turn his head. “He came from a rental stable and knows every trick in the book. No, I’m not an archaeologist. I just spend the summers here keeping everything running, feeding the horses, irrigating the hay fields, putting up the hay, repairing things, that kind of stuff. I’m a Jack of all trades. I’m from Wellington, near Price. We’re shutting the place down soon. I’ll be hauling these dang animals out over the pass and back home, and not a minute too soon for me.”

“The sheriff here’s from Price, too,” Mrs. Jensen now said from atop a mule named Abe.

Bud groaned, but said nothing. Shorty gave him a look, and as if realizing what she’d done, Mrs. Jensen said, “I mean, he used to be from Price, but now he lives in Green River.”

Lonnie laughed. “It’s OK. I know who he is. He’s Emery County

Sheriff Bud Shumway."

"How did you know that?" Mrs. Jensen asked.

"Phil told me," Lonnie answered.

"How does he know?"

"Beats me," Lonnie replied. "He just told us all before dinner that Bud was the sheriff. There's a bit of skepticism about your geology expedition. Or did you become a geologist all of a sudden?" Lonnie now looked at Bud with suspicion.

Shorty replied, "We never said Bud was a geologist. *I'm* the geologist. I taught at Stanford and also worked for the Yukon Geological Survey for many years. Bud's my helper, and Mrs. Jensen here is coming along because she knows the country. Why is that so unusual?"

Lonnie just shrugged his shoulders, then asked, "Exactly where are we going, anyway?"

"We're going to Choo-Choo Rock," Mrs. Jensen answered. "Since I'm the one who knows the country, I'm making the decisions, and that's where we're going. I've wanted to go back there for years."

"What's there?" Bud asked.

"Ask our guide," she nodded towards Lonnie. "He knows."

Lonnie looked surprised, then said, "Well, I don't know about anything special there, but I can tell you about Range Creek, it's like the last 1,000 years never even happened here. The petroglyphs here look like they were created yesterday, and the cliff-side granaries are still stocked with dried corn. At the peak of the Fremont occupation, hundreds if not thousands of Indians lived here. They grew maize, which they stored in the granaries high above the canyon floor. They lived here from 900 to 1200 AD, then they supposedly mysteriously disappeared, though we all know they're probably the ancestors of the Utes, just like the Anasazi are probably the ancestors of the Hopi and Puebloan people. But things here are so well-preserved that the field archaeologists have found perfect sandals, woven baskets, and strands of ancient human hair. Harvey Driggs bought the ranch in the 1950s, but it was at one time part of the Nutter Ranch holdings. Some of Nutter's cowboys took things, but Harvey was pretty good at making sure everything was left intact."

"You sound like a tour guide," Mrs. Jensen said.

"I am, part-time, anyway. The state lets 28 people come in per day, and I'm the one who gets to accompany them when the ranger's off-duty, though we never have that many. But what are you looking for at Choo-Choo Rock? It's a bit of a ride—a good 10 miles or so. We should go back and get the ATVs, they're faster and less of a hassle."

"Let's just ride up the canyon a ways," Mrs. Jensen said. "I can't tell you how much I'm enjoying being back on a mule, though I've actually never been on one. Harvey always had horses."

Bud was surprised at how agile she seemed to be, riding as if she'd been on a horse just yesterday, even though it had been many years.

He was even more surprised when a branch came crashing off a nearby cottonwood, making everyone jump, including Tucker, who took the element of surprise as the opportunity to take the bit between his teeth and run back towards the ranch house, leaving a trail of dust and Lonnie's cussing in his wake.

A fat porcupine ambled across the road in front of them, which Bud figured was probably the source of the breaking branch. He and Shorty both called the dogs.

"You think Lonnie will be OK?" Shorty asked, porcupine now gone on down to the creek.

"All he needs to do is hang on," Bud replied. "We're not all that far from the ranch. But let's use this little twist of fate as an excuse to do some exploring on our own. How far is Locomotive Rock again?" He asked Mrs. Jensen.

"It's a ways, but if we hurry, we have plenty of time," she replied. "There's water in the creek and plenty of grass for the horses, and I packed us all lunches, so we're good for the day. Let's roll 'em on out, Rawhide."

Bud grinned as they all took off, Shorty's muscular little cowpony Teton in the lead, Shorty bouncing along at a slow trot.

"Wait up, Shorty, and I'll teach you how to post," Mrs. Jensen yelled. "It'll save your rear end from destruction."

She was soon riding alongside him, showing him how to go up and down in the stirrups in unison with the horse's gait. Bud brought up the rear, wondering if Lonnie was OK, though it really didn't look like it was his first rodeo. The dogs happily trotted behind them.

They eventually slowed to a walk, enjoying the autumn golds and reds of the cottonwoods and sumac along the creek, as well as the burnished buff cliffs that pulled back from the canyon sides.

Now, Bud pulled Spirit to a stop, saying, "Don't look now, but we're being watched."

As the others stopped, he pointed up into the cliffs where a skull looked down on them, the empty eye sockets black as night in the shadows.

"Creepy," Shorty said, shielding his eyes from the sun.

"Oh, wow," Mrs. Jensen said. "I forgot all about that one. That skull was there even when I was a kid. We need to climb up there—rather, *you* need to climb up there and take a look. I'll stay down here and hold the horses."

"Why should we go up there?" Bud asked.

"Because that's where one of the mummies lives. It's in that alcove right behind the skull."

"How do we know it's still there?" Shorty asked, thinking of the photo Bud had shown him.

"Well, I can't imagine anyone taking it. Why would someone want a mummy?" Mrs. Jensen asked.

"Well, maybe they just wanted the burial items," Bud said.

"One of the archaeologists told me over dinner that the Fremont didn't put artifacts with their dead like some cultures did," Shorty replied. "He also said that, out of respect to the Utes, the archaeologists here leave human remains alone, even though they'd like to study them, as they could reveal a lot about the health, diet, and genetics of the Fremont. When they discover bones, they record the location, notify the BLM or the state and move on. But we might as well climb up there, Bud, though I suspect we'll find the mummy's gone."

"Why would it be gone?" Mrs. Jensen asked as they all dismounted.

"It decided it was finally old enough to leave home," Shorty joked.

Bud and Shorty scrambled up the steep canyon side, soon at the ledge where the skull seemed to be watching them. Puffing, they both leaned back for a moment, then Bud reached out and picked the skull up from its resting place in a small nook.

"Just as I thought, Shorty," he said, handing him the skull. "It's fake."

"It's too white, isn't it?" Shorty replied. "Plastic. Made in China." He returned the skull to the small rock shelf.

"Why would someone put a plastic skull up here?" Bud asked. "But let's crawl up to the alcove and see if the mummy's still there. I have a feeling it's long gone."

"No, I can see something up there, Bud," Shorty replied, now making his way up the steep slope. Bud waited, not wanting to be on Shorty's heels in case he started sliding backwards. He could see Mrs. Jensen holding the horses below, Abe the mule shaking his head up and down, wanting to graze.

Shorty was soon in the alcove, shouting, "Bud, I'm coming back down, stand aside."

He slid back to where Bud waited, then said, "There's something that kind of looks like a mummy, but when you get closer you can see it's a bunch of weeds and grasses all rolled together. Weird."

"Not really," Bud replied.

"Not really what?"

"Not so strange when you think of what the archaeologists said last night about how they record the location of remains and leave them there. If someone were looting, they'd want things to look untouched. Like that skull. You can bet the archaeologists know it's there, and if it were to go missing, they'd climb up to see why. If you leave plastic junk in its place, nobody suspects anything."

"Makes sense, I guess," Shorty replied. "And this is probably the final resting place of that mummy you have the photo of. But Bud, we need to get down off here. There's an ATV coming, and it's probably Lonnie."

They slid down off the rocks, barely making it back to the horses before an ATV drove up. But instead of Lonnie, it was Phil, and Bud noted he didn't look too pleased.

27

"Just what exactly are you doing here?" Phil asked, involuntarily glancing up at the skull.

Bud replied, "Are you asking me or the skull? We were wondering what kept it from blowing off that ledge."

"It's been there for a thousand years. Why would it blow off now?" Phil asked suspiciously.

Bud, watching Phil closely, said, "Because it's plastic, and plastic's much lighter than bone."

"Plastic? I've been up there and seen it myself. That's ridiculous. The Fremont didn't have plastic. It's bone."

Mrs. Jensen now said, "There's been a mummy up there for a long time, down behind that skull. We used to climb up there as kids and scare ourselves looking at it."

Bud replied, "And someone smuggled it out of here, which I would suspect was no easy task."

Phil said nothing, looking incredulous.

"It had to be someone who has a gate key," Bud added. "Or maybe they took it past the ranch house and out the river, but surely someone would notice, unless it was someone who worked here and no one thought anything of it, then you might get away with going out that way."

"That mummy's been there since I was a child," Mrs. Jensen said. "But it's not like you would know it unless you climbed up there for some reason."

"We have over 400 recorded sites here, so far, and we haven't even begun to touch this place," Phil said. "I'm sure there's stuff all over we don't know about. But we did know about that mummy and recorded it."

"It could've been someone from outside who was dressed to look like you, Phil," Bud continued. "Maybe wearing a mask that kind of resembles you. No one would think anything about seeing you on an ATV. I think they drove down the canyon to the river, stole a raft, and took the mummy to Green River. Unless maybe it actually *was* you."

Phil looked shocked. "Me? Steal antiquities? Never in a million years! My job is to protect them. And someone wearing a mask to look like me? Ludicrous!"

He now climbed up to the skull, disappeared into the alcove, then slid back down.

"I can't believe this," Phil said. "I just can't believe it. Someone wadded up a bunch of detritus in there to look like a mummy."

He sat down on a rock, catching his breath, then added, "I knew you were up to something, being a sheriff and all. That geology thing just didn't ring true."

"How did you know Bud was the sheriff?" Shorty asked. "Being that you guys are from Salt Lake and all."

"He pulled me over in Green River for speeding once. You don't remember that, do you?" Phil asked Bud.

Bud replied, "I thought you looked familiar. If I recall, I gave you a warning."

"You did, and I appreciated it, as I was close to losing my license. I drive too fast. But your geology thing is a ruse to look for looters?"

"It's no ruse," Bud replied. "We're looking for the iridium layer. Finding this was unexpected."

Bud felt uncomfortable, though it wasn't exactly a lie. They were looking for the layer and hadn't known they would find a plastic skull and the home of the missing mummy. He took the aluminum arrow from his pocket and began fiddling with it.

"The iridium layer here? In Range Creek?" Phil asked. "It's the wrong formation. Look, my training's in geo-archaeology. I'm the guy who studies the soils and sediments at a site to help determine how old things are. I studied a lot of geology, and these layers are too young. They're all Tertiary, laid down long after the big asteroid."

"True," Shorty replied. "But the Book Cliffs are Cretaceous, some 145-65 million years ago, and there's an unconformity here that nobody really knows the extent of. I'm hoping to find some of the North Horn Formation or something similar here."

"Well, good luck," Phil said. "This is all from about 58 to 48 million years old, the Flagstaff and Colton formations. Finding it here would be the last thing I would expect. I hope you don't, as we don't need a bunch of geologists roaming around the canyon."

"Well, they're generally a good bunch, even if they drink too much beer, and I know they'd get permits," Bud replied. "You know we have permission from the BLM."

Now Phil noticed what Bud was fiddling with and said, "Where did you get that? Mind if I look at it?"

Bud handed the aluminum arrow to Phil, who turned it over, then asked, "Where did this come from?"

"I don't know, maybe China," Bud replied.

"It belongs to me. I lost it when I was working on a dig somewhere here in the canyon about a week ago. See, it has my initials on it, *PM* for *Phil Masters*. One of my grad students gave it to me as a gift."

Shorty frowned, saying, "When I taught at Stanford, accepting gifts from students was taboo."

Phil, looking embarrassed, said, "She ended up becoming my fiancée. We're getting married after the canyon shuts down for the winter. She's moving to Salt Lake from Price after the wedding, though she'll probably end up helping me here next summer."

"You can keep the north arrow," Bud said. "Since it's yours anyway. I have no use for it, other than fiddling, which helps me think, but I'll find something just as good. And don't let Shorty give you a hard time, because he also ended up marrying one of his students."

Shorty laughed, "Yeah, Cassie, but about 30 years after she was my student."

Bud now said, "It's been nice talking with you, Dr. Phil, but we have work to do, and we need to get on it, especially with a storm coming in. We'll let you know if we find anything else missing, though I'm not really sure how we'd know."

With that, he helped Mrs. Jensen onto Abe, then he and Shorty got onto their horses and began riding up the canyon, the dogs at their heels.

Phil sat there for awhile, then turned the ATV around and headed back to the ranch headquarters.

"I guess he's going to let us do our own thing without a guide," Shorty commented, now riding alongside Bud, Mrs. Jensen in the lead.

"I think he's a bit shaken about the mummy," Bud replied.

"Are you sure he's not in on the looting?" Shorty asked. "I mean, telling him about someone wearing a mask that looks like him? Wouldn't that tip him off to change his tactics if he is helping someone loot stuff?"

"I wanted to see his reaction," Bud replied, slowing Spirit down a little, as the horse was beginning to live up to his name with his long energetic stride.

"I sure wish I knew what you boys are talking about," Mrs. Jensen said, now riding alongside them. "Is someone taking stuff from the canyon? If so, they're going to have to answer to Harvey."

"I thought he died some years ago," Shorty said.

"Harvey's ghost," she said. "But is this the real reason we're here, to look for looters? I'm going to have some great stories for Frosty."

Bud sighed. "Mrs. Jensen, you know you can't say a word to Frosty or anyone else until we're done here. Agreed?"

"For the umpteenth time, call me Eileen, and I won't tell anyone if you say not to. You just have to say not to."

"OK, don't tell anyone anything about this trip or what we're doing," Bud replied.

"I can't tell Frosty I went riding in Range Creek? That's no fun."

"OK, you can tell him about that, and that we're doing geology, but mum's the word about anything to do with looting and antiquities. Agreed?" Bud tried not to sound exasperated.

"Agreed. But Sheriff, can I tell him about the missing mummy and the skull?"

Bud groaned as she added, "I'm just teasing you. I won't say a word, I promise. I can't tell you how much I appreciate being able to come in here, and I don't want to do anything to expose your undercover spy operation. But let's get going on up to Choo-Choo Rock."

"Choo-Choo Rock?" Shorty asked.

"That's what everyone called it when I was a kid," Mrs. Jensen replied. "Nobody called it Locomotive Rock—the archaeologists were the ones who named it that. It looks like a big steam engine."

She now touched Abe's side with her heels and took off at a canter, leaving Bud and Shorty in the dust, Bud now thinking of the note in his pocket that read *Choo-Choo Rock* and wondering if it hadn't been written by someone local, now recalling that Lonnie had also called it that.

28

Bud and Shorty scrambled up and up, climbing the steep hill that held the remnant of a cliff that had eroded away until all that was left was a tall band that resembled a train engine, complete with smokestack.

The hill was thick with tall pine trees, testament to their altitude, and the pair had to make their way around thick piles of undergrowth and debris. Finally at the base of the rocks, they stood for awhile, catching their breath, when Shorty said, "Mrs. Jensen told me there's a nice granary up here in the rocks. How in hellsbells can she remember where all this stuff is after some 50 or more years? She's got a darn good memory."

Bud replied, "It wouldn't surprise me one bit, Shorty. My dad was like that—razor-sharp memory for things he did in his youth, though he got to where he couldn't even remember when his own birthday was. He could draw you a map to places he'd been as a youngster, complete with the trees and rocks, but he was good at getting lost on his way to the grocery store."

"I've heard that you have somewhat of a photographic memory yourself," Shorty remarked.

"I do for some things," Bud replied. "Landscape stuff, like trails and roads and that sort of thing. But when I'm in a city, I can only remember which street leads out. But look, isn't that the granary Mrs. Jensen told us about way up there?"

High above, tucked under an overhanging ledge in the rocks and clinging to the cliff face was a small curved wall of stacked rocks that had been tightly fit against the cliff face and mortared to keep rodents out. Bud suspected the small granary was filled with corn cobs, possibly seed corn for future planting in the valley floor. It was a precarious location, as were most of the granaries in the canyon, the archaeologists having to rope up and rappel back down.

"How in heck did they get up there?" Shorty asked.

"I've read that they sometimes used wooden ladders and ropes, or chiseled hand and toe holds into the rock face. But there's no way I'm going up there."

"Afraid of heights?" Shorty asked.

"I have this condition where my knees get wobblier and wobblier proportional to how high I am. If I go high enough, things start spinning, and they give out completely."

"It's called vertigo," Shorty replied.

"My knees are kind of chicken shaped," Bud commented. "But you're going up there?"

Shorty was now gingerly edging his way onto the cliff, saying, "Didn't Mrs. Jensen mention that there's this one crack in the ledge that you have to follow?"

Bud replied, "Yes, and she said after you reach the granary, there's a crack you can chimney up to get on top. There's a pit house up there with a pile of rocks still stacked by it, like they'd collected them for defensive protection. Be careful, Shorty. I can't believe she actually climbed up there at one time."

"Kids have no brains," Shorty replied, trying not to look down.

Now at the granary, Shorty yelled down, "I can't get close enough to look inside without going on up."

Instead of watching Shorty, Bud looked back down to where Mrs. Jensen sat on a log, holding the dogs on their leashes so they couldn't follow them. Bud had hobbled Abe and the horses, their reins tied up around their necks so they could graze.

Seeing Bud looking down, she waved. Bud waved back, and feeling as if he were about to float away, looked back up to see that Shorty was gone. Now gazing back along the canyon, taking in the contrast of colors—the reds, yellows, greens, browns, and buffs, all under a bluebird sky—Bud noticed a few wispy clouds coming in from the west. He could make out the slow-moving dark blue water of the creek below winding its way through what had once been cultivated hay fields but were now fields of tall yellow native grasses.

Now he thought he could hear Shorty yelling high above, and he yelled back, wondering what he would do if Shorty got himself in a pickle and needed rescued. He guessed he'd have to ride back down to the ranch headquarters and get help, for he knew there was no way he could climb up the narrow shelf.

Shorty was soon inching back down the ledge, and Bud could see he was carrying something that looked like a small pouch. Unable to watch, he reached for the aluminum arrow to fiddle with, then remembered he'd given it to Phil, so instead started humming.

Finally back, Shorty leaned against the cliff wall and took a deep breath.

"Man, that was hairy. That's why I brought this back to show you, because I know you'll never go up there, and I'm sure as heck not going back."

He handed Bud the small pouch, which Bud could see was made of a deep-purple velveteen with a gold drawstring and the words *Crown Royal* embossed on it in gold.

It was heavy, and Bud carefully opened it and looked inside.

"Shorty, this is going to turn the world of archaeology upside down, you realize that, don't you?"

Shorty laughed. "You think it could be a thousand years old?"

"Where exactly was it?"

"Tucked inside the rocks of a pit-house wall. Do you think it's real?"

Bud replied, "Well, it's real enough, but the question is whether or not it's valuable. It could be costume jewelry, but to my untrained eye, it looks like the real deal. Looks like someone robbed a jewelry store."

"There's a fortune in diamond earrings and gold necklaces in there, Bud, as well as bracelets. But why would someone leave it up in a pithouse in the sky like that?"

Bud said, "Maybe because it's so hard to get to. They know it would be safe, especially if it's a site the archaeologists have already studied. Nobody would be going back up there."

Shorty added, "And they could leave everything until things cooled down, then hock or sell it all. Maybe come back and retrieve it in the spring."

"Kind of the opposite of what's going on with the looting, eh? Bringing what's probably stolen goods into the canyon for safekeeping. You know, Shorty, this is the most protected canyon in Utah outside the national parks. Phil told me at dinner that most of the sites here are on rises above the creek's flood plain or even high on cliffs like this. Range Creek has a dozen tributaries, and most are untouched. If one had a list of the places that have been studied, you could hide things with complete impunity, knowing the sites won't be touched again. All you'd need is a list of the archaeologists' GPS coordinates. It's a paradise for hiding stuff, as long as you didn't need it back for awhile, as you can't get in here half the year or more."

"The perfect hiding place," Shorty replied. "But there are lots of good hiding places around Utah where nobody goes and that you can reach year-round. Why Range Creek?"

"Familiarity. If you worked here, you could keep an eye on things and it would feel much safer than out somewhere in the desert," Bud said. "And nobody's going to accidentally come upon things you've hidden. But it's getting late. We need to head back. What are you going to do with the pouch?"

"Give it to the sheriff," Shorty said, handing it to Bud.

"I'll have to find a safe place for it until we leave," Bud replied. "Any ideas?"

"You could hide it in a pithouse," Shorty kidded. "Or your saddle bags."

"Good idea," Bud replied as they began their trek back down the hillside. "And when we get back, I'll need to find out exactly what store or who was robbed. Do rich people have these kind of jewelry stashes?"

"You're asking me?" Shorty laughed. "The only jewelry I've ever owned is my gold-nugget belt buckle, and I found the nugget in the Yukon."

"Would that aluminum arrow qualify as jewelry?" Bud asked.

"Probably not," Shorty said. "It's more of a tool. But I wonder if Phil knows a lot more about what's going on than we do, since it was with the note and mask."

"Food for thought," Bud replied. Just then, the dogs ran up to greet them, Mrs. Jensen having seen them coming and unhooking their leashes.

"And Bud," Shorty added. "There's another plastic skull up there."

29

Bud, Shorty, and Mrs. Jensen all sat in camp chairs on the front porch of the old cabin, wrapped in warm blankets and watching the glow of the sunset lighting the canyon rim, the last of the crickets now beginning to mourn the oncoming winter, their chirping slower than usual.

"I know Halloween's close, but where did this come from?" Shorty asked, eyeing a plastic skull that decorated a nearby wooden table.

"I think Phil must've left it there," Bud replied. "It's the same one we saw by the mummy."

"How can you tell?"

"It has a crack by where its ear would be," Bud replied. "Probably ran into a tree or something, as it couldn't see too well."

Shorty frowned. "Why would he retrieve it and leave it here?"

"Maybe he's making a statement," Mrs. Jensen replied. "Maybe he wants us to leave."

"We might as well," Shorty said. "I don't think I'm going to find the iridium layer."

"Why not?" Bud asked.

"I think Phil's right. It's the wrong formation. Besides, I need lots more time than we have. It's going to take some serious looking if it is here."

"Can't you just look up at the canyon walls and see it?" Mrs. Jensen asked.

"Well," Shorty replied. "The layer's only about three centimeters thick over in the North Horn Formation by Emery, so it's not quite that simple."

Just then, Lonnie came by, carrying what looked to be a portable heater.

"You folks can use this," he said, placing it at their feet. "It's propane and will keep you warm. Just be sure to turn it off when you go to bed."

With that, he pulled out a firestick and lit it, the flames immediately putting out a welcome warmth, Lindie and Freckles both lying down by it.

"Might as well join us," Bud said. "Pull up a chair and tell us how the rodeo ended."

Lonnie sat on a nearby log, shaking his head. "That dang Tucker. Fortunately for him, one of the ranch hands has been wanting to buy him from me. He thinks he can work with him and make him into a nice cow pony. So, Tucker's leaving the canyon tomorrow in my stock trailer, along with Abe, Spirit, and Teton, but he's going to a different destination than they are. Good riddance to him."

"Are you OK, dear?" Mrs. Jensen asked.

"He smacked my leg against a corral pole when we came running back, but other than that, I'm fine. Thanks for asking," Lonnie said, looking disgusted.

"So, it looks like we're going to be walking tomorrow, eh?" Bud remarked.

Lonnie replied, "I think you guys might want to head on out. That storm's coming in a bit early. If you don't leave tomorrow morning you're going to get rained in here, or worse, snowed in, for who knows how long. The ranch is about ready to shut down for the winter anyway. You can come back next summer and look for that layer or whatever it is."

Now, as if encouraging them to heed Lonnie's advice, a stiff breeze came in, quickly dropping the temperature.

As everyone scooted closer to the propane heater, Bud asked, "Lonnie, any idea why this skull would be here on our table? Is it a Halloween decoration or something?"

"Halloween?" Lonnie asked. "Nah, I went out to check a site we'd cleared and found it there. It's kind of weird. I thought you might know something about it."

"Was it at Locomotive Rock?" Bud asked.

"Choo-Choo Rock? No, this one was at a pithouse near the creek. Phil asked me to go double-check a GPS reading, and the skull was just sitting there. Bad thing was, someone had been digging in the pithouse, and I know it wasn't any of our crew, because they left a big mess. That particular site was one they were saving for next summer when some of Phil's new grad students were coming out. He wanted to use it to teach them how to dig and stuff, as it was so accessible."

"Do you think whoever it was got anything of value?" Shorty asked.

"Who knows? It's never been excavated. But they left a big pile of dirt, a real mess. They're lucky I didn't see them."

"Any idea when they dug it?" Bud asked.

"Recently. You guys weren't there today, were you? I mean, after I left on Tucker."

"Lonnie, we'd never do something like that," Shorty said. "We're professionals."

"What does that mean?" Lonnie asked suspiciously. "That you take notes while looting?"

"I'm going to forget you said that," Shorty replied, irritated. "Or maybe pretend I never heard it."

"Now, Lonnie," Mrs. Jensen interrupted. "You're a grown man, and I don't want to hear another insinuation from you that these boys would take anything out of here. After all, you're talking to the Sheriff of Emery County and one of the top geologists in the country. We're here looking for some layer or other, and if you want to cause trouble, you're going to have to answer to me."

"So let's get out our guitars and sing Kumbaya together," Lonnie answered sarcastically. "Kumbaya, my Lord, kumbaya..."

"I don't believe I know that one," Mrs. Jensen said. "But yes, go get your guitar. That's a great idea."

"You're joking, right?" Lonnie asked with surprise.

Now Bud asked, "Lonnie, do you have any idea who might be looting out here? Have you seen anything or anyone suspicious looking?"

"Just you guys," Lonnie replied, then added, "But are you insinuating I know who's doing it? And maybe that I'm a part of it? Like they say in the old Westerns, them's fightin' words."

"First of all," Shorty replied, "You just accused *us* of looting a few minutes ago, am I correct? And second, *them's* not a real word, it's grammatically incorrect. And third, fighting words are, according to the Supreme Court, words which, by their very utterance, inflict injury or tend to incite an immediate breach of the peace, and fighting words are a category of speech not protected by the First Amendment. My words didn't inflict injury or breach the peace, so they're not fighting words."

"Do you even have a guitar?" Mrs. Jensen asked, ignoring Shorty. "Or were you just making that up?"

"I never said I had a guitar," Lonnie answered.

"Yes, you did. You said, and I quote, 'Let's go get our guitars.' Go get it. We'll wait," Mrs. Jensen persisted. "And if you have any Irish Cream or anything like that, bring it along, too."

Lonnie, now looking incredulous, stood and headed for the main ranch house across the way.

"Grab yourself a warm jacket!" Mrs. Jensen yelled as he disappeared. She then turned to Shorty and said, "You're sure a smarty-pants, Mr. Doyle. How did you get to be so knowledgable?"

"There's a difference between smart and knowledgable," Shorty answered, Freckles now by his side, the wind picking up even more, "I don't think I'm smarter than other people, I just have a different set of tools, since I have a graduate degree in geology. A lot of my tools aren't even that useful in day-to-day life. But I enjoy learning, and I think happiness comes through knowledge. You see, to me, every bit of knowledge I learn makes the world a bit less intimidating. So, I like to share my knowledge."

"Your wife's a lucky gal," Mrs. Jensen mused. "I wish Frosty was more like you. All he wants to talk about is the good old days or food."

"Nothing wrong with either of those," Bud said, Lindie at his feet. "But before Lonnie comes back, assuming he does, do you remember when you said Harvey didn't have any children? Wouldn't that mean he didn't have any grandkids?"

"I'm pretty sure that's how things work, Bud," Shorty replied. "No kids, no grandkids."

"Did he adopt someone?" Bud persisted.

"Why do you ask?" Mrs. Jensen asked.

"Because I met a woman who claims to be his granddaughter. She's the interim director of the museum in Price, and she said the canyon here rightfully belongs to her archaeology team, since her family once owned it. Are you positive he had no children?"

"I'm positive, Bud. I spent a good deal of my childhood with the Driggs family. I would know, if anyone did. He had no children. But did you hear her actually say that? Be careful of second-hand reports, though as sheriff, you already know that."

Now Shorty, who'd been examining the skull, said, "Bud, you said this was the skull from Locomotive Rock, but Lonnie said he found it at some pithouse site. But it does have that same crack by its ear. What's up with that?"

"I think it's from the same mold. Someone bought a bunch of them at Wiggins Diggins, and they probably all came from the same manufacturer."

"Why would someone want a bunch of plastic skulls?" Mrs. Jensen asked.

"So they could leave them laying around Range Creek," Shorty answered.

Bud now replied, "Actually, Shorty, I think you might be right. But

Lonnie's coming back, and I think we should listen to him and get out of here tomorrow."

"How about tonight?" Shorty asked. "Did you feel that? It's starting to spit a little snow."

"Oh my," Mrs. Jensen said. "I'll vote for tonight. I can't get stuck in here."

Just then, Lonnie walked up with a guitar and a bottle of what looked to be Crown Royal whisky.

"We're leaving tonight," Shorty said. "Maybe you'll want to go out with us."

"I can help you load up the horses while Shorty and Mrs. Jensen get our stuff packed up," Bud offered.

Lonnie replied, "I already have my tack and everything packed in my truck, and I'm all hooked up. All I need to do is grab a few personal things, tell Phil we're leaving, and load the horses. They're easy loaders."

Now Mrs. Jensen held up her hand, saying, "We have time for one important thing. I want to hear this song Lonnie was talking about, and I think a shot of whiskey would do us all good. I'm beginning to feel like my life has been revived, and I want to celebrate."

"You can have my shot, Mrs. Jensen," Bud said. "It will make you even more revived."

Lonnie played Kumbaya while everyone but Bud sipped whiskey, then, as if a fire had been lit under them, they all got busy getting ready to go.

Finally on their way out, Bud rode with Lonnie, and Shorty drove Bud's FJ, Mrs. Jensen in the front and the dogs in the back. They slowly made their way up Range Creek Canyon to the gate, then on up over Horse Canyon Road, which was already starting to get wet.

As they topped over the pass, Lonnie said, "Well, that's a relief. I was worried we wouldn't make it up. Now to see if we can get down without sliding over the edge."

"You're doing great," Bud encouraged him. "Just take it slow and easy, and we'll be down before you know it."

"I'm glad to be getting out of there," Lonnie said. "I'm starting to get crotchety. Actually, everyone is, especially Phil. I guess it's rough when you're in academia and don't meet your goals. Too much pressure."

"What kind of pressure?" Bud asked.

"He was hoping to find the shield," Lonnie replied, glancing in the rearview mirror to make sure the stock trailer was still there.

"What shield?"

"After he sold the ranch to the state, Harvey Driggs told Phil he'd stopped one of Preston Nutter's cowpunchers carrying a buffalo-hide shield. It apparently had some kind of design on it that was really unusual as it had some kind of marine symbol. See, everyone says the Utes were descendants of the Fremont, but nobody can prove anything, since it was so long ago and there doesn't seem to be any continuity. This marine symbol might show a connection to some other group, maybe an oceanic bunch, or maybe some kind of trade route. If so, it could change some ideas about the Fremont."

"And finding this shield would make him famous, right?"

"I'm sure, at least in the world of archaeology. It would be significant. He and the director of the museum in Price have spent a lot of time looking for it. But so far, nobody's found anything."

"Here comes somebody, Lonnie, stay over," Bud said as a Jeep came up the switchbacks. He strained to see who it could be, but they passed without slowing.

Finally down and at the pavement where the road met the highway, Lonnie called his wife, then said, "Bud, I want to apologize for insinuating you guys were looters. I feel real bad about that. And thanks for helping me get out. I would've been stuck in there for a week or more if I'd waited until morning. And my wife's real tickled I'm coming home. She says she's not gonna let me sell Tucker. She's soft hearted and says Tucker would miss the others, so we're both going to work on his training. Anyway, call me if there's anything I can do to help you out."

With that, Bud said goodnight, and Lonnie pulled out, headed for his place near Wellington, as the snow started coming down hard.

Now headed for Green River and happy to be going home, Mrs.

Jensen and Shorty sang the words to Kumbaya over and over as the snow came down, the FJ's wipers keeping time, Bud straining to keep the vehicle on the slick road. Even though it was tense driving through the storm, he felt a sense of relief, knowing they'd all survived the spy mission.

And in the back, snuggled on their comfy dog beds, Freckles and Lindie slept the sleep of the innocent while a plastic skull watched over them and a velveteen Crown Royal bag of jewelry.

30

"Bud, I'm not sure how I'm supposed to work with that thing staring at me," Howie said. "Why is there a skull on your desk, anyway?"

"That skull's there to remind me to figure out why someone would leave skulls sitting around, Deputy. But go ahead and stick it in the bottom desk drawer if you want."

Bud and Howie were both in the office catching up on paperwork, as there was nothing else going on. Bud had searched for reports of stolen jewels and found nothing. The rain was coming down hard, and he felt that he would be forever grateful to Lonnie for suggesting they leave Range Creek the previous evening.

Howie gingerly picked up the skull, putting it in the desk drawer, then said, "It feels like it's made out of plastic. Where did you get it?"

"Range Creek. There's another like it where that mummy came from."

"Why would there be plastic skulls out there?"

"I don't know. That's what I'm trying to figure out," Bud replied.

"It makes me want to replace my plastic water bottle with a stainless steel one," Howie said. "They say plastic is bad for you. Maybe it made their skulls soft."

"Howie, the Fremont didn't even have plastic—well, not as far as I know, and I kind of doubt if it would affect their skulls, even if they did. But what were you doing that the skull distracted you from?"

"Well, Sheriff, I got a call the other day from a gal saying her neighbor's wind chimes kept waking her up. I did some research, and I can't find anywhere that says it's illegal to have wind chimes. So I'm trying to see if anyone sells silent wind chimes, the kind that don't make any noise. If I can find some, maybe I can persuade her neighbor to replace them."

Bud looked at Howie, trying to figure out if he was kidding or not, then said, "Howie, if you can find some, I'll personally pitch in to help buy them."

Howie replied, "Just kidding, Sheriff. Sometimes I get the impression you think I'm kind of gullible."

"Closet geniuses can sometimes have that effect, Deputy," Bud grinned.

Howie was quiet for awhile, drumming his fingers on his desk, then said, "Bud, I can't figure out if that's a compliment or an insult. It's kind of like when Maureen told me I had a million-dollar voice and a ten-cent brain."

"Howie, you know she was kidding—she even said so. That's what Roy Acuff said to Hank Williams—he was warning him about his drinking."

"I don't even drink, Sheriff," Howie replied. "But do you think I'm gullible?"

"Deputy, I could ask you the same question about myself. We all do things sometimes that make us look that way. It's just part of being human—like me losing sleep trying to figure out how a dinosaur could stomp someone and kill them, when dinosaurs don't even exist anymore."

"They still haven't figured out what killed that guy in Sunnyside?"

"Not as far as I know," Bud said. "Well, actually, they did—the medical examiner said he was crushed by something heavy that left a three-toed print on his back. I'm not sure what he actually put on the death certificate, as that seems a bit iffy."

"You know, if you were sitting around wondering how you might die, I think being stepped on by a dinosaur would be pretty far down on the list," Howie mused. "Maybe a dinosaur statue fell on him or something. Like that big metal Utahraptor statue they have in front of the museum."

Bud was silent for a moment, then said, "There was nothing like that near the guy, though that's as good a guess as any. But are you ready for the car show? It's coming up soon, isn't it?"

"Next week," Howie replied. "I found this pompadour gel that has glitter in it. I hope it gets here in time."

"I can't exactly picture James Dean with glitter in his hair. Is the band all set?"

"We've been practicing a lot, but Maureen says I smile too much. She says rebels don't smile. But I wrote a song for you that we're going to debut at the concert. Wanna hear it?"

"Sure."

"It's called *Bud's Song*."

"Seems appropriate," Bud replied.

"OK, here goes."

Have another cup of coffee,
To start a brand new day.
Another cup of coffee,
To see us on our way.
Is it ritual or addiction?
I couldn't really say.
Another cup of coffee,
With ice cream like Monet.
It's called a Shumway Latte,
The best way to start your day.

"Howie, that's fantastic," Bud replied. "I like it. But did Monet put ice cream in his coffee?"

"I'm working on that line still, Bud. It's hard to rhyme sometimes, things get tangled up. For example, I started one about that mummy that I called *The Dehydration Blues*, but got stuck."

"Maybe for the best," Bud replied.

Just then, his cellphone rang.

"Yell-ow."

"Bud Shumway?" A woman's voice asked.

"Speaking."

"Bud, this is Bailey, up at the museum. The one you left the figurine with. I'm cleaning out my office as we speak."

"Well, that sounds like a good thing to do, Bailey," Bud replied. "I wish I had your ambition."

"No, no, you don't understand. Cleaning out as in I've been fired. Renee found out I sent the figurine up to the university, and she fired me for insubordination."

"I'm really sorry to hear that, Bailey. But, as interim director, can she actually do that? Insubordination sounds like a military thing, not like something a museum employee could be fired for."

Bailey was silent, then said, "I don't know. That's a good point."

Bud asked, "Is Renee there right now?"

"No, she left unexpectedly for a few days. She didn't say why or where she was going, but she left me in charge, then said I should be ready to leave when she gets back."

Bud sighed. "Since I'm somewhat involved here, why don't you hold out on cleaning out your office and let me call Judge Richter, who's on the board of directors. My uncle's a friend of his, and I also know him from a few cases he's presided over in court. I'll see if she can legally do that or not. In the meantime, did you hear anything back as to whether the figurine is authentic or not?"

"It's real, but Renee has it. I told her it belongs to you, but she's saying you had to have collected it in Range Creek, and it's illegal. One of the university people I trusted with it returned it to her instead of me. She said she's going to have charges filed against you."

"Tell her to have Sam Wiggins file them," Bud replied. "But I'll get back to you as soon as I can get ahold of Judge Richter, who would, incidentally, oversee the case against me. But she sounds like she's having a bad day."

"She's *always* having a bad day," Bailey replied. "And she loves making sure that *you* do, too. Oh, and one more thing—I just discovered that the piece that would be the match to the figurine you brought is missing from the Pilling display."

"Bailey, do you think the missing figurine might have more to do with your being fired than insubordination?" Bud asked.

Bailey answered quietly, "It never occurred to me. I would never take anything from the museum."

"I'm not thinking it would be you," Bud replied. "But more because you know it's missing."

"You're right, maybe she thinks I did it. I'm going to do some more looking around before she gets back and escorts me off the premises."

"Call if you need anything," Bud said.

They said goodbye, and Howie said, "That sounded like an interesting call."

"I just found out I'm going to be charged with stealing antiquities from Range Creek."

"You mean the plastic skull?" Howie asked.

"No, a figurine that I bought up in Price. I have the receipt."

"Do mayors have the authority to pardon things like that?" Howie asked.

"I don't think so, Howie, but thanks anyway."

"Well, if I win, I'll make sure you get pardoned somehow."

"But Howie, I didn't steal it."

Ignoring Bud, Howie replied, "I just found a silent wind chime on the Internet. It's called a Mandala Wind Spinner. Listen to this."

> *Is it just us, or is meditating easier on a beautiful, breezy day? Set your intentions—whether to find inner calm or pay attention to nature—in motion with these mesmerizing designs. Inspired by Buddhist mandala imagery, the twirling metal pieces pop out in layers to reveal a vibrant three-dimensional design. When the wind blows, they spin blissfully.*

"I could use a little inner calm right now, Howie. But how's the mayoral campaign coming?"

"Actually, Bud, I'm kind of losing interest and hoping I don't get elected. I've decided I'd rather be a rockabilly star—or am I being gullible to think that could ever happen?"

"I don't know, Howie," Bud replied. "You guys have the talent, no question about it, but it's more a matter of being discovered, however that works."

Howie added, "I don't think I'm going to get any votes anyway."

"Why's that?"

"Well, Larry Digham's signs say, *Vote for the Future, Digham for Mayor*. Mine just say, *Back to the rockin' good old days. Howie McPherson.* I forgot to put the words *vote* and *mayor* in there."

Bud laughed. "Howie, you're joking again, right? But I need to make a call, then let's go get some lunch at the Chow Down."

"Sounds like a plan," Howie replied. "As long as I don't come off as being gullible by thinking we'll actually do it."

"I don't think it's a bit gullible," Bud replied, "When you can stake your life on something actually happening."

31

The rain had stopped, and Bud sat in his FJ out at the farm, debating whether or not to let the dogs out. He knew they felt pent up like he did, yet he wasn't sure he wanted to have to clean mud off everything.

He finally decided to let them go into the nearby equipment shed where he worked on the tractors and implements. They could sniff around in there while he made sure the battery trickle charger he'd put on his old pickup for the winter was working.

The shop was cold, so Bud turned on the big oil heater by his workbench, then scooted his wheeled office chair up to the big window that looked out over the fields. He could see fog drifting up from the nearby river, and everything felt damp and wet.

He knew winter was just around the corner, and he wondered what it would bring. He hoped it would be mild, and the winds that sometimes plagued Green River would blow themselves somewhere else, like maybe up over the top of the Tavaputs.

He now wondered if the archaeology crew was stuck in the canyon, though he knew they probably were, considering the amount of rain that had come down. They'd probably gotten a bit of snow, as the canyon was surrounded by high country and it had been snowing when he and Mrs. Jensen and Shorty had fled with

Lonnie. And who had been in the Jeep, going in instead of out in a storm?

And come to think of it, he hadn't heard a word from Mrs. Jensen, though they hadn't been back all that long, but he half-expected her to be calling for something or other. Maybe she was busy enthralling Frosty and Eldon with her stories of adventure in the canyon, though she'd have to do some pretty good exaggerating to have much to talk about. He hoped her ride-along penchant was over now that he'd taken her out for some real riding.

Lindie came and lay down next to Bud, bored, while Hoppie and Pierre sniffed around, hoping to find a mouse or two. It would soon be time to take them home for dinner, but he knew he badly needed some time to himself to think and try to process everything that had been happening. He again reached for the aluminum arrow in his pocket, then remembering it was gone, he picked up a wrench and began tapping it on the desk.

His first thoughts went to Jimmy Johnson and what Howie had said about how a dinosaur statue or something must've fallen on him. This made a lot more sense than an actual dinosaur running amuck, but where was the evidence? Sam Wiggins had said there was nothing nearby when they'd found his body. Had someone been out there with him, helping him load coal, and some kind of accident had happened, killing Jimmy? Had they then removed the evidence and fled?

And what about the strange sounds his Aunt Ginger had heard, and the ones he himself had heard that night in their porch room? What was the source of that? Even his Uncle Junior had heard something. Was all this related to Jimmy's death or was it something completely different?

He now thought of Phil, the archaeology field team leader, and wondered if he was somehow involved in the looting. He'd acted suspicious from the start, but Bud had eventually written it off to Phil in turn being suspicious of him, knowing he was the sheriff. Had their geology story been convincing enough? One nice thing about having Mrs. Jensen along, at least in Bud's opinion, was that they would seem more innocuous with her there, as most people wouldn't suspect a nice older woman like that to be involved in anything questionable.

And what about the guy they'd seen in Whitmore Canyon carrying the boombox, the one named Sandy who'd told Bud he was working on a jukebox? Why would he be working on something that was pretty much a thing of the past, though a lot of stuff in Sunnyside seemed to be that way? Did he know anything about Jimmy's death?

Bud now began rolling his chair back and forth, nearly running over Lindie, who jumped up, looking hurt.

"Sorry," he said absent-mindedly, patting her head. He now began thinking of the guys on the raft out by the geyser and the mummy they'd had with them. It was pretty likely it was the same mummy missing up near Locomotive Rock. Were they the same two guys who'd met Rod Ruff in the canyon and tried to sell him back his own tires? Had they brought the mining memorabilia into Wiggins Diggins, which Bud was pretty sure had been stolen from the Sunnyside Museum?

Bud suspected the pair was somehow involved in the looting Ranger Carl had told him about, though come to think of it, Carl hadn't provided much in the way of details, other than that the thieves were taking Fremont antiquities. For all Bud knew, it could be pots or any number of things. He'd even heard of people blasting chunks of rock art off cliffs. But the two guys, who'd called themselves Trevor and Cory, had certainly acted like they were doing something illegal when Bud had overhead their conversation.

And those names, there was something vaguely familiar about them, but he couldn't quite put his finger on it. It would make sense that they were taking stuff from the canyon and drifting it down in stolen rafts to the geyser boat launch, and their voices had sounded similar to the ones who'd taken Rod's whitewalls. And who was Lucy, AKA Rita Brown?

And why was Renee, who was claiming to be the granddaughter of Harvey Driggs, so confrontative, accusing Bud of stealing the lost Pilling figurine and then firing Bailey? And what the heck was going on with the plastic skulls? And what was all the fuss over a lost shield?

And the jewels—he'd almost forgotten about them, which he'd put in the evidence safe at the sheriff's office. Where did they come from? Was Lonnie somehow involved? The jewels were in a Crown Royal bag, and he'd passed around a bottle of Crown Royal the evening they'd left Range Creek.

And another thing—Mrs. Jensen had told them that Choo-Choo Rock was what Locomotive Rock had been called by the locals, and Lonnie had also called it that. Was the looting some kind of inside job with Lonnie involved? And what about the Hercules Dynamite box and its strange mask that looked like Phil?

Bud's head was starting to spin, and he knew there was no way he would ever figure everything out. He wondered if Ranger Carl's mom was doing any better, and if Carl would be coming back soon, wanting Bud to go back into Range Creek with him. Of course, now that everyone knew he was the sheriff, Carl probably would have to fund a new undercover assistant, or at least so Bud hoped. He wouldn't have to worry any more about spying and getting shot, nor try to figure out who was looting.

He sighed, feeling overwhelmed, then got up and kicked an old tennis ball Lindie had left in the shed from last summer, but she didn't seem very interested. Hoppie and Pierre were now sitting by the door, and Bud figured their internal clocks were telling them it was almost dinner time.

He'd go back to the bungalow, feed the dogs, then wrangle up something to eat, as Wilma Jean was again working at the bowling alley. As he opened the shed door, ready to load everyone up, he saw something in the bushes. Worried it might be a coyote, he quickly put the dogs into the FJ, then turning to chase it off, saw that it was Freckles.

He groaned, loaded the dog in with the rest of the gang, then headed for Shorty's place.

32

Bud was soon at Shorty and Cassie's ranch, where he saw Cassie's car and knew she'd come home. Shorty was unloading a suitcase from the trunk, and upon seeing Bud, he came over and got Freckles, opening the door to the house and pushing the dog inside.

"I'm really sorry, Bud," Shorty said. "I made the gate dog proof, but he slipped out during the excitement of Cassie coming back. At this point, I'm wondering if it wouldn't be prudent to find him a home he likes better before he gets himself into trouble running around."

Just then, Cassie came outside, Freckles at her heels.

"Don't let him out!" Shorty exclaimed. "He'll take off again."

But instead, Freckles seemed fascinated with Cassie, following her every step. She said hello to Bud, retrieved something from her car, then went back inside the house, the dog dutifully at her heels.

"Looks like he's taking to Cassie," Bud commented.

"Figures," Shorty replied. "I hope so, anyway. Dogs usually do like her better, but at least Whiskerbiscuit likes me. Thanks for bringing Freckles back."

"It's okay, Shorty," Bud replied. "I read a study in *Popular Science* that says cats bond with humans just as much as dogs do, even if they don't show it much. And they're pickier about who they bond with. I need to talk to you about what's going on in Range Creek, but I'm too tired right now. I'm going to go home and crawl into bed with a good book and promptly fall to sleep."

"I hear you," Shorty replied. "I'm glad we came out when we did because of the weather, but also because Cassie came back early. Are you thinking about going back in there?"

"I don't know at this point. I'm kind of hoping not. It's pretty much beyond me what's going on, and I need some time to think about it all."

They said goodnight, and Bud was soon driving through the inky night back to the bungalow, the last remnants of the dark clouds from the storm hiding the stars.

Suddenly, he thought he saw something on the road ahead and slowed, thinking maybe someone's cow or horse had gotten out. As he got closer, he was surprised to see it was a man walking along, wearing a white jacket and carrying something.

"Evening," Bud said, slowing down. "Everything OK?"

He could now see it was Sandy, who was carrying his boombox with headphones covering his ears. He removed the headphones, turned off the boombox, then said, "Nice seeing you again, Bud. Actually, I wouldn't mind a ride back to my truck. I kind of overestimated how far I came and am getting tired."

"Hop in," Bud said. "Just tell Lindie to scoot over. Where's your truck?"

"It's down the road a ways."

"I don't remember passing it on my way out."

Sandy replied, "It's actually back in town. I parked by that little cafe."

They drove along in the dark, Bud asking, "Are you still doing jukebox repair?"

"I never said I was doing that," Sandy replied.

"Really? I was pretty sure you told me that at the Sunnyside Cafe."

Sandy laughed. "Not to get fussy, but I said I was working on a jukebox."

"What's the difference?" Bud asked.

"Well, the difference is quite major."

"Then you build jukeboxes," Bud replied, sensing the guy didn't want to talk about it. "But did you make it into Range Creek?"

Sandy replied, "I did, but I didn't stay long. The place had bad vibes."

Bud was curious, but didn't want to pry. They were almost at the Melon Rind Cafe when Sandy said, "I didn't realize you were the sheriff when I talked to you up at Sunnyside until your aunt said so. But there's something you should perhaps know."

"Oh?"

"Well, you probably think I'm nuts with my jukebox talk, but I just prefer people don't know what I'm doing. I run into a lot of sarcasm and such, as most people just don't get it. But I'm with the university, and I study soundscapes. I record the sounds of an ecosystem for future generations, as well as for the ecologists that study them. I'm what's called an acoustic ecologist. I'm creating what's called the Acoustic Atlas. So far, it has more than 2,500 recordings of species and environments from throughout the West. I record the planet's jukebox of natural sounds—the music of insects and owls, of rivers and streams, of rustling grasses and forests moving in the wind."

"That's actually kind of poetic," Bud replied.

"Thanks. And every sound has a purpose. Did you know that male cicadas produce the loudest sounds in the insect world, and entomologists believe that the sound protects them by hurting predators' ears? I call each soundscape my jukebox. I have a lot of jukeboxes, all in different landscapes, and they have a scientific purpose beyond having a record of the sounds of the natural world. I study an area, then come back again later to see how things have changed."

"I've never heard of an acoustic ecologist," Bud replied. "It sounds really interesting. And to get to wander around nature like that..."

Sandy continued. "We know that noise pollution harms animals. Human-made sounds threaten the feeding, migration, and communication of mammals, birds, fish, reptiles, and amphibians. But noise pollution is also bad for our own health. It can lead to high blood pressure, heart disease, stress, and insomnia."

"Maybe that's why I like being in the Big Empty so much," Bud replied. "It always makes me feel good."

"It's a really quiet place in terms of human sounds," Sandy said. "Thanks for telling me about it—I've been out there a bunch now. My Big Empty jukebox has lots of birds and other sounds. You're healing yourself when you're out there, Bud. Those who seek solitude in the woods are on a medicinal path—writers and hermits and people like you. Silence promotes the regeneration of brain cells in the hippocampus, which is key for learning, memory, and emotion, and it's also therapeutic for certain types of depression and dementia."

Sandy paused, seeming pensive, then added, "I heard that the Sunnyside power plant was going off-line for a few weeks to install some kind of scrubber or something. I'm thinking of going back up there when it's quiet to work on the Whitmore Canyon jukebox some more."

Bud now pulled up in front of the Melon Rind Cafe. It had only a few patrons this late in the evening, and he could see Maureen inside, wiping off tables, probably getting ready to close down and go home. A Chevy pickup with a nice camper sat in front. Bud recognized it as being the same one he'd seen parked at the gate in Range Creek when they'd all gone in and knew it was Sandy's.

Now Bud asked, "What if you're out someplace really quiet and you have a song stuck in your head, say something like *Found a Peanut* —is being out in nature still restorative?"

Sandy groaned. "Now I'll have that song stuck in my head. But no, I think that may be the opposite of restorative." He hesitated, then added, "But Bud, that's not what I wanted to tell you, I just got carried away with my jukebox thing."

"Go ahead," Bud replied. "I'm listening."

"Well, since you're sheriff, there's something you should know. When I was in Range Creek, I was up in the rocks trying to record two ravens at their nest when I saw a woman come in on an ATV. She had a guy with her. They got out shovels and proceeded to dig in one of the pithouse sites, then put a bunch of stuff from it into bags and drove off. It was like they knew exactly where to dig. I couldn't really see that well, but it looked like they took out several pots and what looked like some woven sandals."

"Would you be able to identify them if you saw them again?" Bud asked.

"Yes, easily. The woman was a middle-aged woman with shoulder-length brown hair, and the man had longish white hair."

"Could you tell if he was wearing a mask?"

"A mask? No, I couldn't tell something like that. I was too far off."

"Thanks for the information, Sandy. It may turn out to be very helpful," Bud replied.

"Thanks for the ride, Bud," Sandy now said, getting out of Bud's FJ, Lindie scooting back onto that side of the seat.

"Not a problem," Bud replied. "But I should probably get some kind of contact information from you in case we need to call you as a witness. You would be willing to do that, wouldn't you?"

"I'm Professor Sandy Young at the University of Utah. You can get my contact info online."

Bud had pulled a pen and business card from his pocket. "Mind if I write it on here?"

Sandy, now looking conflicted, walked around to Bud's window, saying, "Bud, I almost didn't tell you that for a reason. I'm hesitant to get anyone into trouble."

Bud replied, "So let me get this straight. You're willing to tell me a possible crime's been committed, but not who did it?"

"Alright, give me one of your cards."

Bud handed him a card, and Sandy wrote down a number and handed it back.

"That's my cell," he said. "It's turned off when I'm out recording, but you can leave a message if you need to contact me. And I kept seeing these creepy skulls everywhere in there, that's what I meant when I said Range Creek had bad vibes. I decided not to finish my Range Creek jukebox."

Sandy then got into his pickup and drove off, leaving Bud relieved that he now knew what Sandy was doing but also wondering at what he'd said about seeing the dark-haired woman and white-haired man.

33

Bud sat in his office, wondering how Judge Richter's Museum Board of Directors meeting would go. He'd just got off the phone with the judge, explaining the situation with Renee firing Bailey, and the judge had expressed concern, though he said he couldn't talk about it until after the meeting. Apparently there was a rumor making the rounds that Renee was going to fire everyone and replace them with friends, which was highly unethical.

Bud decided to call Bailey and tell her what the judge had said about insubordination, as well as the meeting, though she of course couldn't attend. He dialed her number at the museum, wondering if she'd finished cleaning out her office yet.

"Price Museum, Bailey Miles speaking."

"Hi Bailey, this is Bud. How's everything going?"

"Well, given the current situation, OK, I guess. I was just getting ready to call you."

"You were?"

"Yes, I went into the curation room and found a big box. It has a mummy in it. And there's all kinds of new stuff—pots, sandals, beads, even a cradleboard made from willow, rabbitbrush, and rabbit fur. That in itself is worth a fortune. And there's a ladle made from the horn of a bighorn sheep, as well as a deer antler with a hole in it used to straighten arrow shafts to make them fly straight. It's major stuff, Bud. I have no idea where it came from."

"Does it look like it could've come from Range Creek?"

"Yes, but all their stuff is going to the university for curation, not here."

"Well, I'm sure Renee knows and will tell you when she gets back. But I had a talk with Judge Richter, and he says there's a board meeting this afternoon."

"There's a board meeting? They usually have Renee there. She's going to be mad."

"They're calling it to discuss museum staffing. That's all I can say about that. But the judge said that in order to prove insubordination, an employer has to show that the supervisor made a direct request or order, the employee understood the request, and that the employee refused to comply with it. I wrote it all down, and it doesn't sound to me like any of those were your case."

"They definitely weren't. But Bud, I've been wondering. You said earlier that you knew the judge from a few cases he's presided over in court. Have you been in trouble a lot or something? I've been thinking about this ever since you said it, and quite honestly, I'm wondering if maybe I've shared too much about all this with a complete stranger. And did you really buy that figurine?"

"Bailey, I can answer your questions about why I've been involved with Richter, and yes, I have a receipt to prove I bought it, but first, was the archaeologist friend you gave the figurine to a fellow named Phil?"

"Yes. How did you know that?"

"I didn't, or I wouldn't have asked you," Bud dodged. "But let me ask another thing. Does the museum have any kind of security cameras where you might see who took the figurine's mate from its case?"

Bailey snorted. "We can barely pay our janitor, yet alone install something like that."

"I thought the museum was doing well," Bud replied. "Last time my wife and I visited, you guys had just remodeled one wing of the building."

"That was before Renee came on board. She's lost us a number of donors."

"And you know Phil from your time at the university?"

"No, I went to Idaho State, not the U. of Utah. I met him at a conference in Poky."

"Poky?"

"Pocatello, Idaho."

"Have you known him long?" Bud asked.

"Just a few months."

"Are you sure Phil returned the figurine to Renee?"

"I'm sure. I saw her open the package, and then she lost it and started yelling at me. What are you thinking?"

"Has Renee ever told you anything about how she feels about Phil? I mean on a professional level."

"Not really, but he supposedly was on her PhD. committee and almost failed her."

"Well, that would be a good reason to not like someone, for sure," Bud replied. "Do you have any idea who brought all the new donor stuff to the museum?"

"It was a couple of guys who Renee said have a moving company. She said the donor was some old guy down in Torrey whose grand-parents collected from the Capitol Reef area before it was illegal. That's where the original Fremont Indian name came from, you know, the Fremont River down there. She hired these two guys to go get the stuff."

"Were their names Cory and Trevor by any chance?"

Bailey sounded surprised. "How do you know all this?"

Bud replied, "Just a lucky guess. I'm getting the idea there's a lot going on here."

"I personally think this stuff is looted from Range Creek, and I think Renee's behind it. I hope you don't think *I'm* involved," Bailey said nervously. "And I'm beginning to wonder if *you* aren't involved."

"I'm not, and I'm going to rely on you to keep all this to yourself. Don't say anything to Phil."

"You can bet on that," Bailey replied. "I still can't believe he returned the figurine to Renee when I explicitly told him not to. It was like he wanted to get me fired or something. And I'm really questioning why I'm telling you all this. I really hope you haven't been in trouble with the law, given what you said about all those court appearances. And I still haven't seen your receipt for the figurine."

"Well," Bud replied, thinking of when he'd gone to the Klondike once to help Shorty, "I once had a Canadian Mountie looking for me, but nothing came of it. But don't worry, I'll explain everything when the time comes."

"OK, but I'm about ready to take some time off anyway. I have some money saved, and I want to go look for the Sunnyside Shield."

"What's that?" Bud asked.

"Well, rumor has it there's an old Fremont buffalo-hide shield in an alcove in Range Creek. Phil and Renee have both been looking for it like crazy. But I was doing some research, and I don't think it's there at all. I think it's somewhere around Sunnyside. Even though Fremont rock art has plenty of shield-bearing warrior figures, there's never been an actual shield found."

Bud asked, "How do you know the shield actually exists?"

Bailey replied, "There's an old photo in the Brigham Young University Lee Library Special Collections that shows a cowboy on his horse holding a shield like a warrior. The caption reads *Buried Forest, Sunnyside.*"

"Buried forest? As in petrified trees?"

"Yes, and the cliffs have giant circular features, a bunch of them, and they're huge. They look like mounted shields or targets, or even fossilized cross-sections of huge trees. It's an actual photo, in black and white, so I know it's real."

Bud asked, "And nobody's found the cliffs? Have you guys looked?"

"They should be fairly recognizable, but nobody's been able to find them. I've personally spent days looking, as well as hours pouring over maps and looking at Google Earth. I think the shield is stashed in some crack or alcove. Whoever finds the shield is going to make their name in archaeology, that's for sure. Plus it'll be worth a fortune. A person could retire on it—but of course, you wouldn't sell it, it would go in a museum somewhere."

"I wonder why the cowboy in the photo didn't keep it," Bud replied. "It was probably too much of a hassle, riding horseback and looking for cattle, trying to carry a shield. But I heard that Harvey Driggs took it from him and hid it and then told Phil about it."

"That's what I was told, also," Bailey replied. "But I don't think the story's true. Why would Harvey talk about it then not tell him where it was? He'd just sold the ranch and wanted to protect things, after all. But I'd like to find it just to irritate Renee. It would really torque her to not be the one who gets the accolades from it. Bud, I'm sure this stuff she brought in here is illegal. I know she's behind the looting. What better place to hide looted antiquities than in a museum? And I think Renee stole your figurine. But I need to go lock up the museum and go home. You have a good night."

They hung up, Bud hoping Bailey was better at keeping secrets than Mrs. Jensen was.

34

It was a beautiful bluebird day, the kind after a storm clears the air, and Bud was restless. Instead of being on duty, he wanted to get the dogs and head out for a drive into the backcountry, taking his rented Nikon along. He knew he'd soon have to return it, and he wanted to try it out some more, as he hadn't used it at all in Range Creek.

He fiddled with his coffee cup, wondering if he could somehow talk Howie into covering for him for just a few hours, even though he knew he was busy at Howie's Drive-In, Maureen probably home with the baby. He knew this because the drive-in was across the street, and he could see Howie inside, doing something in the kitchen.

Just as he'd decided to buckle down and do some paperwork, his phone rang.

"Sheriff's office, Bud speaking."

"Bud, this is Carl Chapman. You got a minute?"

Bud replied, "Of course. How's your mom doing?"

"She's fine, but it was a bit touch and go there for awhile. But she's home now, and my dad and sis are there, so I'm back in Radium. I'm wondering if you guys went into Range Creek while I was gone."

"We did," Bud answered, not really sure what to say. "But we didn't have much luck, though we did find where that mummy came from."

"Did anyone figure out who you were?"

"Well, kind of. The head guy, Phil, knew I was the sheriff from a traffic incident a few years ago, but I think we did OK convincing them we were doing geology. Problem was, we didn't get to stay long because the weather turned."

"So you really accomplished nothing?" Carl asked bluntly.

"Probably about right," Bud said. "Should I send the camera gear back to the place in Salt Lake?" Bud was now anxious to be rid of it before Carl proposed another spy mission.

"Yeah, go ahead and return it. Be sure to insure it. That's all you have to report?"

"Pretty much," Bud replied, beginning to feel like he was being interrogated. He was about ready to tell him about the mummy and other artifacts at the museum, but before he could, Carl said, "The undercover guys at the other end of the pipeline made an incredible purchase while I was gone. They're still trying to track down its origin."

Bud, unsure if Carl was free to say more, replied, "Something from Range Creek?"

"Yes."

Bud was now feeling frustrated. He paused, then said, "So, Carl, I take it you no longer want my help with all this? Since it's in my territory, I'm more than willing to proceed on my own, but we might have better luck combining our forces."

Carl laughed. "Your forces aren't any bigger than mine. I have one ranger and you have one deputy, though there are two rangers in Price I can call if I have to. But Bud, I wasn't trying to be standoffish. I'm just disappointed that you didn't have much luck up there."

"Do you want to share with me what your guys recovered?"

Carl replied, "It was a Fremont figurine pilfered from the museum there in Price. Someone sold it to an art dealer down in Durango, Colorado. Do you know anything about one being stolen?"

"I do. Someone took one of the Pilling figurines. I'm not sure if the museum has even reported it stolen yet, as the director is gone."

"You're on it, Bud," Carl said. "The guy paid a fortune for it. Our informant reported it, and we confiscated it. The dealer says he had no idea it was illegal, but we think otherwise, especially since he was eager to pay so much to get it. He's currently under arrest for buying and selling stolen goods, but we want whoever sold it to him. We're pretty sure there's some kind of intermediary between him and whoever looted it."

Bud thought of Renee going AWOL for a few days, not telling Bailey where she went. Had she taken the figurine to the dealer in Durango?

He then thought of Sam and Dottie Wiggins. Would the law view them in the same light as they had the antiquities dealer, even though Bud knew they were nowhere on the same level? Maybe it would be best not to mention he was the owner of the second figurine, as they would want to know where he got it.

"There's more," Bud said.

"More what?"

"Carl, I think the museum in Price may have some stuff from Range Creek. It was supposedly donated, but I think they have the mummy I sent you a photo of. I think it's the looted antiquities and someone's using the museum as a hiding place."

"The mummy that went rafting?"

Bud grinned. Carl seemed to be loosening up. "Yup, the lucky stiff. I'm about ready to get a search warrant from Judge Richter and go have a look."

"I thought you said you didn't accomplish anything. Sounds to me like you have some good leads."

"I have some leads on stolen goods, but not on who stole them, at least not anything definitive."

Carl said, "Well, keep working on it. It looks like Range Creek's going to be shutting down soon. It sure would be nice to figure all this out before winter hits and the case goes cold, no pun intended."

"I have some ideas. I'll stay in touch," Bud replied. "Glad your mom's doing better."

They hung up just in time for Bud's cellphone to ring.

"Yell-ow," Bud answered.

"Buddy, it's your Uncle Hank. Everything going OK down your way?"

"So-so," Bud replied. "It's a nice day and I'm stuck inside, but other than that, it's fine. Hows about you guys?"

"I have some interesting news I thought you might like. Me and Junior were going through Jimmy Johnson's things, at the request of the sheriff, mind you, and we found his will. All legal and done up by an attorney and everything, which sure wasn't like Jimmy. He was a free-ranger kind of guy."

"That *is* interesting," Bud replied.

Hank continued, "He gave Ginger and me his house. I can't believe it! It needs some work, but we're up for that, and your Uncle Junior has offered to help. As soon as we give notice on our rental and get some things done, painting and stuff like that, we'll be moving. It has a nice big yard."

"Did he mention Freckles?"

"He did. He wanted us to take him."

Bud wasn't sure what to say. Finally, he replied, "You know he'll just break out and start roaming, and who knows what will happen then? Don't you think Jimmy just wanted him to have a good home?"

"I'm sure he did, Buddy. Did you find him one?"

"Maybe," Bud replied. "I'll report back. But congrats on the new house. Did you also get his lift truck?"

"I did, along with all his junk. But that's OK. He had a whole carport full of rocks he'd collected, and guess what I'm going to do with them?"

"I don't know, find a glass house?"

"No, I'm going to fix up the back part of the old gas station and open a rock shop."

"That sounds like fun," Bud replied.

"But Bud, I'm wondering if you can't come up here. We found a few things that might be of interest, considering you've been looking into some looting in this area."

"Who told you that?" Bud asked with concern.

"Your Aunt Ginger."

Bud sighed. He had no idea how she knew, but he did know the grapevine flourished in Sunnyside.

"I need to come up your way anyway," Bud replied, thinking of the search warrant he needed. Judge Richter lived in Castle Dale, but Bud knew he went to Price regularly and he could meet him there.

"When can you come?" Hank asked. "Maybe you'd like to go through Jimmy's rock collection before we move it to the station—actually, you could go through it while helping us move it."

"I think tomorrow would work," Bud replied. "I'll give you a call."

"That would be great," Hank said. "And Buddy, just so you know, Jimmy collected all kinds of stuff, some of which probably wasn't too legal, so hold onto your hat when you come up. See you tomorrow."

With that, they hung up, Bud wondering exactly what kind of illegal stuff Jimmy had supposedly collected. He'd find out tomorrow, he figured, dialing Judge Richter's number to request a search warrant for the Price Museum.

35

It was late afternoon, and still unable to get out, Bud had resigned himself to hanging around the office. No one had come in or called, and he'd almost nodded off when the office door opened and Howie walked in.

"I thought you were working at the drive-in," Bud said.

"I was, but I decided to close it down early. I'm too blue to work. It kind of drags the place down when I get like this."

"I'm sorry to hear that, Howie," Bud replied.

"After I closed up, I went in the back there and wrote another song. Sometimes I get creative when I'm depressed."

"Run it by me if you want."

"I don't have any music for it yet, but just imagine Johnny Cash's *Folsom Prison Blues*. It'll be kind of like that, same rhythm, similar sad story, except with no chorus."

"I'm listening, Howie."

"OK, you start with a *well* like Johnny Cash does in his version:

> Wellll,
> I like sad songs in minor keys,
> And saying my goodbyes,

I like the lonesome train whistle,
Birds calling through gray skies.

OK, here you have some guitar strumming for awhile, and remember, there's no chorus. I don't want to get sued by the Cash estate so I'm trying to make it sound a little different.

They say life's like a river,
You float so sweet and free,
Until you hit those rapids,
And then you're lost at sea.

Now more guitar, though you could have a bass riff here, too.

Sometimes I really wonder,
What it is I want to say,
When I try to write these lyrics,
And I'd rather go and play.

And now you sing *well* again.

Wellll,
Tomorrow will be better,
When a new day comes around,
I'll send everyone a letter,
Sayin' Maureen's back in town.

And now you end with a bass riff like *do dee do dee do do*, kind of slowing it down with lots of tremolo on the last note."

Bud grinned, then asked, "Did Maureen go somewhere, Howie?"

"Bud, she took off to her parents' house down in Hanksville. She said her mom was making a lot of noise about not seeing little Malcolm. Wilma Jean gave her a couple of days off. I wanted to go, but I'm too busy. I really miss her and the baby. I woke up in the middle of the night at his feeding time, but he wasn't there, so I fed the cats instead."

"How long have they been gone?"

"The cats didn't go anywhere, Sheriff, but Maureen left yesterday afternoon. You remember that old Hank Williams' song, *I'm So Lonesome I Could Die*? Want me to sing it for you? Or how about that old Righteous Brother's song with the lyrics, *Time goes by, so slowly...*"

"That's alright—I remember the first, and I'm trying to forget the second, kind of like *Found a Peanut*. But when are they coming back?"

"Well, like I say in my song, tomorrow."

"You better hurry and get the music part written, 'cause it sounds to me like your song has an expiration date that's coming up real soon. But I thought you were doing rockabilly now."

"Yeah, you're right. I need to forget my sorrows and get back to the good stuff—no offense to Johnny Cash, he was a fine musician. Man, I loved *How High's the Water Momma*."

"You're welcome to come out to the house tonight for dinner."

"Thanks, Sheriff. I may take you up on that. But you know, I've been kind of getting back into the mayor thing. I've had a few people come up and ask me what kinds of things I'm going to do to keep my campaign promise of taking Green River back to the rockin' good old days. I've decided that, if I get elected, I'm going to make the first Saturday night of each month Rockabilly Night."

"What would that entail?"

"Well, Howie and the Ramblin' Road Rangers will give a free rockabilly concert at the park, as long as the weather's willing and the electricity's not off. And other people are welcome to come and dance and sing and play instruments or whatever they want, but the main idea is to be hep cats and have fun. And if you can't come, or you just want to stay home, you should still do something that's fun. If nothing else, at least make some popcorn."

"Howie, that's a great idea. I hope you're telling people about this. It might help you get elected, assuming you still want to."

"I know Old Man Green and Junkyard Goldie are endorsing me, because they told me so. But I'm thinking they just see it as a venue to sell watermelon spritzer. Do you think we should let people sell stuff?"

"Why not, as long as it's legal?"

"Yeah, remember when I got all bent out of shape thinking the Cinco de Mayo bunch was illegal because their permit was for May 5th and they were holding it on the wrong day?"

"I remember that," Bud laughed. "It was delayed because of rain. You were a rookie then, but you were a very conscientious deputy. I knew you had the right stuff, even back then."

"I was sure wet behind the ears. I've come a long way since then, Bud, thanks to you—oh, and thanks to that *What Would Bud Do* bracelet Maureen got me. I kind of hate to leave the force behind if I get elected mayor."

"I guess if it's just me I'll have to rule by law instead of by force," Bud replied.

"Very funny, Sheriff. But did you know that in physics, a force is something that changes the motion of a body? Force is measured by multiplying the mass of the body by its acceleration. So, if Junkyard Goldie and Old Man Green were arguing, as they're prone to do, and Goldie threw a bottle of spritzer at Green, you could weigh the bottle and—well, never mind, 'cause it would be impossible to tell how hard Goldie threw it. I guess even physics has its limits when it comes to those two."

"You should take up writing word problems for math books, Howie. But it would be kind of hard to weigh the bottle after it's broken—not at all like throwing the book at someone."

"If I'm elected, I'll decree it illegal to tell bad jokes. And Maureen's parents have to come here next time. We have plenty of room."

"Sounds good. But come on out for dinner."

Howie asked, "You want me to bring some sandwiches? I heard about the enchiladas and wine thing."

"Sure, sandwiches would be good. Make those ones where you put pickles and chocolate on them or however that went. Those were tasty."

"They were roast beef, pickles, mayo, hot mustard, and pepper jack cheese, with white chocolate and almonds on top."

Bud replied, "Kind of sweet and spicy. But who told you about the wine?"

Howie answered, "I was talking to Shorty down at the American Legion."

"You guys go to the Legion? I thought that was for veterans."

"No, I pulled him over in front of the Legion for speeding."

"Did you give him a ticket?" Bud asked.

"I was going to, but he told me that Cassie was in charge of the election parade and wanted to know if I would lead it in the sheriff's vehicle, since I would probably be mayor by then, and I could kill two birds with one stone—a parade led by both the mayor and the deputy. I told him I'd clear it with you, and by the time we were done jawboning, I forgot to give him a ticket. I wasn't going to give him one anyway, maybe just a warning."

Bud replied, "Well, no harm done, and it's fine with me if you lead the parade. But if you're elected mayor, will you dress as the mayor or as a deputy?"

"I never thought of that. I guess I'd be both until I resign as deputy. How do mayors dress?"

"You have to wear a top hat," Bud replied, grinning. "Actually, I think they dress pretty much like their constituents."

"Say, Bud, I almost forgot. Shorty wanted me to give you a message. He says they're keeping Freckles, as he's really taken to Cassie. She's starting agility training with him and he loves it. He doesn't even try to run off now."

"That's great news, Howie!" Bud said. "Thanks for relating it. But I need to get home. I'll see you in a bit, and don't forget the sandwiches."

36

It was the next day, and Bud stood in the living room of Jimmy Johnson's house, eating antacids, amazed at how much stuff Jimmy had managed to stack in the room. He'd come up to Sunnyside that morning to help his uncle, but he was beginning to think the project was way more than Hank could manage, even with Bud's help.

"Where's Junior?" Bud asked.

"He's down at Rod's shop, working on *Rockabilly Hound Dog*."

"What's that?" Bud asked, thumbing through what looked to be a stack of *Lost Treasure Magazine*, thinking of Howie.

"That's Rod's old 1942 Ford Coupe. They're trying to get it ready for the show down in Green River."

"What happened to fixing up Junior's old pickup?"

Hank replied, "We're done. You should see it, Buddy. It's a thing of beauty, a work of art, and I'm proud to say I helped. It has a new paint job, a pretty powder blue. It'll be the star of the show. Rod named it *Summertime Blues*."

Bud laughed. "That's a perfect name. I can't wait to see it. But man, did Jimmy Johnson used to own a junk store or something? Where'd he get so much stuff?"

Hank replied, "He had even more, but someone broke into his

house a few days before he was killed. Most of Jimmy's stuff isn't of much interest except to us oldtimers, but they did take an old guitar and his grandmom's costume jewelry. Actually, I don't really know what they stole, he has so much junk, but those two things I did notice were missing."

"What did the jewelry consist of?" Bud asked.

"It was in a velveteen sack, just necklaces and some earrings and bracelets. It was really pretty stuff, but not worth anything," Hank replied.

"How do you know?" Asked Bud.

"Well, he offered it to Ginger. She's not much for that kind of flashy stuff, but she took it down to the jeweler in Price and had him take a look, and he said it was just costume jewelry. She brought it back to Jimmy. But one other thing I noticed they took was this little statue—I'm not sure what to call it—it looked like a pagan doll or some such thing. It was about six inches tall and was very unusual, made of clay."

"Did it have a circular design on it with a red crab-like thing in the center?"

"Yes, it did. How did you know that?" Hank asked.

Bud replied, "They took it to Wiggins Diggins and sold it to Sam and his wife. I saw it there and bought it."

"Why would you want something like that?"

"It reminded me of one of the Pilling figurines. And I think I have the costume jewelry, too. I'll have to show it to Ginger and you. It's in my safe back in Green River. I thought the jewelry was the real deal," Bud replied.

"The jewelry? Where did you get that, Wiggins Diggins, too?"

Bud said, "I found the jewelry where someone tried to hide it, or rather, Shorty found it. I'll tell you about it later. I know someone who would love to have it, if it's the same stuff."

Bud thought of Mrs. Jensen and her freshly-dyed platinum-blonde hair and cashmere sweater.

Hank, now going through a box of old books, said, "Well, I installed a security system after I found out Jimmy had been robbed."

Bud asked, "You invested in a security system for what looks like a bunch of junk?"

"It's not all junk, Buddy, well, at least so I think. But I didn't pay much for the security system. I got it at Wiggins Diggins for three bucks."

Hank now pointed to a sticker on the front window that read, *This Property Is Under 24 Hour Video Surveillance.*

Bud grinned, then opened a box with *Wiggins Diggins* stamped on the lid. It contained a small assortment of sheriff's badges.

"Can I have one of these?" he asked Hank.

"Sure, take them all if you want. They're kids' toys."

"It's a hard choice—should I go with U.S. Marshal of Deadwood, Dodge City, or Tombstone?"

Hank replied, "I'd go with Dodge City—didn't everyone get shot at Tombstone? And I don't think Deadwood is a happening place. I never thought of taking this stuff to Wiggins Diggins. I bet they'd buy it all."

Bud stuck the Dodge City and Tombstone badges in his shirt pocket as Hank continued. "Buddy, there's more here. You need to look at some of this stuff Jimmy had. I have no idea where he got it, but it looks pretty authentic to me, and neither your aunt nor I want anything to do with old Indian stuff. It's illegal to have, you know."

Bud replied, "I do know that, Uncle Hank. But let's take a look."

Now Hank showed Bud to a small back room filled with even more stuff—an old stiff lariat, several pairs of old worn out cowboy boots, a set of vintage glasses with John Wayne pictures on them, and even an old saddle with a deep seat and wooden stirrups.

"That's an old McClellan saddle," Bud said. "The kind the calvary used. It's probably worth some money."

Hank replied, "I think Jimmy somehow got ahold of some old rancher's estate. I think he bought it at an auction over in Colorado. But that's not what I want to show you."

Hank pushed more stuff aside until he uncovered what looked to Bud to be an old piece of stiff cowhide. Gently pulling it out, Hank said, "Look at this, Buddy. It folds up for storage. I know it's Indian, and I betcha it's pretty darn old."

Bud unfolded the stiff leather, then whistled.

"It's a shield, Uncle Hank. Probably buffalo. It does look really old, and what a strange design it has painted on the leather. It looks vaguely familiar."

"It's the same design that was on that figurine thing," Hank replied.

"That figurine thing is a thousand years old, Uncle Hank."

"How do you know that? You suppose this is an old Fremont shield?" Hank asked.

"It very well could be, in fact, I would go out on a limb and say it is, even though I'm no archaeologist. I suppose it could be Ute, which would make it much younger."

"Take it to the museum and have them check it out, Buddy. We don't want it. Donate it to them."

"I think it might be better off at the university," Bud replied, thinking of his cold reception from Renee. "That's who's studying Range Creek. But let me take it home and put it in a safe place where nobody will bother it. It's probably worth a fortune."

"Not the kind of money I want," Hank replied. "Too many strings attached."

"Strings?" Bud asked.

"You know, weird things happening. I've heard enough stories about people who find these old Indian things and then have bad luck."

"You suppose that's what happened to Jimmy? Bad luck because of this shield?"

"Nah, you know I'm not superstitious, I'm just talkin'. Just go ahead and take it. We have no use for it, unless you'd prefer I take it to the museum or whoever."

"I'll take care of it," Bud replied. "I just wonder where he got it."

"He told me one time he got some Indian stuff from a yard sale over in Kenilworth. He was real excited about it, then kind of lost interest. That's how he was—he loved going to auctions and yard sales and things, then he'd just stick stuff away. Kind of a hoarder, but some of it's pretty good stuff. But come on out back and look at the rocks he collected. His whole darn carport is practically filled up."

"He was quite the rockhound, eh?" Bud laughed, seeing the size of the pile, then paused when he remembered he'd promised to help move it.

"I pulled this one out to show you," Hank said, tapping a large circular rock with his toe.

"What the heck?" Bud said, puzzled. "It looks like a concretion, but I've never seen one so big."

"It's definitely a concretion," Hank replied. "We need to get Shorty to come up here to take a look. But you can see something there in the center, a fossil or something, which was what the concentric circles formed around. The darn thing weighs a ton—it's over three feet in diameter!"

Bud stood, studying the rock, thinking. Since he no longer had the aluminum arrow to fiddle with and his harmonica was at home, he started humming *Found a Peanut*.

"Great, now I'll have that dumb song stuck in my mind all day," Hank said.

"Uncle Hank, if you look at this rock and think about the shield and the figurine all at the same time, which I admit is hard to do, you might start believing there's a connection between them all, though I'm not really sure."

"I see," Hank replied. "But could you stop humming that song? The words are starting to come to me, and I thankfully haven't thought of it since I was a kid."

Now Hank started singing:

Found a peanut,
Found a peanut just now.
It was rotten...

"OK, OK," Bud said, taking one of the marshal's badges from his pocket and rubbing the metal. "What do you think this badge is made of, anyway? Is it something toxic if I handle it?"

"It's probably some kind of zinc alloy, would be my guess," Hank replied. "But Buddy, I know where there's a lot of big concretions like that, right in the cliffs. That's probably where it came from."

"Where is that?" Bud asked, thinking of Shorty.

"It's called the Buried Forest by the locals, but it's not really petrified wood. The concretions just look like the ends of big logs sticking out of the cliffs. It's over along the Mounds Reef, you know, that big anticline. You take off just about two miles out of Wellington, turn to the right, and the road follows the upper part of the reef. The concretions aren't far along that road, just down below the rim. There's an old drill site right off the road and the trail takes off from there. You should go see it sometime, it's quite the sight. But let's go get some lunch at the Sunnyside Cafe, then we'll go find Junior to start helping us load these rocks."

"I have a free lifetime tab over there, as long as I don't bring Freckles back," Bud grinned.

"So that's how that works," Hank laughed, showing Bud to the gate. "But just don't ever hum that dumb song around me again, OK?"

37

It had been a long afternoon, Bud helping Hank and Junior haul rocks to the gas station, where they tried to categorize them in piles according to type—agate, petrified wood, selenite, jasper, chert, celestite, and an assortment of marine fossils. If one could be rich in rocks, Bud figured his Uncle Hank was now a millionaire.

He'd finally said goodbye, wanting to go meet Judge Richter in Price. Bud was tired, and just wanted to get his museum search over with. As a member of the board of directors for the museum, the judge had made Bud a key, and after the judge, who'd been in a hurry, had handed it and the search warrant off, Bud then dialed the number for the Carbon County Sheriff's Office.

"Sheriff's Office," a voice answered. Bud felt fortunate to get Sam Wiggins on the first try, as he figured he'd be off duty soon, as it was getting late, and he was typically up in the Sunnyside area.

"Sam, this is Bud Shumway. How're things going?"

"OK, Bud. I'm just about ready to call it a day."

"Sam," Bud continued. "I have a big favor to ask of you. Would you mind doing a standby in case I need to execute a search warrant? I'll be over there soon."

"Where's it at, Bud?"

"The museum."

"Judge Richter gave you a warrant to search our museum?" Sam asked.

Bud replied, "Yes, and that's why I need your help. You're the law in these parts. I can legally do it, but it gets sticky if I don't run it by you guys first. But I'm actually also acting on behalf of the BLM."

"What are we looking for, Bud?"

"Stolen artifacts, and they appear to have come from Emery County."

"You have good reason to think the museum is stealing things?" Sam asked.

"I think someone there is, or at the very least helping. I can go into it all later, but if we get busted, I need to rely on you to do something which you won't feel comfortable doing, but which there's a good reason for."

Sam now sounded perplexed. "It's not something illegal, is it?"

"No, not at all, but maybe a bit unusual. By the time I get there, the museum will be closed with hopefully no one around. I have a key and will let myself in. I'm going into the collections room to take photos. If all goes well, I'll get the photos and be able to get right back out."

Sam now said, "Sounds pretty easy. What's the problem?"

"Well," Bud replied. "If I get caught, I need you to come in and arrest me for breaking and entering."

"What?" Sam asked incredulously.

"You tell whoever finds me that you just happened to be in the parking lot and saw lights come on and came in to investigate. I'll leave the door unlocked. Don't hesitate to pull your gun, as I'll make it look like I don't want to go."

"Bud," Sam protested, "Is this some kind of practical joke? I don't think it's a good idea for me to arrest you. You're legal—you have a search warrant."

"Look, Sam," Bud replied. "I have a good reason, and I'll fill you in on it later, but I don't have time right now. But if you see the museum lights come on, then you can be assured I've been caught, and that will be your cue to come in and arrest me. Got it?"

Sam groaned. "Bud, it's time for me to go home. I really don't want to do this. By the time I book you and do all the paperwork, dinner will be cold. Dottie will have a cow. And what's Wilma Jean going to say when she finds out I threw you in jail?"

"Sam, I don't want you to book me. You can just drop me off at my vehicle. Consider it like a skit or drama that you have a part in. The whole thing shouldn't even take a half hour. I need your help, just like you needed my help trying to figure out what happened to Jimmy Johnson, which I'm still working on, by the way. But you have to pretend you don't know me."

Sam now sounded eager to help. "Bud, if you can figure out what happened to Jimmy, I'll arrest you any time you want."

"OK, let's go. Operation Museum Sting. I'm heading over there as we speak. Give me 10 minutes, then roll into the parking lot and watch for lights. No lights, nothing to do, I'll come back out, shake your hand, and we'll call it a night. Lights? Well, then, camera, action! And remember, you don't know me."

"OK, Bud, but I hope you have a good explanation for all this."

"I do, and Sam?"

"Yeah?"

"One other thing. Are you aware that you're selling stolen goods?"

"What? Me? You mean at Wiggins Diggins?"

"Yes. I'll explain later." Bud hung up, knowing Sam would be there soon, if for nothing else, to find out what he was selling that could get him in trouble.

Now in Price, Bud parked in a shadowy area near the side door of the museum that led into the storage and curation part of the building. He sat for awhile, lights off, assessing the situation.

A light lit the main door into the museum, and he could see the small gift shop next to the entry also had a small light on its display, but it didn't appear anyone was still there. He could make out a dim light on the second floor where the staff offices were, but it didn't really worry him, as the rest of the building was dark, and even if there were someone up there, he was confident he could get inside and get photos before anyone noticed.

He could now see a white SUV pull into the lot on the other side of the parking area and cut its lights. A streetlight lit up the words, *Carbon County Sheriff.*

Bud got out of his FJ and opened the museum's side door, the warrant in his pocket, while instinctively touching his Ruger in its shoulder case. He had put it on after leaving the Sunnyside Cafe, knowing he was coming here. His other shoulder carried the rented Nikon, ready to take photos.

Now inside the dark building, he pulled out a small penlight and found his way through the door of the curation room. He'd been here a number of times, both as a kid and as an adult under various scenarios, from volunteering to archive dinosaur bones to helping paint the inside of the building with his scout group.

He now scanned around the room, looking for the refrigerator box Bailey had said was holding the mummy. He soon found it next to a number of other boxes, then opened the lid and shone his penlight inside, the mummy looking even stranger than before in the bluish light.

Bud now turned on the camera and held it up to take a photo, but soon realized that, like most higher-end DSLR cameras, there was no internal flash. Even if he upped the ISO, there was no way he was going to get anything definitive in the photo department without at least some light. He tried holding the penlight on it, but all it did was make the mummy look even more distorted and weird.

He stood there for what seemed like forever, not sure what to do, then walked over and turned on the main lights and began taking photos.

But before he'd barely even started, he felt something cold and hard pressing into his back as a voice said, "You're under arrest. Put your hands up."

Bud groaned. It was Sam, and he was doing exactly what he'd told him to do.

"It's OK, Sam," Bud protested. "I had to turn on the lights to get the pictures I need. Hold off, and we can leave in a bit."

But Sam now had him in a vise grip and was dragging him out the door to the sheriff's vehicle, even though Bud was protesting. Sam opened the back door of his SUV and pushed Bud inside while asking if he shouldn't maybe also handcuff him.

Bud sat in shock for a moment, then, trying his best not to laugh, said, "Sam, I screwed up. I turned on the lights so I could see to take photos, forgetting that was your cue. Now I need to go back inside and finish the job."

Sam, now in the front, said, "Bud, I'm totally confused. You told me you were going to resist arrest, so what exactly am I supposed to do now?"

"Well, I guess you could open the door so I can get out, then you might as well go on home."

Sam let Bud out, then asked, "I really don't understand what our little play here was about."

Bud replied, "It's good practice—practice for you for arresting someone, and practice for me for getting arrested."

Sam thought about it for awhile, then asked, "But what was this about me selling stolen goods?"

Bud replied, "I was in your shop the other day, and it appears you have stuff that came from the Sunnyside Museum robbery. Go take a look in the back of the shop. It's all mining memorabilia."

Bud could see Sam turn white, even though it was dark.

Bud added, "I think you might want to get a list of what was stolen and compare it to what's in your shop, then return it all to the museum."

"But they'll think I stole it."

"Maybe not, if you can prove someone else did it," Bud replied. "You might want to get right on that, and thanks for your help tonight."

Bud turned and walked back through the museum door to finish taking photos, leaving Sam even more confused.

38

Bud was feeling pretty good, as he'd almost finished taking all the photos he needed, and he hadn't even had to execute his search warrant, though he knew he would need it if the photos became evidence.

He also hadn't needed his ruse, which Sam was a part of, since no one had noticed he was there. His plan was that, if someone came in—and that someone was most likely to be Bailey, though Renee was also a possibility—he would have Sam arrest him and take him away. That way, he could legally take photos, since he had a warrant, but he would look illegal, and it would fit right in with Bailey's apparent assessment of him as a crook, which might come in handy later.

He would then be set up to become part of future enterprises, assuming she wanted an accomplice. What better way to solve a robbery than to make the thieves think you're one of them? And if Bailey wasn't in on the looting, she'd never be the wiser. In any case, the thieves wouldn't be tipped off that their loot was under suspicion and had been photographed.

And now, he would soon be able to hit the road and go home, where he knew Wilma Jean was fixing something good for dinner, or at least so he hoped. He now began softly humming, going through the last of the boxes and taking photos.

Finally done, he noticed one last small box on a nearby shelf and took it down. As he did so, he kind of forgot where he was and, thinking of homemade enchiladas, began singing:

Found a peanut,
Found a peanut just now.

He opened the box and was suddenly silent, for there, in all its glory, was one of the Pilling figurines.

He held the small box up to the light. He could now see that it was the same figurine he'd bought at Wiggins Diggins. What was it doing here with what appeared to be stolen artifacts from Range Creek? Having nothing to fiddle with, Bud again began singing:

Found a peanut,
Found a peanut just now.

Now a voice said, "You can put that peanut right back where you found it, buster."

Bud turned to see one of the men from the raft—if he recognized the voice correctly, the one called Cory—pointing a gun at him. He carefully put the small box back on its shelf.

Now Cory yelled out, "Trevor, get in here right now!"

The second man soon appeared, and Cory said, "This guy's stealing our stuff."

"Be careful, he's a smooth talker, Cory," Trevor replied.

"How so?" Cory asked.

"I saw a deputy arrest him out there in the parking lot, and he talked his way right out of it. He and the deputy acted like they were buddies before it was all over and the deputy left. Be careful. What are you going to do with him?"

"Good question. Just what exactly are you doing, buster?"

Now Bud said, “I was just taking photos of all this stuff. That way, I have a record of it.”

“He’s lying, Cory,” Trevor said, then asked Bud, “Why would the sheriff arrest you if you’re supposed to be here?”

“He let me go, didn't he?” Bud replied. “And I could ask the same of you guys. What are you doing here? And for Pete’s sake, put the gun down. There’s two of you and only one of me. If I were to try anything, you could easily out-muscle me. When’s Renee coming back?”

Cory, putting the gun away, said, “I don’t know anyone named Renee. But you need to hurry up and finish with the photos so we can get this stuff out of here.”

“Where are you taking it?” Bud asked innocently.

“Where we always take stuff,” Trevor evaded, giving Cory a look of concern. “The museum has a bunch of different storage units. But we don’t have to tell you anything. We don’t even know your name.”

“I’m Buddy,” Bud replied, holding out his hand. They all shook, Trevor and Cory introducing themselves.

“Are those your real names?” Bud asked. “They sure remind me of something, but I can’t quite put my finger on it. Where’s Lucy?”

“How do you know Lucy?” Cory asked.

“I guess I should say Rita,” Bud answered. “I met her up in Salt Lake. We got to be pretty good friends. I know those aren’t your real names. Rita told me what they were, but I forgot.”

“He’s the Sock Hat Bandit,” Trevor replied.

“I am not,” Cory protested. “But if I were, you’d be Attila the Bun.”

“Why’s that?” Bud asked.

“He sometimes wears a man bun, puts his hair up. You know what a man bun is, right?”

Bud replied, “You put your hair up in a bun, and you’re a man?”

“Well, it doesn’t *make* you a man—some would say the opposite. But our real names are Doyle and Eugene. We have a moving business.”

“Why carry a gun?” Bud asked.

"In case we get robbed," Trevor said. "Isn't that usually why people carry guns?"

"I don't know," Bud replied. "But why don't any of you use your real names? I was going to ask Rita that after she said to call her Lucy, but I didn't have a chance."

"Well, if our parents had given us nice names like Buddy, we'd use them. But who wants to be called Doyle and Eugene?"

"I don't see anything wrong with either," Bud replied. "But fellows, I need to get going. It would be nice if you told me where you were taking this stuff, because I got kind of flustered when the deputy showed up, and I don't think I cataloged everything. That way I could double check if I needed to."

"We take stuff to the Sunnyside..."

"Don't tell him!" Cory interrupted. "Sorry, but it's not a place where we can lock things up, and we need to be extra careful. If you have any problems, call us and I can go check it out for you or something."

"Sounds fine," Bud replied, pulling a pen and business card from his pocket. "Can you write your number on here?"

Trevor wrote it on the card and handed it back to Bud.

"You boys gonna lock up?" Bud asked. "You have a key?"

"Oh sure, Lucy trusts me like a brother," Cory replied.

Now standing to go, Bud asked, "Mind if I ask where you got your new names? They sound vaguely familiar."

"From a sitcom, a mockumentary," Cory replied.

"Canadian?" Bud asked.

"You a fan?" Asked Trevor.

"I've watched it a few times with my Aunt Rhoda. Is it about these guys who are always in trouble and end up in jail?"

"Yeah, it's great," Cory replied. "They like it there. We'll go out the back door. Can you lock this side door?"

"You bet," Bud said, turning out the lights as they all walked out, grabbing the small box with the figurine when they weren't looking and stuffing it in the front of his jacket. He was soon in his FJ, glad he'd parked it in the shadows, for he knew the pair would immediately recognize it, just like they had down at the geyser.

He was soon on the road to Green River, the box with the figurine resting on the passenger seat, the buffalo-hide shield from Jimmy's in the back. He was glad he didn't have the dogs, as they'd want to chew it up.

He would put everything in his office, where it would be secure from robbers like the Sock Hat Bandit and Attila the Bun. He would then call Carl and tell him there would soon be stolen artifacts hidden at the Sunnyside coke ovens, since Trevor had said it was in Sunnyside, and Cory said it wasn't a place where they could lock things up.

In the meantime, he'd go home and have dinner, then see if he could trace the number Trevor had written on his business card, right under the name *Bud Shumway, Sheriff of Emery County*.

39

"Sheriff, it says here that *Big Daddy* is used to address older guys, while *Daddy-O* is for younger guys. You can also use *Clyde* for a normal person, though I don't know if by normal they mean a regular guy or a hep cat. And *nest* is a hair-do. Maybe I should start calling my pomp my nest. And *agitate the gravel* means someone spun out real fast, while *Shoot low, they're riding Shetlands* means watch out and be extra careful."

"What exactly are you reading, Howie?" Bud asked, examining the cover of an old copy of *National Geographic* with a picture of King Tut, one of the many magazines he'd rescued from Jimmy Johnson's house.

"It's a list of rockabilly words and what they mean. I got it off the Internet."

"Probably put together by some hep cat, eh?" Bud remarked.

"You think it may be a bogus list?" Howie asked with concern.

"Howie, even if it is, your coolness wouldn't be affected."

"Well, I don't feel very cool right now," Howie replied. "First of all, I'm kind of nervous about our upcoming concert for the car show, but that's not unusual, I always feel like that. But the election's coming up, and now I'm just wanting to stay a deputy. I don't want to be the center of anything, and Maureen says that if I win I should steel myself for criticism, as the mayor's responsible for everything, good or bad, at least in the eyes of the people. What was I thinking?"

"It'll all work out either way," Bud replied. "If you get elected, you'll be a good mayor. If not, you'll be a good deputy. Looks to me like you've got it covered regardless."

"Thanks, Bud," Howie replied.

"But Howie, right now you're still my deputy. I have a conundrum I need help solving."

"Sure, Sheriff, go ahead. I'll do my best."

"It's kind of like a puzzle, or maybe Whack-A-Mole is more like it. See, someone's lying, and I can't figure out who it would be or why. I bought this figurine and took it to the museum, and the curator supposedly sent it to the university for analysis. She then told me a fellow at the university, who also happens to be the head honcho at Range Creek, said it was authentic, the mate to one of the pairs that had gone missing. That same fellow gave it to the head of the museum, and it then went missing again. But I found it in the museum last night."

"Jeez Louise, Bud, you're giving me a headache!"

"The puzzle is, who lied? Did the curator possibly make the whole story up? Maybe she didn't even send it in."

"Why would she do that?"

"Good question. The museum director is supposedly out of town, and she may have been the one who sold a different figurine, one that was stolen from the museum, to a dealer. Or it could've been the curator, who somehow got it down there. Her name is Bailey, and she seems to hate the interim director, whose name is Renee, so maybe she's trying to frame her."

"And you have no idea where this Renee happens to be?"

"I think she may be in Range Creek. I have a witness, a guy named Sandy, who may have seen her there, and it may have been her who I saw in a Jeep going in. If so, she's currently stuck in there with Phil, the head honcho who supposedly examined the figurine and said it was authentic."

"Bud, I think you need to take a break. Go out in the desert and hang out with the dogs. I'll cover for you. This is all too complicated."

"The funny thing is, Howie, the curator, Bailey, doesn't know I'm the sheriff. In fact, I think she has the idea that I'm doing something fishy."

"How'd she get that idea?"

"Well, I think it started when I told her I knew Judge Richter because he presided over some of my cases. She thought I meant cases where I was the defendant. She didn't make the connection that I was the sheriff. So, I decided to run with it. My reasoning was that maybe if she thought I was on her level, she would ask me to do something illegal, assuming *she* was doing something illegal. That's why I told Sam to arrest me."

"Bud, I'm totally lost. But like Shorty always says, the simplest solution is usually the right one. Occam's razor."

"Do you think I'm overthinking this?"

"I don't know. Someone is looting in Range Creek and selling invaluable antiquities. It would make sense that someone on the inside, like an archaeologist, would be doing it. It looks like you have three archaeologist suspects, but only one is really on the inside, and that would be Phil, because he's actually in Range Creek. But the other two, because of their relationship with the museum, have access to people and resources that Phil may not have. So I guess what I'm saying isn't really very helpful, as it could be any one of the three. Or even all of them."

"Thanks, Howie. I guess that's helpful, though not very definitive."

"In other words, helpful, but not. Do you have any evidence that would point to one over the others?"

"Not really," Bud replied. "I think I'm pretty sure who their helpers are, two guys who call themselves Trevor and Cory, but I don't actually know who they're helping. The number they gave me was for the local pizza place in Price. But if I could figure out who Lucy was..."

"Sheriff, go ahead and take a break for awhile. I'll cover for you.

Go home and kick back. The dogs probably miss you. Go have a soda at Howie's Drive-In, Daddy-O."

"Thanks, Howie," Bud laughed. "I think I'll do that. I need to quit taking things so seriously. This is really Carl's case, not mine, but I haven't been able to get ahold of him lately. And don't you worry about the concert or the election—just like this looting case, it'll all work out."

With that, Bud put on his hat and jacket and headed for the bungalow. Pulling into the drive, he was happy to see the porch light was on, and he knew Wilma Jean was home. He knew she'd probably have something good going for dinner, even if it was just that day's special at the Melon Rind Cafe.

As he got out of the FJ, he could indeed smell something cooking —something that smelled like freshly baked pie of some kind. Even though he considered himself somewhat of a pie aficionado, he couldn't quite put his finger on it.

As he walked in the door, little Pierre automatically grabbed his pant cuffs, dragging along with each step, growling as if he'd just caught a badger, while Hoppie watched on, wagging his tail, happy to see Bud. Lindie stayed back, recognizing the danger she was in when around a wiener dog in for the kill, then gladly came to Bud when he called, patting her on the head.

Wilma Jean had indeed just taken a pie from the oven, and Bud was sure it had to be some kind of berry.

"Blueberry?" He asked, putting his arm around her waist.

Wilma Jean replied, "No, it's blackberry, freshly picked from Mrs. Jensen's bushes out in her back yard. She dropped by with a bunch and said to tell you hello. She said to tell you she and Frosty are getting engaged."

"No kidding?" Bud replied. "It was nice of her to bring the berries, and even nicer of you to make it into a pie. But what's for dinner?"

"Today's special, leftover chili," she answered. "But you have a call you need to return from some guy named Carl. Bud..."

"Don't worry, I'll call him back later. Nothing's going to tear me away from a peaceful evening alone with you and the dogs and a big bowl of blackberry pie a la mode."

"I hope not," his wife replied. "But I have a feeling..."

"I have a special gift just for you, assuming you're into costume jewelry." He handed her the purple velveteen Crown Royal bag.

"What is this?" She asked, opening the bag. "Oh, Bud," she added, looking through the jewelry inside. "It's very nice, but it's way too gaudy and flashy for me. Where did you get it?"

"It belonged to Jimmy Johnson. Uncle Hank gave it to me. I know it's not your style, but it may be something Mrs. Jensen would like."

"Oh, it would suit her perfectly," Wilma Jean said. "Anyway, the chili's ready, so let's go out on the back porch and eat under the stars."

"Isn't it a bit cold for that?" Bud asked.

"Not when you see what I bought today at a yard sale over by the grade school."

Bud followed her outside, where she put the pot of chili and bowls on the patio table, dogs now following along. Bud gave them each a biscuit as Wilma Jean fiddled with something near the table.

"Well, darn," she said. "I can't get it to light. I tested it before I bought it, and it worked fine."

"It's a propane heater, isn't it?" Bud asked. "We had one of those up at Range Creek. I'll take a look at it later, but for now, I guess we'll have to stay warm the old-fashioned way."

He handed his wife a bowl of hot chili, then grabbed himself a bowl and took Wilma Jean by the hand, leading her to the settee as the dogs, now giving up on handouts, headed inside to snooze by the warm heater.

40

It was cold, and even though Bud was dressed warm in his heavy down coat and Wolverine boots, he just couldn't seem to shake the chill.

He wished he'd brought along the propane heater Wilma Jean had bought, though he knew it wouldn't serve well to keep his location secret, which is what one needs when doing a stakeout, as its burning light and noise would instantly give him away.

He pulled up his coat sleeve just enough to see his watch, and noting that it was four a.m., sighed and leaned back against the cold bricks, hoping that whatever critters that might make the Sunnyside coke ovens their home were either gone for the night or hibernating.

It was funny how he'd managed to avoid spying at Range Creek only to end up doing it here at the coke ovens. Maybe spying was his destiny, as they say, but he sure wasn't going to embrace it.

He now recalled what Sam had told him—something about there being about 400 ovens left, stretching clear across the countryside, though there were originally over 800.

He knew there were a lot, as he'd now personally searched through at least a fourth of them, along with Ranger Carl and two BLM rangers from the Price office, who'd searched the others. It had taken hours, and he could still see the strange sight of their flashlights bobbing and reflecting off the red bricks under the clear starry sky.

Carl had eventually found what they were looking for—or rather, found *more* than they were looking for—as three of the ovens he'd searched held priceless artifacts presumably from Range Creek, including the mummy and other stuff Bud had photographed at the museum. Bud wasn't sure why the thieves had taken the stuff to the museum, then hid it out here, but he knew it had something to do with Renee being gone. Maybe they'd just needed an interim place, or maybe someone was trying to frame Renee—or maybe Renee wasn't really gone and had something to do with it.

Bud had been right in suspecting they were hiding everything in the coke ovens, and even though he'd intended to spend a peaceful night at home, Carl had finally called again and, upon Bud telling them where he thought the stuff was hidden, had persuaded him to come help them look, as they were worried someone might come and collect everything right away, especially if they'd already sold the stuff.

Time was of the essence, and Bud had come along, even though his heart was home with his wife and the dogs.

The others had loaded the artifacts into their SUVs, leaving Bud to hold down the fort until they could take everything to Price and unload it. It was imperative they protect the irreplaceable artifacts, yet they needed someone to stay and try to arrest whoever might come to retrieve everything, or at the very least, to identify who it might be.

Bud looked again at his watch—ten after four. He knew it would take them a good half-hour to travel the 25 miles to Price, then they'd have to unload everything, which would be no easy task, then take another half-hour to get back. They'd left around one, so he hoped they'd be back soon, or at least before anyone else showed up, as he didn't feel awake enough to make an arrest single-handedly. He found himself actually wondering if he shouldn't call Sam and see if he would come help, putting to good use his practice session with Bud in arresting techniques.

Now Bud slipped down against the bricks of the nearby oven, then realizing the cold was seeping from the bricks, he leaned against a small nearby tree, soon warming up a bit.

But he immediately stood up straight, for the sound he heard in the distance had taken away all thoughts of being cold and tired, making his adrenaline kick in. He was all ears, alert and wide awake, listening to one of the strangest sounds he'd ever heard.

It appeared to be coming from the distance in the direction of Whitmore Canyon, and since the power plant was offline, he had no trouble hearing it through the crisp cold air. Later, when he tried to describe it to Howie, he realized how much his words fell short, and he could only say it sounded like one of the dinosaurs in *Jurassic Park*, which was exactly how his Aunt Ginger had described what she'd heard.

Whatever it was, it made his blood run even colder than it already was, and he quickly ran to his FJ, which he'd hidden behind the ovens, and jumped inside.

He rolled the window down partway, locking the doors, again listening, deciding if he heard it come closer, he would flee, as his life was more important to him than making an arrest.

Finally starting to shiver, he decided to turn the engine on and get the heater going until he warmed up, then he could shut it down again for awhile. He could see even better from his FJ than by the coke ovens, but the element of surprise would be missing if anyone were to see it.

The heat felt good, and Bud savored it, knowing he'd have to turn the FJ off soon, partly to save gas, as he was almost out, the gas stations in Green River having been closed when he'd left town late that night.

After he'd gotten good and warm, he cut the engine, then wrapped up in an old blanket he kept in the back for the dogs. He again rolled the window down a crack, listening, hoping to soon hear the sound of Carl and the BLM rangers returning.

He could see the stars through the windshield, and even though he was again getting sleepy, they took his breath away. So many, and what was that he could see to the north that looked like a distant galaxy? Could it be Andromeda? Howie had told him it was visible to the naked eye and looked like a distant smudge with an oblique fuzzy halo around it, an amazing 2.5 million light years away.

And look! Wasn't that Mars, high in the northeastern sky, all ruby colored like the redrock down in the canyons in the Big Empty? And over there, the Pleaides or Seven Sisters? And Taurus the Bull, with his triangular horns?

Bud again heard the strange sound, but now it was much closer. He shivered, and deciding it would be prudent to leave, he turned the FJ key, yet the engine didn't respond. He tried again, but it was dead without even the tiniest bit of spark.

He now felt a chill go through him, but it wasn't the chill of the cold, but was rather the chill of fear, something he rarely felt. He sat for awhile, trying to figure out what to do, when he finally decided it was time to face his fears. He'd never been one to fall prey to irrational superstitions, and he knew it was impossible for a dinosaur to be making the noise. It had to have a logical explanation, and he was going to figure out what it was.

He put on his gloves, grabbed his flashlight, made sure his Ruger was handy in its shoulder holster, and stepped into the black night, wondering if he would ever see his wife and dogs again, noting that his least favorite constellation, Orion, was on the horizon, foretelling not only the oncoming winter, but his own possible doom.

41

Bud wasn't sure where the sound had come from, but he knew it was somewhere towards the Books, so he carefully started out in that direction. It was hard to see in the inky darkness, but he didn't want to use his light and tip whoever or whatever it was as to his location, so he moved very slowly.

He could see the faint forms of the coke ovens stretching towards Sunnyside, so he stayed close along their backs, where there seemed to be the remnant of an old road. Thinking back, he recalled seeing an old photo where a train actually ran on top of the ovens in order to dump the coal inside them, so maybe he was on an access road. Whatever it was, it made the going much easier, and he could now see the moon rising high over Bruin Point, which would make it easier to see where he was going, but also for others to see him.

As he walked along, tired, he began to assess where he was and how he got there. It had all started with taking Wilma Jean's used stove to Ginger for the Sunnyside Cafe—if he'd known what he was getting involved in, he probably would've hired someone to bring it up from Green River and stayed home and played ball with the dogs on the farm. Things would've been much easier, as he never would've known about Jimmy Johnson's death and dinosaurs and all the looting going on.

It then occurred to him that Ranger Carl would've called him regardless, but if he'd had any sense he would've told him he was too busy to get involved with looting in Range Creek and instead gone fly-fishing, even though he didn't fish.

He sighed. At least he'd gotten to try out some fancy camera gear. He'd returned it the previous day, and he was glad to be rid of it. It was nice having expensive gear, and he'd gotten some outstanding photos, but the responsibility and worry that something might happen to it had made it less enjoyable.

Sometimes it was better not having nice stuff, he thought, the moon now almost up over the rim, lighting the landscape. He stumbled on a rock and nearly went down, which made him realize he was so tired he was almost sleep walking. He stopped for a moment, trying to wake himself up.

And as he stood there, leaning against an old post, he heard it again—a roar so loud and ominous sounding that it made him flinch. He knew it was close, and even though he wanted to turn and run, he stood his ground, then turned a little more towards the steep jutting ramparts of the Books and again started out.

He could now see something softly glowing in the moonlight in the direction the roar had come from, and he carefully and stealthily made his way towards it. What would glow like that? It took some time, but he was soon standing on the edge of a small swamp, its water shining in the moonlight.

Bud was puzzled. This area was a desert, so where in hellsbells did a swamp come from? Maybe it was wastewater from the power plant, which wasn't all that far away. He thought he heard something coming, so he slipped behind a clump of trees at the edge of the water and waited breathlessly.

What emerged from the shadows was beyond his wildest belief! He was looking at no other than a large upright dinosaur! He knew it was a therapod, which meant it was carnivorous and from the late Jurassic. As he stood watching it in shock, he realized it was an

Allosaurus, one of the fiercest predators to ever walk the planet. He knew this because he'd been many times to the nearby Cleveland-Lloyd dinosaur quarry, where the remains of a number of the great beasts had been found.

Bud now held his breath as the giant looked towards him, then began walking his direction through the swamp. He could see it had red and green feathers all along its neck that glistened in the moonlight. It was heavy, and its feet made a sucking sound as it left its giant tracks in the mud, tracks that Bud could now see had three toes.

Ginger was right—there was a remnant dinosaur walking the Earth. Where had it come from? Surely someone would've seen its ancestors through the years, though it was vaguely possible its kin had lived in one of the remote deep canyons of the Books where no one ever went. Like Shorty had said, extremely unlikely and improbable, but possible.

Maybe it had discovered the fountain of life and was very old—millions of years old. That would account for its wrinkly skin, which reminded Bud of the mummy.

As the beast advanced towards him, Bud was astounded to think he was looking at the very species that birds had evolved from—theropods, the fierce, three-toed predator family that also included Tyrannosaurus rex. He knew the Allosaurus was every bit as fierce as the T. rex, and he also knew his puny Ruger would only serve to irritate it, like a fly.

Now, just when Bud was ready to panic and run, the Allosaurus turned, heading towards the faint lights of the town of Sunnyside. Bud envisioned the creature raining havoc on the sleeping town, just like in some movie, and his stomach turned at the thought—or maybe it was just the chili he'd had for dinner.

The dinosaur now stepped from the swamp, long plant tendrils and murky water dripping from its legs, moving quickly and leaving Bud behind, amazed at how fast it could move, especially given its size. It was soon gone, and Bud again heard its roar, which made him shiver.

He wanted nothing more than to jump in his FJ and head for

Green River, but he knew he had to somehow warn the people of Sunnyside. He paused, pulling his cellphone from his pocket, and dialed Ginger and Hank's number, but there was no service.

He felt a sense of urgency like he'd never felt before, and was soon running as fast as was prudently possible, following the *thump thump* of the beast's huge feet pounding the ground. Before he knew it, he was near the power plant, which sat silent.

He'd completely lost the Allosaurus, but he could now see its tracks clearly in the loose dirt, and he thought of Jimmy Johnson. He *had* been killed by a dinosaur after all, in spite of Bud's pooh-poohing of the idea. He recalled Ginger's words: *A dinosaur. I knew it. A real live dinosaur.* Even Sam had been convinced: *Jimmy Johnson was killed by a dinosaur. I know it in my gut.*

It now seemed as if the giant had turned to bypass the town, but Bud still felt a sense of urgency. He needed to somehow follow it and find out where it was going so he could help track it down later. He was amazed at how well he'd been able to follow it and how far he'd come without feeling a bit tired. Maybe he was in better shape than he'd thought.

For a brief moment, he saw his face on the front page of the worlds' news as having discovered an extinct creature, just like in the movies, and he hesitated. Maybe he could get Howie or someone else to take the credit, for he knew he wouldn't be up to the fame.

Back to the task at hand, he could still see the tracks, but they now seemed to be entering Whitmore Canyon, and he could make out something shiny in the distance. He was soon there, the moon lighting up what appeared to be a big sign that read *Sunnyside Mine #1*.

Hadn't the mine been reclaimed? Sam had told him it had, and yet here was its big open portal, and the tracks went right inside. And now, he could hear a faint roar coming from the depths, echoing and far away.

Bud turned and high-tailed it out of there. He now knew where the dinosaur hid out, and he would go to Ginger and Hank's and get help. They could take him back over to his FJ, and he could then come back and have breakfast at the Sunnyside Cafe when it opened and try to figure out what to do.

As he walked down the highway coming out of Whitmore Canyon, he looked at his watch. It was only four-thirty in the morning. How could that be? And he could hear people talking, but there was no one around. What was going on?

Now the sound of a car door slamming jerked Bud awake. His neck was sore from where he'd been slumped over the steering wheel. It was still dark, and there was no full moon. He could still see Orion, and it hadn't risen all that much from when he'd last seen it.

It had all been a dream, and now someone was here, and he could tell from the voices that it wasn't Carl and the BLM guys.

Bud knew the dream had been his subconscious telling him what he already knew but wasn't able to process at a conscious level, and he now knew what had really killed Jimmy Johnson. All he needed to do was to get Jimmy's lift truck and go prove his theory. But the original sound, the one he'd heard before he fell asleep, was no dream, and he again shivered.

But now, there was trouble at hand, and he needed to wake up and gather his wits, for he thought he recognized the voices.

42

Now a voice Bud knew was Trevor's said, "I know it was here. I counted the ovens. It was seven in. I'm positive of it!"

Cory said, "Trevor, I don't think you even know how to count, you idiot! If it was seven, then why's the stuff not here?"

"I know it was seven, but maybe it was eight. Let's keep looking."

"This is just like when you hid all that jewelry at Choo-Choo Rock and we couldn't find it again—and the mask and stuff in that wooden box that you let fall off the side of the raft. Idiot."

"That box walked the plank all by itself, it just slid right off. Besides, I was tired of that dumb mask. It was creepy."

Now the voices became muffled, and Bud assumed the pair had continued on down the line. He couldn't see if Lucy was with them or not, and he cringed to think they might come around the back side of the coke ovens and see his FJ. If so, he'd just hightail it out, hopefully before they recognized who was driving. He pulled his hood up around his face.

Now the pair had returned.

"I know it was here, Cory. I just know it! Someone's been here and taken it. Lucy's going to be furious with us!"

"Furious with *you*, you dimwit. Just let her stay in the SUV, and don't say a word. We'll tell her we have to leave for some reason."

"For what reason? She's no dummy. We need a good excuse."

"We'll tell her someone's watching the place and we don't want to be implicated. It's a stakeout. Then we'll come back without her and see if we can find the stuff. We'll take the back road to Columbia like we think someone might be following us. Hopefully that will convince her."

Bud had his hand on the ignition key, ready to roll, when he heard two car doors slam and their SUV drive off.

Relieved, he started the FJ. He'd get back to where he had cell service, then he'd call Carl and tell him what was going on.

Pulling out with his lights still off, he could see their taillights in the distance, heading down the back road to the tiny town of Columbia. Bud had driven it a couple of times, as it was the old railroad grade for the trains that brought some of the coal to the coke ovens from another mine there and now served as a shortcut to the small town.

As their vehicle rounded a curve out of sight, Bud turned on his headlights and started the half-mile or so back to the main highway. He got about half way when his engine sputtered and died, out of gas.

He'd have to walk to the highway, and the odds of getting a ride were slim to none this time of night. It was a good five miles or so to Ginger and Hank's, but maybe he could get a cell signal before long and call them to come pick him up.

Soon at the highway, there was just enough starlight to see the black asphalt stretching both directions into what seemed like infinity. He suddenly felt very alone, thinking again of the strange dream he'd had. Reminding himself it was just a dream, he took the *U.S. Marshal-Dodge City* badge from his pocket and began fiddling with it as he walked along, which made him feel better. He looked at his watch—it was now five a.m. and was shaping up to be the longest night ever. Surely Carl and the boys would be coming back soon.

Sure enough, he could see headlights in the distance, but they were coming from the wrong direction. Had Carl come around the long way over by Horse Canyon? The highway formed a big loop, so it was possible, and it would account for their delay, but why would they do that?

As the vehicle came closer, it now occurred to him that he could be seeing Trevor and Cory, as they'd had enough time to circle around to Columbia and get back on the highway. By the time he thought about hiding, it was too late, and a black SUV was pulling over.

Now Trevor hung out the passenger window, saying, "You need a ride, buddy?"

"You idiot, it actually *is* Buddy," Cory said. "What are you doing out here? Trevor, get out and let him ride in the front."

Bud was conflicted, but he was tired of walking and just tired in general. A ride would be nice, though he had no idea what he should tell them he was doing. But if he took a ride, maybe he could finally figure out who Lucy was.

He said, "I was over at the coke ovens spying. A ride would be great."

"Hop in," Trevor said, getting into the back. "What were you spying on?"

Bud got in and said, "I was watching somebody. You guys told me that's where you stored stuff, so I went out to see what was going on. I ran out of gas."

"We never told you we store stuff there," Cory protested, glancing towards the back seat, where Bud could see a shadowy figure who seemed to be intentionally making themselves even more shadowy.

"Well, not in so many words," Bud replied. "You kind of hinted at it, though. Somebody was out there, but since you gave me a fake phone number, I had no way of calling you. I'm sure glad you showed up when you did."

"Thanks for looking out for us," Trevor said. "Did you see who it was?"

"I did," Bud said, thinking he was doing pretty well so far, not even lying. "Actually, I think that's them coming back." He nodded at three sets of headlights coming towards them. "Because there were three vehicles."

"Bloody thieves," Cory muttered, stepping on the gas. "We're outnumbered. Let's just get out of here. Where do you want us to take you, Buddy?"

"My aunt and uncle live in Sunnyside, so it's not far out of your way. Just swing into town and take me to the last house before the canyon. I really appreciate the ride."

He nodded towards the person in the back, knowing it was Lucy, but she didn't say a word.

As they approached Ginger's, Bud added, "They found a shield, and I think I know where they're hiding it."

Cory asked with surprise, "You know? What, did they say something?"

"Yes, they said they were going to take it out to the Buried Forest and hide it there. So, you might want to go out and see if you can find it, but give them time to get it out there."

"Where's the Buried Forest?" Cory asked.

Recalling what his Uncle Hank had told him, Bud said, "I've never been there, but I think I can find it. It's on the first road to the right a couple of miles east of Wellington, just a dirt two-track. You hike down from an old drill site. They called it the Sunnyside Shield. Be there by say, mid-afternoon."

"Do you think that's a good idea, Lucy?" Trevor asked. "You know Buddy, don't you? He said he knew you. Isn't he the guy you said was maybe also taking stuff and could maybe help us out?"

Bud was now on high alert. If Lucy wasn't who he suspected she was, he could be in trouble, but he now knew in their own words that they were indeed looters, even though he'd suspected it all along.

A muffled voice now said from the back, "We'll be there."

"Sounds good," Bud replied, getting out. He then added, "And guys, just so you know, you beat me to the Sunnyside Museum, and that's not fair. I never even got to see all that cool mining stuff before you sold it to Wiggins Diggins."

Trevor said, "Sorry, but you have to seize the moment. Someone left the door unlocked."

Bud said goodbye and watched as they turned around and drove back down the street in the darkness, wondering how he'd managed to land on his feet again, hoping he could keep his good luck going for just a couple more days.

Tomorrow was the election, but he'd slip away with Shorty and go find the Buried Forest, hiding the shield he'd gotten at Jimmy Johnson's. Hopefully it would entice Lucy and the gang to come looking, just in time for Carl and his boys to show up.

43

Bud had tried to sleep on the settee in Ginger's front porch room, not wanting to wake them, but he'd finally given up and slipped inside to make some coffee. Remembering the maté, he finally dug out a metal container of Folgers, but upon opening it, found it was full of screws and nails and bolts and such.

He accidentally dropped it and the lid came off, hardware flying all across the room, the tin banging against the refrigerator. As he crawled around picking it all up, he noticed his Aunt Ginger standing at the kitchen door in her robe, watching.

"Morning," he said, smiling as he picked up the last washer.

"Good morning, Buddy," she replied. "Want a cup of coffee?"

"Sure," he said, putting the Folgers tin back where he'd found it.

Ginger set to making a pot of coffee as Bud sat down at the kitchen table, waiting, neither saying a word.

Finally, Bud said, "If you guys would open the cafe earlier, I'd be down there instead of bothering you here. Just a suggestion."

"Buddy, it's five-thirty in the morning. There's no way I'm going to open anything at this hour, not even my eyes, except when you show up. Where's your FJ?" she asked.

"Out of gas," Bud replied.

"Does your wife know you're out galavanting around in the wee hours of the night?"

"Kind of."

Ginger soon handed him a cup of coffee. "Do you mind if I ask what you're doing?"

"I can't say," Bud dodged.

"Why not?" Ginger persisted.

"The Sunnyside grapevine grows far and wide. I mean, even Uncle Junior knew about Jimmy Johnson's death way over in Colorado mere hours after it happened."

"Nobody told me it was a secret," Ginger protested.

Bud changed the subject. "Have you heard any more dinosaur sounds?"

Ginger replied, "It was quiet for a long time, then I heard them again last night. Buddy, it's real. I can't wait to move into Jimmy's house so we're not right here at the mouth of the canyon. But is that why you're here? You're following up on his death, aren't you? I won't say anything."

"Well," Bud replied. "I do want to figure that out. I need Uncle Hank to get Jimmy's lift truck and go out with me, but I need to get back home today, so it won't be until later."

"Everything going OK there?" Ginger asked, getting Bud a refill.

"It's fine. Today's the big election, and my deputy's running for mayor, so it should be interesting. But when does the cafe open?"

Ginger looked at the green melamine clock above the sink. "Soon, at six."

"Shouldn't you be getting dressed, or did you turn it into one of those come as you are places?" Bud kidded.

"LuAnn's there opening up. She and Junior are staying in the back of the old gas station in their new RV. But yes, I need to get down there before long."

"They sold the Paradox Cafe and General Store?"

"You didn't know? They've already moved out, though most of their stuff went with the sale. But they bought an RV on their way back through Grand Junction. It's really nice. Makes me want to travel. Wilma Jean talked to them the other day. I thought she told you. I guess the grapevine's not as robust as you think, my boy."

Ginger stood and put her hand on his shoulder. "But come on down and have breakfast. You're not bringing Freckles back, are you?"

"I think he has a good home with a friend. She says she's going to start doing agility training with him. He sure seems to like her."

"Well, I'm getting dressed, then we'll go to the cafe. I can hear Hank getting up. He can join us. You go wash up and comb your hair. You look like you've been up all night."

They were all soon on their way to the cafe, where Bud and Hank ordered breakfast while Ginger went into the kitchen to help LuAnn. They would take some gas out to retrieve Bud's FJ after they ate.

The cafe soon began to fill up, and Bud noticed Rod Ruff come in.

"Come on over and join us," Bud offered.

Rod pulled up a bistro chair, saying, "Nice to see you again, Bud." He then turned to Hank saying, "Where's Junior?"

"Probably sleeping in out back," Hank replied.

"Say, Rod," Bud said. "Can I have a word with you before breakfast, maybe outside?" He nodded at Hank, saying, "We'll be right back."

Rod followed Bud around to the back of the cafe, then asked with concern, "I know you're the sheriff in these parts—did I do something wrong?"

"No, no," Bud replied. "And I'm not the sheriff here in Sunnyside, just in Emery County, and the county line's a ways down the road."

He then explained how he'd been walking out of Whitmore Canyon and had overheard Rod's conversation, then continued, "It seemed to me like you knew those two. Is there anything you would care to share about them? They sounded like they'd taken your tires and tried to sell them back to you."

Rod shook his head in disgust. "Yup, that was Doyle and Eugene. They live in Price, but they grew up here. They kept getting themselves into trouble and had to leave town, but every once in awhile they come back and we run them off again. There's a number of things missing that most people attribute to them."

"Do they seem like the type to steal stuff from Range Creek?"

Rod thought for a moment, then said, "Probably, though that would be going for the big stuff. They were pretty much petty thieves when they were here. I wouldn't put stealing things from there past them, but neither has the savvy to know where to sell antiquities like that. They'd definitely need help."

"Any idea who such help might be?"

"No idea. I don't run in those circles."

"Ok," Bud replied as they walked back around to the cafe. "I appreciate the information. I'm looking forward to the car show and to seeing *Summertime Blues*."

Rod grinned and held the door open for Bud, saying, "You're going to flip your lid, Daddy-O, when you see *Rockabilly Hound Dog*."

Bud replied, "I can't wait to see it agitate the gravel."

44

Bud sat in his office, desperately trying to stay awake. He'd managed to call Ranger Carl and let him know what was going on, and he'd also called Howie to wish him luck with the election, and now he was sitting up as straight as he could, fiddling with the *U.S. Marshal-Tombstone* badge, for he knew the minute he leaned back in his chair he would drift off.

He finally decided to boot up his computer and see if he could learn anything new about the Buried Forest. He keyed in "Buried Forest Sunnyside," and immediately brought up a page about some poor fellow named George Forest who had been buried in the Sunnyside Cemetery in 1922.

Trying again, he keyed in "Buried Forest Mounds" and got something about some strange molds that grew in mounds in a forest in Brazil.

He was beginning to think he was out of luck when he tried "Buried Forest Mounds Reef Utah." The first page started off with *Location: Mounds Reef; Fossils: pelecypods and cephalopods*, then went off on some tangent using geologic terms that Bud could barely pronounce, so he gave up and went to the next page.

Bingo! He actually found an article in a regional paper that even had an old photograph with it. He studied the photo, which was in black and white and had *Buried Forest, Sunnyside about 1899* written at the bottom in a florid script, and under that the words *BYU Lee Library Special Collections.* The picture showed a cowboy on his horse holding a shield like a warrior, looking up at what looked like huge trunks sticking out of a cliff, each easily the height of a person.

Bud now slowly read through the article.

> *This old photograph from the historical collection at the BYU Library suggests that the stumps sticking out of the cliffs are fossilized trees, though they're actually huge sandstone concretions. The name "Buried Forest" has stuck, and the locals still call it that, though they now often modify the name by the addition of the word "concretions."*
>
> *How concretions form is still somewhat of a geological mystery, but they're thought to form around some kind of organic nucleus, such as a fossil or shell while the sedimentary rocks are still forming.*
>
> *Some of the Buried Forest concretions are several feet in diameter, and often their inner faces are etched with fascinating detail, and sometimes fossils can be seen inside.*

Bud again studied the old photo, now sure it was the same one Bailey had mentioned earlier.

He found himself nodding off, so he stood up and walked around, wondering what the daily special at the Melon Rind Cafe was. Maybe he should go to the Chow Down, he thought, try something different. He hadn't been back all that long from the Sunnyside Cafe, yet he was hungry again. Maybe he should just go home, say hello to the dogs, and take a short nap.

But he'd told Cory and Trevor to meet him later, and he needed to go out to the Mounds Reef and find a good place to hide the shield. He wanted Shorty to go along, but he hadn't been able to get ahold of him. He also needed to call Carl so he'd know where to find everyone and make his arrests.

It wasn't like him to put something that important off, but Bud was beginning to realize he was exhausted. He knew that he needed to sleep or he risked crashing and burning. There was a time he could easily stay up all night and not feel any effects, but he wasn't getting any younger, he decided. He then noticed he had a note from Howie to call Judge Richter, but he was too tired, it would have to wait.

Just then, the phone rang.

"Sheriff's Office, Bud speaking."

"Bud, it's Maureen. I hope you're doing well, because I have a huge favor to ask of you."

"I'm fine, Maureen. What do you need?"

"Is there any way you could get Howie out of my hair for the day, or even part of the day? He's a nervous wreck, and he's driving me nuts. Even little Malcolm is on pins and needles."

"It's the election, isn't it?"

"Yes. I've never seen him like this. Don't you have some kind of project you need help with?"

Bud replied, "Can you put him on the phone?"

Bud soon heard Howie say, "Sheriff, I know I'm driving them crazy. I can't help it."

"Howie, can you come on over to the office? I actually do need your help. I want to go up by Sunnyside, but I'm too tired to drive myself, plus I don't want to go alone. We may be gone awhile. I'll get us lunch at the Melon Rind, but bring a warm coat in case we're out late."

Howie replied, "But Bud, if we're out late I won't know how the election went."

"Maureen can call us, but we probably won't be all *that* late."

"OK, I'll be over shortly."

"Thanks. I'll give you an extra day off to make up for it, Deputy."

"Nah, Bud, you don't need to do that. It's probably a good idea to get me away from here before Maureen leaves and goes down to Hanksville again. I don't want that."

"Sounds like a plan," Bud said. "And Howie, don't come in uniform, but bring your gun, concealed. Just in case."

"Just in case what, Bud?"

"Well, just in case someone else decides to join us."

"This is all very cryptic, Sheriff," Howie said. "Is it going to be dangerous?"

"Probably not, Deputy, but one never knows when they're in law enforcement what might come up. But I'm going to call the State Patrol to cover for us for a bit, then order some sandwiches and lock up. Meet me at the cafe. I'll get us some coffee, too."

"OK, Bud, but just be aware that after this escapade, you may be calling me Mayor McPherson instead of Deputy McPherson."

"That would be great, Howie, though I'd miss working with you," Bud said.

Howie paused, then added, "Jeez Louise, Bud, what am I doing? I don't really want to be mayor. Is it too late to back out? What if someone tries to sue me because there's a pothole in their street or something—or worse yet, puts me on some Mafioso hit list?"

Now Bud could hear Maureen say, "See what I mean? I'm sending him right over. Good luck, and thanks."

Bud said goodbye and hung up the phone, wondering if Howie's nervous energy would help wake him up or just make him more exhausted.

He'd find out soon enough, he guessed, taking the carefully wrapped shield from its hiding place.

45

"Howie, wear this hat. Pull it down over your forehead if we meet anyone."

Bud handed Howie an old straw hat he wore when plowing to keep the sun off his face.

"What's this all about, Sheriff?" Howie asked.

"We're going incognito. I don't want anyone to recognize you, since you're my deputy."

"What about you, Bud?"

"I've already been recognized."

"So we're like spies?" Howie asked.

Bud grimaced. "No, we're just incognito."

"Is that why we're going in your old farm pickup?" Howie asked.

"Pretty much. They would recognize my FJ, and we for sure don't want to be in a sheriff's vehicle. We're undercover, don't forget."

Bud tried to outline where they were going and why, but he was too tired to really go into detail and was soon fast asleep, Howie driving, the old truck bouncing along, badly in need of new shocks.

After a good 45 minutes, Howie woke Bud, saying, "Sheriff, wake up. We just passed the turnoff to Sunnyside, and I need you to tell me exactly where to go."

It took Bud a few minutes to figure out where he was, Howie handing him a thermos of coffee. Studying the road, Bud finally said, "It's up here about a mile on your left, just before the highway starts down the hill into Cat Canyon."

"Did you have a nice nap?" Howie asked.

"It was good, Howie. I really needed it. I think I might be able to function now, whereas before it was marginal. You want some coffee while I'm at it?" He pulled a cup out of his pack.

"Sure," Howie replied, turning off the highway onto a dirt road that immediately began a gradual climb.

"We'll climb up this hill, then be on top of the Mounds Reef," Bud said. "The road follows along the reef, then goes through a break in the cliffs down to the railroad and the Price River."

"Oh sure," Howie replied. "I know this area well. We used to come out here and rockhound when I was a kid. Lots of marine fossils and concretions."

Bud, now sipping hot coffee, was surprised. "You know this area?"

"Sure, Bud," Howie said. "I grew up in Sunnyside, remember? My mom worked for the coal mine and my dad was a postman. We spent almost every weekend out and about, exploring the country, at least when it wasn't too snowy and cold. But I wonder why someone has a stock trailer out here this time of year. All the cattle should be gathered up by now."

"Howie, do you know where the Buried Forest is?"

"Sure."

"Wait! Slow down by this trailer. I think I know who it belongs to," Bud said, then added, "Sure enough, it's Lonnie's. He lives in Wellington and is the wrangler for the Range Creek bunch. I wonder what he's doing out here."

"Looks like horse tracks," Howie replied. "Probably out riding."

"Probably," Bud said. "I forgot you grew up in Sunnyside. Did you ever hear any strange noises, kind of like a dinosaur might sound?"

"Only when my dad caught me getting into his home brew," Howie grinned. "But does where we're going have something to do with that dinosaur that killed Jimmy Johnson?"

"I think it's something different," Bud replied. "But Howie, can you take us to the trail that drops off the reef and goes to the Buried Forest? That's where I want to hide this shield."

"Sure, it's not very far up the road. You stop at an old drill site."

They bounced along for a bit, then Bud said, "Howie, did I tell you I saw the Andromeda Galaxy when I was out at the coke ovens?"

"You mean you saw M31? That's pretty cool, Sheriff. You have to have really clear skies to see it."

"Maybe we can go out sometime with your telescope and look at it," Bud said. "I'd really like to see what it looks like a little closer. All I saw was kind of a smudge, like you needed to clean your glasses."

"It's amazing one can see it at all with the naked eye, considering how far away it is."

Howie now turned off the dirt road, parking at the old drill site. Gathering up the shield, they then took a well-trodden game trail through a break in the cliffs and were soon on the cliff talus below. There, Bud stood in amazement, for he could see large, round, embedded concretions halved along the face of the rock. He counted 20 in just a couple of hundred yards.

"They're up too high to really get a good look at what's in their centers," Bud said. "I wish I had a pair of good binoculars. Let's find a good place to hide this shield and get out of here."

"Are you worried Lucy's gang will show up early?" Howie asked.

"I am," Bud said, unwrapping the old shield. "I sure don't like the idea of leaving this out here, as I don't want anything to happen to it, but Carl and his guys are supposed to be on their way."

Howie studied the unwrapped shield, looked up at the cliffs, then back at the shield, then said, "Bud, look at that one concretion up there, the third from the crack in the cliff. Then look at the shield."

Bud studied both for awhile, then said, "I see it, Howie. It can't be a coincidence. The design is too unusual. And it's the same design on the little figurine I bought, which is one of the Pilling bunch if I was informed correctly. It had the same yellow concentric rings with the red middle."

"It's odd, Bud, that's for sure. That concretion has the strangest center, it looks like a giant crab or something, and the shield is exactly like it. Someone modeled the shield after the concretion, Bud."

"How do these things form, anyway, Howie?"

"Well, I'm no geologist, and Shorty could probably explain it better, but think of sand immersed in water that has concentrations of minerals floating in it. Sometimes something like calcite will precipitate out of this watery solution around some sort of nucleus, which can be anything. This in turn attracts more of the calcite, which forms in concentric, well-cemented masses that harden. The nucleus, which is often a sea critter of some kind, gets fossilized, and this circular mass then weathers more slowly than the softer, surrounding rocks, leaving what looks like a tree trunk."

"Sounds pretty complicated," Bud replied, recalling what Lonnie had said about a shield on their way out of Range Creek that night, which now seemed long ago.

"Lonnie told me there was a shield that had some kind of design that was really unusual and that finding it would make a person famous in the archaeological world."

"How would that work?" Howie asked.

"I don't know. But Howie, something's coming back to me. He also said that Phil and the director of the museum in Price had spent a lot of time looking for it. That would be Renee. I wonder if she isn't in Range Creek with Phil and is the fiancee he mentioned."

"Would that be important, Bud?"

"Yes, because it means that Renee wasn't the one who took the Pilling figurine to Durango to sell. If she was involved, she had an accomplice. And it also means I might know who's lying about everything."

"Bud, it seems to me you have it figured out. You seem to know who this Lucy person is. But let's hide this shield before they come out here. I'm going to shimmy up into that crack and stick it way back in there. Hand me your GPS so I can get a good reading."

Howie carefully put the shield under one arm, then climbed until he was up at the crack, where he carefully hid the shield. He then took a GPS reading and slipped back down.

"Nice job," Bud said. "Put this handheld recorder in your pocket and be sure to record everything if they show up while we're still here. But Howie, why would someone leave plastic skulls all over Range Creek? I just can't figure it out."

"Maybe it's exactly the same as what we just did with the GPS, Bud, a way of marking a place."

Bud was silent for awhile, then said, "Bingo! I think you're on to something. The skulls we found were at sites that had been looted. Someone was making a statement."

"A statement like *neener neener*?" Howie replied.

"Exactly. It was a way to say we're doing this right under your nose. But how did they know where the sites were that hadn't yet been dug?"

"Didn't you tell me the archaeologists had a map with GPS markers for everything?" Howie asked. "Someone got ahold of this map and was looting the undug sites and leaving a skull at each one to taunt the archaeologists, especially Phil, as he was the head of the whole thing."

"It's like they had a grudge and were gigging him," Bud said. "And they obviously hired Cory and Trevor, AKA Eugene and Doyle, to do their dirty work. These guys would dig a site, load up everything on an ATV, then one would take their truck back, which they had to park by the gate, and the other would haul the goods down to the river, wearing a mask that looked like Phil in case anyone saw them, steal a raft, and take it out to the Crystal Geyser boat launch. And seeing a good place to hide their own loot, like the jewelry, which they'd stolen from various places, Cory and Trevor would bring stuff in and hide it in places here in Range Creek they'd already looted. Pretty handy."

"But why did they have the stuff at the museum?"

"Either they thought it would be a good holdover place for a day or two or they were hoping to implicate someone."

"And who is Lucy?"

"I thought it was Renee for awhile, but now I'm not sure. Sandy the ecologist said he saw someone with Phil who could've been her, and they were digging a site, but it's possible they were legit. But we'll soon find out, because I hear a vehicle coming. Pull your hat down, Howie, and let me do the talking, but have your gun handy, as I know they're armed."

"You mean as in *Shoot low, they're riding Shetlands*?"

Bud laughed. "Exactly."

46

Bud could now hear the sound of car doors slamming on the road above.

"Howie, if that's the Lucy Bunch, be cool, and if I give the signal, be ready to make a fast arrest."

"What exactly will the signal be, Bud?" Howie asked, pulling the straw hat even further down on his head.

"I'll probably say something like 'You're under arrest.'"

"Got it!" Howie replied. "And record everything."

Now Bud could see two men and a woman coming down the trail that led to the Buried Forest. As they got closer, he could see that the men were indeed Cory and Trevor, but like Howie, the woman was wearing a hat that hid her face, though hers was a felt cowboy hat.

Upon seeing Bud and Howie, the group came over to them, and the woman said, "You came out ahead of us to find the shield? Sneaky."

Bud, now recognizing her voice, said, "Hello Lucy, I mean Rita—Rita Brown."

Rita asked with surprise, "How do you know that?"

"I ran your plates."

Trevor and Cory looked at each other with suspicion, then Cory said, "You told us you already knew Rita."

Bud didn't miss a beat. "I did."

Rita asked, "How do you have access to info on license plates?"

Bud replied, "I know how to get into information systems."

Rita seemed to relax. "You *are* good. And who's your friend?"

"He's a friend," Bud said, nodding at Howie.

"Very funny," Rita said.

"Don't worry. He's trustworthy. He's going to be the Mayor of Green River in a few hours. I brought him with me so he'd forget about the election for awhile."

Rita, looking dubious, said, "Right. Who is he, really? He could use a new hat."

"His name is Howie. He's the hep cat who hangs around keeping me from getting bored."

Rita smiled. "Nice to meet you, Howie."

Bud continued, "What I'm wondering, Rita, is what you're going to do with the stuff you guys stored at the coke ovens. You know, the stuff Cory and Trevor got from Range Creek. Since they stole it, I assume it belongs to them, right?"

Rita scowled and said, "It's not theirs, it's mine. They were paid well for it. Are you interested in any of it?"

Bud said, "I'm definitely interested."

Rita replied, "There's more available, if the weather cooperates. Right now we need to find that shield."

"I think it's up there, in that crack," Bud said, pointing to where Howie had hid the shield.

Rita nodded at Cory, who nodded at Trevor, who then climbed up to the crack and pulled the shield out, sliding back down.

Rita said, "That was easy—maybe too easy. How did you know where it was?"

"Just a lucky guess," Bud replied, noting she was getting suspicious. "That's where I would hide it, if it were me."

Trevor was now holding the shield for everyone to see. As Rita examined it, Bud could see that her demeanor was changing from being reserved and careful to being exuberant, though she was trying to hide it.

Now Bud said, "See that concretion up there? It's what the shield was modeled after. The supposed marine connection is just them copying an unusual marine fossil from millions of years ago."

Everyone looked up, then down at the shield, nodding their heads.

"It's a petrified crab," Trevor said. "Right out of Davy Jones' locker."

Rita replied, "It's still a significant find and worth a fortune. You told us it was here, but we're the ones who actually found it, so it's ours. But I'll be fair and give you a finder's fee."

Bud replied, "I showed *you* where to look. I should give you a finder's fee and keep the shield."

"What would you do with it? I'll have my people sell it and give you part."

Bud asked, "Who exactly are your people? I'm not having just anyone sell my shield. I probably already know them anyway, if they're who I think they are—down in Durango?"

"You know Jens Anderson?" Rita asked.

"Jens? Oh sure. That's who sells your stuff? Anyone else involved?"

"Why do you want to know?"

"So we're not overlapping or competing, Rita, you know how it works."

Rita replied, "Jens works alone. He picks up my stuff and takes it down there to a dealer."

Bud was tired. It suddenly hit him like a ton of bricks. Now, with the recording and with Howie as a witness and with the artifacts from the coke ovens, he had enough to convict Rita and the whole bunch. He didn't know what was holding Carl up, and he knew he didn't want to play the game any longer, but Cory had gone and sat on a rock in the shade behind him, and he needed to be able to see everyone to arrest them, as things just worked better that way.

He could now see someone else coming, someone on horseback,

a black-and-white horseback named Tucker, and with Lonnie was a woman who Bud assumed was his wife, riding Spirit, both with rifle scabbards on their saddles.

Cory, now on alert, jumped to his feet and came around to where Bud could see him, and Bud, nodding to Howie, pulled out his gun, saying, "You're all under arrest!"

Howie quickly had his gun out also, training it directly on Trevor, saying, "Put 'em up."

"You can't arrest us!" Rita said in surprise as Cory and Trevor put their hands up. "You're not even the law!"

Bud pulled Jimmy's badges from his pocket and tossed them to Rita, his gun now trained on her. She caught them, then laughed.

"U.S. Marshals of Dodge City and Tombstone? This is a joke, right?"

But Lonnie, now pulled up on Tucker behind her, his rifle trained on her back, said, "It's no joke, Bailey. Bud's the Sheriff of Emery County, and the other guy's his deputy. Put your hands up, 'cause my Remington speaks way louder than words when it gets irritated."

47

Bud and Howie leaned against Bud's old farm pickup, watching as the taillights of Ranger Carl's vehicle went down the road on its way to the Carbon County Jail with Rita, AKA Lucy, AKA Bailey, handcuffed in the back. It was followed by another vehicle carrying Cory and Trevor and two BLM rangers, and not far behind was Lonnie's pickup pulling his stock trailer, the couple on their way home with the horses.

Bud would be forever grateful to Lonnie and his wife Jane, whose timing had served Bud and Howie well, for Bud had not only not brought handcuffs, but had no way to transport anyone in his old truck. Lonnie had helped keep everyone at bay by locking them in his stock trailer until Carl showed up.

"That worked out pretty well," Bud said. "You did a great job, Deputy."

"I guess we weren't planning on making any arrests today, eh Sheriff?" Howie replied.

"I was hoping Carl would show up sooner. I'm glad it's over with, is all I can say. There's a few loose ends to tie up, but it shouldn't take long. I just want to go home and go to bed."

"Sheriff," Howie said, "There's several more hours until the election's over. If we go back now, I'll probably get served with divorce papers by the end of the day. Maybe we should go into Price and see a movie or something until the tally's over."

"Howie, there *is* one more thing I'd like to do, which you could help me with, if you're up to it. Let's go to Sunnyside and get a cup of mud at my aunt's cafe. You've never been there, and I think you'll like it. It's kind of like a bistro."

"What's a bistro, Bud?" Howie asked.

Bud grinned. "I'm not actually sure, but I have a little experiment I need help with."

"If it's anything like today's little excursion, maybe I should pass," Howie said with concern.

"Howie, I have a theory about what killed Jimmy Johnson. Let's go get Jimmy's lift truck and my Uncle Hank and see if it works out."

"Is it going to involve guns again?"

"No guns, I promise. But would you mind driving? I'm still pretty tired."

"Sure."

It wasn't far to Sunnyside, and after stopping at Hank and Ginger's, they were soon following Hank to the Sunnyside Mine. He was driving Jimmy Johnson's lift truck, having first stopped and gotten a key to the mine grounds from the city office.

Once through the gate, Hank pulled up next to the pile of coal and asked, "What are we doing here, Buddy?"

"Actually, Uncle Hank, could you back up over here a bit farther —I want to lift this big slab of coal, then have you park exactly where the truck was when you came and got it after Jimmy's death."

Hank backed the truck to the pile and lowered the lift, Bud and Howie wrangling the big belt around the coal. Bud then gave the signal to move the truck, which Hank did, though very slowly so as to not lose the big slab.

"Take a look at the bottom of this thing," Bud directed Howie and Hank. "Do you see anything unusual?"

"Oh man, Sheriff," Howie said. "That's really something."

Hank added, "Just like Jimmy to want something like that. I

remember him talking about getting a big slab of coal to make a fireplace mantle with. I told him it might not be such a great idea, seeing how coal was so flammable. But this, well…"

"If you look over to the left of the truck, you'll see an impression in the ground, which is where I think the slab was when Jimmy actually got it onto the lift. Now go stand over there while I perform the experiment, 'cause I don't want to kill anyone," Bud advised, pointing to the far side of the truck.

He then turned on the lift motor, then jerked the swingarm as hard as he could, making the slab of coal fly through the air, landing on the ground with a thump.

"Jimmy somehow got himself in the way of that slab as it came flying through the air," Bud said. "I don't know if he accidentally hit the swing too hard or if something malfunctioned, but the slab of coal hit him square on, just as he turned to run, slamming right into his back. It was probably instant death, and as you can see, that slab just happens to have a fossilized theropod dinosaur track on it, which are common in coal mines."

"I'll be darned," Hank said. "Yes, tracks are common. Coal miners usually chisel them off so they don't bump their heads on them."

"How did you figure that one out, Sheriff?" Howie asked.

"Well, first, we were talking about all this, and you said that maybe a dinosaur statue fell on him, and that got me to thinking in a different way than it being an actual dinosaur, Howie. So that was a helpful start. I then recalled seeing a coffee table at one of my dad's friends when I was a kid. The guy was a coal miner and had made this table from a chunk of coal that had a big dino track in the center of it. It was pretty impressive to a ten-year old boy. And then the other night I had a dream, and there were these big dinosaur tracks leading right into the Sunnyside Mine. This was the big clue, and when I woke, I had a hunch there was a track on that slab. I'd seen the slab before with Sam Wiggins and knew it had something on the bottom that made it tippy."

"So," Howie said, "It whacked him on the back with such force that it actually killed him. Mass times acceleration equaled death."

"Yes, and then it slipped off the lift belt and landed with the track on the bottom, or it would've been more obvious what had happened," Bud added. "Ginger and Sam were right, a dinosaur did kill Jimmy, though it itself had been dead for millions of years."

"Actually, Buddy," Hank said. "Jimmy was killed by a trace fossil."

"What's that?" Bud asked.

"It's a fossil of something the animal left rather than of the animal itself—like a fossilized footprint, trail, or burrow."

"Killed by a dinosaur trace fossil. What a way to go," Howie said thoughtfully. "Poor fellow. I can see the coroner's report: *He was killed by a lethal trace fossil. We are unaware of any other circumstances where dinosaur activity has contributed to the death of human beings, but we're standing by*."

Hank looked blankly at Howie for a moment, then said,"Boys, I'd like this slab for my rock shop. I'm going to make a memorial to Jimmy and set it at the door for people to look at. Could you help me load it?"

Bud said, "Uncle Hank, no offense, but maybe it's better off here where it landed, otherwise there may be more coroner's reports to write."

Hank looked disappointed, but said, "You're right. It'll be a leaverite."

"What's that?" Howie asked.

"A leave 'er right there," Hank replied.

Bud laughed. "Howie, you just fell for possibly the oldest rock-hound joke in history. But let's go to the Sunnyside Cafe and get some coffee before I go to sleep on my feet."

"I can be a bit gullible, you know," Howie replied, then added glumly, "The election reports should be coming in soon, and I know I lost. But Sheriff, I'll give you this, you definitely took my mind off it all, no question about that."

"Glad to have helped," Bud replied.

48

Bud sat in his camp chair in the screened-in porch room at his Aunt Ginger's house in Sunnyside, sipping lemonade and fiddling with his little pocket harmonica, Lindie sleeping at his feet.

He was tired again, even though it had been a couple of weeks since he'd stayed up all night spying at the Sunnyside coke ovens, and he was well recovered from that.

This was more of a good kind of tired, he mused, the kind you get from physical labor, as opposed to sleep deprivation, though he knew he'd probably be sore the next day. But it felt good to have finally carried the last tub of stuff from his aunt and uncle's rental into their new house, which they now owned courtesy of Jimmy Johnson.

He and his Aunt Ginger were taking a break, thus the camp chairs from Bud's FJ, since the furniture and everything else was gone. Hank, LuAnn, and Junior were at the other house unpacking everything.

It felt good to sit and talk for a bit, and he'd soon be heading back to Green River, where he'd happily don his Scooby Do PJs and climb into a warm bed made even warmer by the presence of Hoppie, Pierre, and Lindie, as well as his wife. The thought was so cozy it made him want to start singing Kumbaya, but he knew better than to go there.

"So you no longer have a deputy, I hear," Ginger said. "Have you considered hiring Sam Wiggins? He told me he'd like to move down your way."

"Yes, I need a deputy now, but I don't think Sam wants the job."

"Why not?"

"He told me he thinks I'm too dramatic for his taste. He wants to work for someone who's, as he put it, nice and steady."

"Why in the world would he think you're dramatic, Buddy? You strike me as the opposite."

"I think it has to do with a little mock arrest I got him involved in. But it's for the best. He'd get bored in Green River. Nothing ever happens there."

Ginger said, "He solved the case of the museum break-in, or at least he recovered the stolen goods. That was a feather in his cap."

"A very good thing," Bud agreed.

"And he and his wife bought most of Jimmy Johnson's junk from us at Wiggins Diggins. We made enough to buy a new washing machine."

"That's fantastic!" Bud said.

Now Ginger added, "I saw in the paper where someone donated the missing Pilling figurine to the museum. They wanted to remain anonymous. It's been missing for years."

"They probably didn't want to reveal where they got it," Bud commented. "Maybe one of those *Mission Impossible* kind of things."

Ginger continued, "And the museum's looking for a new director. I guess the interim one quit and got married to one of the archaeologists working down in Range Creek. That would be quite the job. I wonder who will replace her?"

"I heard the curator got fired and is in jail under looting charges."

"No kidding? That sounds like quite the story. As sheriff, do you know anything about it?"

"Kind of. I guess she has a long criminal history, but they didn't know it when they hired her. She immediately began badmouthing the interim director, Renee somebody or other, spreading all kinds of rumors and such to get her fired, stuff like she was the granddaughter of Harvey Driggs and was jealous of the archaeologists in there and all that. She tried to make her look like she was the one doing the looting and had stolen the Pilling figurine. The interim director and board were starting to figure it out and had actually fired her. She'd hired a couple of local petty thieves to help her. I guess they were digging things up and taking them out by the river, then she'd send them off to be sold. Kind of a bad deal."

"Who told you all this?"

"Oh, some of it came from Judge Richter. He's on the board of directors for the museum, plus he'll oversee the case in Federal Court. There's some good witnesses, so they'll go to prison without a doubt. The two young guys may get off on probation after a couple of years if they're good."

"Buddy, you're really a treasure trove of information. Can I put this on the Sunnyside grapevine?"

"Sure, it's mostly public knowledge at this point anyway. But you know that costume jewelry Jimmy Johnson had? It went to a good home, an older gal in Green River who's dating a fellow she wants to impress. It looks really good on her. They're engaged."

"That's wonderful! It was too tacky for my tastes."

"And that shield Jimmy had? I don't know if you saw that, but it also went to the museum. I guess it was quite the find. Next time you go in there you'll see it on display with you and Hank as the donors."

"Oh my gosh. No kidding?"

"I gave it to the judge and told him it was from you, so he told me that was how they do it. But Aunt Ginger, I have to tell you about the Green River Rockabilly Car Show."

"Oh, Hank and Junior already told me a bunch. They said it got pretty crazy."

"Did they tell you *Summertime Blues* was a big hit?"

"You mean Junior's old pickup?"

"Yes, and Howie and his band had a fantastic concert, all rockabilly stuff. Howie had his hair up in a pompadour with glitter in it, if you can imagine that, the new mayor of Green River."

"Oh, Junior told me about that. He said Howie was up there telling the crowd he was going to play a song dedicated to you, then broke out in this most incredible guitar riff—is that what you call it? —to the tune of *Found a Peanut*. I guess the crowd went wild."

"That actually wasn't one of my brighter moments," Bud frowned. "But it was fun, I guess. I thought he was going to play a different song, one about coffee."

"Oh, you've never liked being the center of attention, Buddy, but I wish I'd gone just to see that. You deserved every minute of it after getting that stupid song stuck in everyone's head."

Bud grimaced, then said, "Howie did his mayoral acceptance speech there at the concert, though it was a song, not a speech. He sang about Green River to the tune of *O Canada!* Everyone at the concert stood and took their hats off, and a few even had tears in their eyes. That's the Canadian national anthem, you know."

Ginger said, "Isn't that something? Did he also sing it in French like they do in Canada?"

She then stood, refilling their glasses from the pitcher of lemonade. "We should close up here and go to the new house, I guess, but it's nice to spend a minute with you."

As she walked by, she squeezed Bud's shoulder, and he took her hand and held it close to his heart for a moment, saying, "You're very special to me—you know that, I hope."

"Likewise, Buddy. You've always meant the world to me. But someone's walking up the highway. Who would be out this late?"

Bud could see a figure coming along the borrow pit in the lengthening shadows. Seeing what he was carrying, he knew it was Sandy. He opened the side door to the screen room and shouted, "Hey, Sandy! Bud Shumway here. If you need a ride I'm going your way in a few minutes."

Sandy veered towards the house, where Bud invited him in.

"Come in and have a going-away lemonade with me and my Aunt Ginger. You know her from the cafe."

"Who's going away?" Sandy asked, setting his giant boombox and headphones down as Ginger handed him a glass of lemonade.

"Nobody, really," Bud replied. "They're just moving into their new house down the road in town. Are you getting a lot done on your jukebox?"

Ginger looked puzzled, so Bud explained what Sandy was doing, then asked, "Are you about done here?"

Sandy replied, "Yes, it's been nice and quiet with the power plant offline. I'm leaving in the morning for Salt Lake."

Ginger asked, "Why not get a smaller recorder? Isn't that a lot to be carrying around all the time?"

"It's not heavy," Sandy replied. "Most of it's a speaker to broadcast sound. The recorder part is actually pretty small."

Now Bud, thinking of the dinosaur sounds they'd all heard, asked, "You broadcast sounds when you're out and about?"

"Sometimes," Sandy replied. "It can get things stirred up to where the animals will make noises, then I can determine what's out there. It especially stirs up the birds, like the ravens and magpies."

"Would that explain why some of us have been hearing dinosaurs?"

"Maybe," Sandy replied. "If the air currents were just right, the sound would carry. I have several odd noises on my recorder I can broadcast pretty loud."

Bud looked at Ginger, then asked, "Do you have a sound kind of like a T. rex?"

"I'm not sure what a T. rex would sound like, but I have a sound of a moose in heat that's pretty wild."

"How about a long siren?"

"Yes, and it actually *is* a siren. That one really gets to the birds. And I have one that's kind of bizarre that's a bird call slowed down to half-speed."

"How about a *thwock thwock* noise?"

"No, but that could be the sound bighorn sheep make when butting heads. I heard them when I was in Whitmore Canyon. It can carry for a mile or more. They fight during the rut, which is this time of year. The males have a triple-thick skull structure that protects their brains when they collide, which can be at up to 20 miles per hour."

Bud replied, "That's amazing, and so is what you're doing out here recording the soundscapes. But some of us thought we were hearing some dinosaur-like beasts. You actually created a rumor or two."

Sandy laughed. "I guess I should tell communities what I'm doing, but someone is bound to not know, even at that. I had a guy come after me with a shotgun once, thinking I was a flock of geese."

"Well, that explains that," Ginger said. "Another mystery solved. But we need to get going. I hope you'll come into the cafe next time you're down this way, Sandy."

"I may be coming back sooner than later," he answered. "I like it here, and if you'll give me your landlord's number, I may contact him about renting this house as a getaway when I'm not working."

Ginger wrote the number on a piece of paper as Bud folded up their camp chairs, Lindie at his side, slowly wagging her tail, ready to go.

"Buddy," his aunt said. "Tell Wilma Jean the stove has been fabulous, and tell her you guys need to come back up here soon. Don't be strangers, and that goes for you, too, Sandy. You're welcome anytime at the Sunnyside Cafe."

With that, she shook out the welcome mat, grabbed the empty lemonade pitcher and glasses, and they all walked out the door and on to better things.

COOPER COBRA

ABOUT THE AUTHOR

Chinle Miller writes from southeastern Utah and western Colorado, where she spends most of her time wandering with her dogs. She has an A.S. in Geology, a B.A. in Anthropology, and an M.A. in Linguistics.

If you enjoyed this book, you'll also enjoy the other books in the Bud Shumway mystery series:

The Ghost Rock Cafe

The Slickrock Cafe

The Paradox Cafe

The No Delay Cafe

The Silver Spur Cafe

The Ice House Cafe

The Rattlesnake Cafe

The Beartooth Cafe

The Melon Rind Cafe

The Cessna Cafe

The Klondike Cafe

The Yellow Cat Cafe

The Swiftcurrent Cafe

The Sunnyside Cafe is the fourteenth book in the series.

And don't miss *Desert Rats: Adventures in the American Outback*, *Uranium Daughter*, *Wandering off the Map*, and *The Impossibility of Loneliness*, also by Chinle Miller.

And if you enjoy Bigfoot stories, you'll love *Rusty Wilson's Bigfoot Campfire Stories* and his many other Bigfoot books, as well as his popular *Chasing After Bigfoot: My Search for North America's Most Elusive Creature*.

Other offerings from Yellow Cat Publishing include an RV series by RV expert Sunny Skye, which includes *Living the Simple RV Life, The Truth about the RV Life,* and *RVing with Pets*, as well as *Tales of a Campground Host.* And don't forget to check out the books by Sunny's friend, Bob Davidson: *On the Road with Joe* and *Any Road, USA*. And finally, you'll love Roger Dean Miller's comedy thriller, *Bombing Hoffman*.

www.ingramcontent.com/pod-product-compliance
Lightning Source LLC
LaVergne TN
LVHW020042110826
845155LV00029B/606

9781948859165